Tempting the Boss

Two wonderful office romances from two top Desire™ writers

Liaisons at the water cooler…
Life would never be the same…

Meet Kate and Maggie—they made sure the temperature in the office was really hot…with a little help from the boss!

Dear Reader,

We welcome you to the new 2-in-1 Desires. Each month we'll bring you three new 2-in-1 volumes from all your favourite authors. A double helping of the most rugged, gorgeous heroes around and all in one value-priced book!

This month kicks off with the first story in a new trilogy from Leanne Banks—MILLION DOLLAR MEN—and a wonderful stand-alone story from Joan Hohl in *Tempting the Boss*; these are two office romps sure to satisfy.

Next, we have the latest book in the SONS OF THE DESERT series from Alexandra Sellers—with a super, sexy sheikh hero—and a fantastic story from Peggy Moreland, too, in *100% Male*. You'll need lots of ice to cool you off after meeting these two strong, stubborn yet loveable rogues.

Finally, *Brides-To-Be* has two stories with a modern twist on the classic fairytale wedding fantasy written by fabulous authors Katherine Garbera and Kate Little. Wedding bells are definitely ringing for these couples.

Do tell us what you think of the new format for Desire™ and do look out for our wonderful new line—Superromance™—which is on the shelves now!

The Editors

Tempting the Boss

LEANNE BANKS
JOAN HOHL

DID YOU PURCHASE THIS BOOK WITHOUT A COVER?
If you did, you should be aware it is **stolen property** as it was reported *unsold and destroyed* by a retailer. Neither the author nor the publisher has received any payment for this book.

All the characters in this book have no existence outside the imagination of the author, and have no relation whatsoever to anyone bearing the same name or names. They are not even distantly inspired by any individual known or unknown to the author, and all the incidents are pure invention.

All Rights Reserved including the right of reproduction in whole or in part in any form. This edition is published by arrangement with Harlequin Enterprises II B.V. The text of this publication or any part thereof may not be reproduced or transmitted in any form or by any means, electronic or mechanical, including photocopying, recording, storage in an information retrieval system, or otherwise, without the written permission of the publisher.

This book is sold subject to the condition that it shall not, by way of trade or otherwise, be lent, resold, hired out or otherwise circulated without the prior consent of the publisher in any form of binding or cover other than that in which it is published and without a similar condition including this condition being imposed on the subsequent purchaser.

Silhouette, Silhouette Desire and Colophon are registered trademarks of Harlequin Books S.A., used under licence.

*First published in Great Britain 2001
Silhouette Books, Eton House, 18-24 Paradise Road,
Richmond, Surrey TW9 1SR*

TEMPTING THE BOSS © Harlequin Books S.A. 2001

The publisher acknowledges the copyright holders of the individual works as follows:

Expecting the Boss's Baby © Leanne Banks 2000
The Dakota Man © Joan Hohl 2000

ISBN 0 373 04730 4

51-1101

*Printed and bound in Spain
by Litografia Rosés S.A., Barcelona*

EXPECTING THE BOSS'S BABY

By
Leanne Banks

LEANNE BANKS

is a number-one best-selling author of romance. She lives in her native Virginia with her husband and son and daughter. Recognised for both her sensual and humorous writing with two Career Achievement Awards from *Romantic Times Magazine*, Leanne likes creating a story with a few grins, a generous kick of sensuality and characters that hang around after the book is finished. Leanne believes romance readers are the best readers in the world because they understand that love is the greatest miracle of all. You can write to her at PO Box 1442, Midlothian, VA 23113, USA. An SAE with postage for a reply would be greatly appreciated.

This book is dedicated to my terrific editor,
Karen Kosztolnyik, a real writer's 'she-ro'.

Prologue

According to the headmaster's speech at the alumni event earlier that evening, they were the Granger Home for Boys' biggest success stories, multi-millionaires, supposedly role models. The role-model comment still got under Michael Hawkins's skin. *They* were Dylan Barrow, Justin Langdon and himself, Michael Hawkins. Uneasily connected by their prosperity, the three men somberly toasted each other's success at O'Malley's bar.

"Congratulations, Dylan," Justin, a stock-market wizard, said, lifting his beer. "I bet you were surprised to find out your father was *the* Archibald Remington, CEO of one of the biggest pharmaceutical firms in the world."

Dylan nodded, his dark eyes glinting with cynicism. Of the three of them, Michael thought Dylan pulled off the wealthy-man image with the most ease. If one didn't look too closely, Dylan gave the appearance of sophisticated wealthy satisfaction. Dylan hid his rough edges fairly well, but Michael could see them just beneath the surface. Easy for Michael to see. He possessed those same rough edges.

"My father was a very wealthy, highly successful coward," Dylan said, downing his glass of Scotch. "He didn't claim paternity of me until he died. He left me a lot of money, a seat on the board of a company that doesn't want me and siblings that are horrified by the scandal I represent. Everything has its price."

Michael couldn't blame Dylan for his attitude. He couldn't recall one boy he'd known at the Granger Home for Boys who hadn't longed for a father. It was one more bitter thread that united the three of them. None had had fathers. He threw off the depressing thought. "How did you celebrate when you made it?" he asked Justin, knowing the man had started out trading penny stocks and advanced to dollars. Nowadays, he only traded in blocks of a thousand or more.

Justin gave him a blank look. "I'm not sure I celebrated. For years, I lived on a shoestring so I could trade stocks and I didn't live in the best area of town. When I first hit seven figures, I didn't do anything. When I hit the second million, I moved to a neighborhood where the windows don't wear bars. What about you? How did you celebrate when your Internet company went public?"

According to the press and the headmaster's speech, Michael was a computer genius who'd founded an Internet business. When his business went public, he'd become, well, rich. According to the press, this seemed to have occurred overnight, but Michael knew years of his life had passed in non-stop work mode.

"I slept for eight hours straight, first time in three years."

Dylan shook his head and spun his shot glass around. "I thought having money would take care of everything."

"It takes care of a lot," Justin said.

"But there's gotta be more than this," Dylan said. "Didn't you feel like a fraud when that headmaster went on and on about what great examples of success we are?"

Michael felt the same emptiness and dissatisfaction Dylan expressed echo inside him. Money had bought him publicity he didn't want, IRS bills and the sense that he would never find what he'd been looking for. Whatever the hell that was. "For all the good it's doing, we might as well dump it all."

Justin choked on his beer. "That's rash."

Dylan tilted his head thoughtfully. "It's not a bad idea. Vegas or Atlantic City?"

Justin looked at Michael and Dylan. "What have you two been drinking?"

"Michael's got a point. There gets to be a time when adding zeroes isn't fun anymore. The most fun things that I've bought so far are a house and car for my mother. None of us is married or has much family."

"Marriage is the giant vacuum cleaner of finances," Justin said ominously.

Michael felt the same avoidance to the big M for different reasons. He'd earned the nickname Tin Man honestly. Although he didn't place his trust in anything emotional, he felt the insistent nudge of an outrageous idea. "Instead of Vegas, we could be the benefactors we always wished we'd had when we were scraping by."

Dylan glanced at him for a long moment and his lips curved in a slow gambler's smile. "If we pool our resources, we could do some big things."

"Wait a minute," Justin said, clearly alarmed. "Pool our resources?"

"Are you sure your name isn't Ebenezer?" Dylan asked. "As in Scrooge?"

"You don't know how many cans of Beanee Weenees I ate."

"It would be tax-deductible," Michael said, and Justin's frown lifted.

"Tax-deductible," Justin repeated, warming to the idea. "Capital gains tax eats into my profits like a killer shark."

"We could make it a sort of club," Michael said, warming to the idea with a wry grin. "A secret millionaire's club."

"A secret millionaire's tax-deductible foundation," Justin clarified.

"Let's do it," Michael said. He hadn't felt this right about something since he'd started his business and hired his assistant Kate Adams. She was one of the few people on the planet in whom he could trust, and if he were a different man, a man with a heart, their relationship might have been more than business. One night it had been, but thank goodness Michael had come to his senses in time the next morning to salvage their business relationship.

"I'm in," Dylan said and nodded to the bartender. "A round of Scotch."

A long silence followed as Michael and Dylan looked expectantly at Justin. "Okay, okay. But if I get stuck eating Beanee Weenees because of this, I'm coming after both of you."

"Cheers," Michael said, lifting his glass. An odd sense of anticipation raced through him. "To the Millionaires' Club."

One

Kate Adams stared at the man she'd developed a monster crush on three years ago and felt her stomach dip and turn. Kate hadn't fallen for Michael Hawkins at first sight. Although she'd been attracted to him immediately, her passion, care and, heaven help her, her heart had taken a deceptively slow slide into the pit where they now resided. It wasn't love, she insisted, but it was something very strong.

The leather chair beside his huge gleaming walnut desk sat empty as usual. Instead he propped his tall, masculine frame against an upright desk with a tall chair to accommodate his need for movement. Michael wasn't the type of man to sit. His blazing topaz eyes belied his detached demeanor. His fierce intelligence and unswerving tenacity challenged her creativity in ways she'd never experienced. They'd worked together closely, and, after a time, she began to long for his low-voiced words of appreciation, the gentle, fleeting touches of approval. Every once in a while she'd felt his gaze on her, and the attraction had shimmered between them, but he'd always been quick to snuff it out.

She had waited for him to look up from his work, see her and realize that she was the woman for him. She'd thought Michael had done that two months ago on that fateful night when he'd looked at her and reached for her.

Kate felt a rush of heat as the memory sizzled through her. It could have been yesterday. They'd both been giddy from lack of sleep over an ongoing project. When Michael had received word of a new contract from a large company on the west coast, he'd pulled a forgotten bottle of champagne from the refrigerator in his executive suite and insisted they celebrate.

He'd opened the bottle and accidentally sprayed her with the cold champagne. She shrieked, he apologized, and they both laughed at her damp blouse. No flutes in sight, so they drank from mugs. One drink turned into two, and Kate couldn't say which intoxicated her more—the wine or the way Michael's gaze had remained focused on her, hungry.

He'd tipped his mug against her lips, spilling once more.

"I'm going to end up wearing more of this than I drink," Kate had told him, laughing and pulling at her blouse. She'd glanced up at him and the look in his eyes stole her breath. Her laughter died, and a lump of fear and exhilaration had formed in her throat. She had longed for him to look at her this way.

His gaze had dropped to her lips. "I can't help wondering how champagne tastes on your mouth."

Still unable to breathe, Kate had licked her suddenly dry lips. She felt as if she were on a precipice, and what she did in the next moment would determine which way she would go. Her heart hammered so hard she knew he must surely hear it. "Maybe," she said in a voice so low it was almost a whisper, "you should find out."

His gaze holding hers, he'd lowered his head and kissed her. His mouth was seeking, yet sure, inviting and aggressive enough to keep her off-balance. One kiss turned into two, and three, and after that, Kate lost count. Her damp blouse was discarded, and she grew hot beneath his touch. His hands seduced and demanded, and there was no place on her body he left untouched. The night had turned into a haze of repeated passion. Deep inside her, a tight bud of hope bloomed that Michael wanted her as far more than his secretary.

By the following morning, however, her dream had shattered: Michael had apologized profusely for stepping beyond the bounds of their professional relationship. He'd been so clearly upset that she couldn't hate him. She didn't know that she could ever hate him anyway.

Even at this moment, she felt the sliver of seductive hope that he would look up and realize he wanted her. The time had come to find out, she thought, and felt her stomach jump with nervousness. She took a calming breath. Time to lay it on the line. Win or lose, she couldn't afford to wait any longer for Michael.

She approached him and opened her mouth.

Michael glanced up with a piece of paper in his hand. "Would you mind doing some research on this home for unwed teenage mothers?"

Kate's heart stopped. *Did he know?* She worked her mouth, but no sound came out.

"I need you to keep it quiet," he said in the same low voice that reminded her of the night they'd shared together, the night he'd shown her with his body and words how much he could want her. "It's a favor for a friend."

Kate sucked in a shallow breath. "Favor for a friend?" she echoed in a voice that sounded high and strained to her own ears.

Michael shrugged his broad shoulders in discomfort. "Yeah, something about a charity thing."

She gripped the piece of paper tightly. "I'll try, but I may be leaving."

"Leaving?" Michael glanced at his watch, then studied her. "It's only ten o'clock. Are you sick?"

"In a manner of speaking," she muttered under her breath and felt her courage slip. Kate locked her knees and lifted her chin. She had to do this. "I can't go back," she blurted out.

"Back where?"

His utterly clueless expression fueled her frustration and stabbed at her heart. "Back to where we were before that night we spent together."

Realization dawned on his face and he rubbed his hand over his eyes. On a long exhale he met her gaze. "I told you I was sorry. Messing up our professional relationship is the last thing I want to do. You're the best assistant," he said, then added, "the only assistant I could ever have."

He was referring to the fact that he'd gone through seven assistants before Kate arrived on the scene. If she hadn't fallen for him, his words might have offered a bit of comfort. Not now. "I can't go back. I have feelings for you," she said in halting tones and felt her heart crack when his gaze slid away from hers.

Determined to give this her best shot, she continued despite her unsteady voice. "I have feelings for you that aren't going away. I don't just care about you as a boss. I care about you as a man."

"Don't," he said bluntly, finally looking at her again with stormy eyes. "I'm not the right man for you. I don't believe in romantic love. I'm not sure I believe in any love. Emotions come and go. You can't depend on them. Your odds of winning would be better in Vegas than with something as capricious as human emotion. I'm not cut out to be someone you can depend on. I'd be a rotten husband and father. Don't get involved with me. Not that way."

Kate's heart twisted viciously and nausea rose in her throat. She was going to be sick. Panic flooded her and she spun around to run to the rest room.

"Kate!" Michael called after her.

Feeling him on her heels, she slammed and locked the door behind her. She flipped on the exhaust fan, jerked on the water faucet, and dropped to her knees until she was finished. Ignoring the pounding on the door, she rose and splashed water on her face and took a few cool sips.

"Kate, you'll get over this," Michael said through the door.

Kate felt like such an idiot. She was humiliated, mortified and pregnant. She thought about the tiny life she carried in her womb, the result of that one night with Michael. A lump formed in her throat, but she shook her head. She refused to cry. Perhaps later, but not now.

Glancing in the mirror, she saw her pale face and hopelessness and hurt in blue eyes her friends once had said always sparkled. Something was terribly wrong with this picture.

"If you always do what you've always done, you'll always get what you've always got." She recited the quote from a book she'd recently read. "Time to do something different," she said and steeled herself once again.

"I'm quitting," she simply said when she opened the door.

Michael's eyes narrowed in consternation. "Quitting? Why would you give up a job you love because of one night when we both made a big mistake?"

Because I'm having your baby. She refused to tell him right now. Sometime later when she was more composed, but not now. Anger burned inside her. She latched onto the hot emotion, letting it chase away the cold chill inside her. "It's impossible for me to stay. I quit," she said and headed for her office.

Michael walked beside her, his long stride easily matching hers. "This is ridiculous. You'll get over it. I'll give you a raise."

"I don't need a raise," she said, barely holding herself in check. She pushed open her office door.

"My company stock options have insured my financial security."

"I'll give you your own project," he offered.

A plum, she distantly thought, but not for her. "No."

"There must be something you want," he said, exasperation swelling in his voice. "Everyone has their price."

His words angered her so she could barely speak. She took a deep breath. "I always believed the people who called you Tin Man were wrong. I always believed there was more to you. That's why I stayed." She turned and looked him in the eye. "I quit. I quit organizing your day, reminding you to eat, being your sounding board. I quit being seduced by your intelligence. I quit wishing you would want me. I quit working for you."

"Your contract specifies that you're required to give two weeks' notice."

She felt the edge to his voice cut inside her. She knew he could be tough. He'd just never been tough with her. Her hands began to shake. She needed to leave before she fell apart, she realized, and decided to return for her belongings later. "Dock my pay. Good-bye, Michael." She slung her pocketbook over her shoulder and left the room feeling his gaze burn a hole in her back.

The sound of her footsteps echoed on the tile office floor of the executive suite as Michael stared after her. *What in hell had just happened?* He had been so careful to put their professional relationship back in place after that night he'd given in to the dark hunger and need he'd so often denied, and they'd made rock-your-world love.

He'd always been physically attracted to Kate, but what man wouldn't be? Her silky dark hair swung in a sexy curtain to her shoulders, her blue eyes glinted with intelligence and humor, her full mouth often formed a secret smile that made him curious, and she moved her lithe feminine body in a way that reminded him of a sensual feline.

She brought out the urge for conquest in a man, but he'd denied himself food and sleep while he'd been building his company. He told himself sex was just one more need denied. Michael had valued Kate for other, more important reasons. She had been the most solid, dependable person in his life during his last three roller-coaster years. She'd treated him the same way when he'd been in debt for the company up to his eyeballs as she did when he became a multi-millionaire. He trusted her. He could count on her, and for a man who'd spent his life not counting on anyone, that was something.

Her scent lingered in the air—a scent that smelled like cookies and sex. That alone could have driven him crazy. She probably had no idea of her importance. But now she was gone. The wild, yet sad look in her eyes haunted him. She was neither impulsive, nor given to irrational displays of emotion. Michael had the uneasy sense that she had meant every word she'd said, and he had not only lost the best assistant he'd ever had, he'd lost his best friend.

The ringing of the phone on Kate's desk jolted him. He picked up the receiver. "Hawkins," he muttered in a rough tone.

"Michael? What are you doing answering the phone?"

Michael instantly recognized the voice of his personnel specialist, Jay Payne. "Good timing, Jay. I need a new assistant."

A long silence followed. "Pardon? Did you say a new assistant? What about Kate?"

"She's gone."

"On vacation?"

"No."

"Temporary leave?"

"No," Michael said, feeling his impatience grow.

"Is she sick?"

"No," Michael answered shortly, then remembered she had in fact appeared sick just before she'd left. "She quit."

Another long silence followed. "Just like that?"

"Just like that."

"But she's required to give two weeks' notice," Jay sputtered. "Did she give a reason? Did one of our rivals steal her? I know she's received offers," he added.

Michael frowned. Something about this didn't add up. "Put her on sick leave and I'll see if she changes her mind. Give me the names of the companies who have been after her. In the meantime, get me an interim assistant."

"Any special requirements?"

"Someone like Kate," Michael said and knew he had just delivered mission impossible.

Two weeks later, when he joined Dylan and Justin at O'Malley's, Kate's departure still bothered Michael.

"Hey, Michael, you're falling down on the job," Dylan said. "You're in charge of the home for unwed teenage mothers, Justin's looking into the after-school program for underprivileged kids and I'm checking into a medical research program."

"Medical research," Justin echoed with an uneasy expression on his face. "Sounds expensive."

"If you don't watch out, we're gonna start calling you the tightwad millionaire," Dylan threatened with wry humor.

"Call me anything. Just don't call me broke." Justin popped an antacid and glanced at Michael. "You don't look too good. What's up?"

Michael paused, then reluctantly said, "I lost a key employee a couple of weeks ago."

Dylan grimaced. "A death? I'm sorry—"

Michael shook his head. "Not a death," he said,

wondering why it felt like one. "My assistant quit. No notice. Just walked out. I'd just given her the assignment to check out the home for unwed teenage mothers."

Dylan raised his eyebrows. "Flighty?"

Michael shook his head again. "Not at all."

"Maybe she got a better offer," Justin said.

"Nah, I checked."

Dylan signaled for the bartender. "Well, I haven't yet met a woman who doesn't act on her emotions every once in a while. PMS, pregnancy... they all get a little crazy every now and then. Maybe she'll come to her senses and come back soon."

Michael's mind locked onto Dylan's words. *PMS, pregnancy.* He shook his head. Not pregnancy, he told himself. Maybe PMS, maybe anything, but not pregnancy. It had been just one night. One night full of making love. Hell, they'd made love at least four times, each time more uninhibited than the previous. Contraception had been the last thing on his mind. Losing himself and his hunger in Kate had been his driving focus.

Michael began to sweat. He'd just figured she wouldn't get pregnant. After all, he'd never intended to be a father or a husband. It wasn't part of his plan. He was cut out for neither role. It wasn't part of his destiny. In fact, he'd nearly convinced himself he was genetically designed never to be a father.

"Earth to Michael, come in," Dylan said, knocking on the wooden bar top. He laughed, but his eyes held a trace of concern. "Something you want to tell us?"

Michael thought of Kate and shook his head slowly. "No. Don't mind me. I'll do the research on the unwed teenage mothers' home myself. I'll see you guys later," he said and rose.

"But your beer," Justin said, clearly uncomfortable with the waste. "Dylan just ordered you another beer."

"Thanks, but I'll take a rain check. You can have it."

"I don't want it," Justin said.

Dylan shrugged. "We'll give it away."

Justin shook his head. "You two take this charity thing too far."

"It's just a beer," Dylan said with a smile tinged with glee. "You'll be writing a much bigger check when the Millionaires' Club makes its first donation."

Justin's queasy expression amused Michael despite his preoccupation with Kate. "You're looking a little green around the gills, bud. You must be so full of money you need to get rid of some. Don't worry, Justin. No cans of Beanee Weenees in your future. Later, guys," he said, and as he left the bar his mind immediately turned to Kate. Was she pregnant?

He drove to his apartment, brooding all the way.

He examined the possibility of her pregnancy, turning it around in his head first this way, then that. Walking into the apartment that was more a place to sleep than a home, he didn't bother turning on a light. The dark suited his mood. Although pregnancy was a physical possibility, every time Michael seriously considered it, he felt a dull thud in his stomach.

Tugging the buttons on his shirt loose, he stood in the quiet dark and swore at himself in disgust. How could he have been so careless? So stupid? Potentially to bring a baby into the same single-parent situation that he'd faced as a child. Granted, Kate was neither ill nor uneducated, as his mother had been, but she was young and alone. A smoky visual of his mother just before she died slithered through his mind.

The memories were poison, he knew, and he deliberately closed his mind to them. Sleep, he told himself. Eight hours would clear his head, and if ever he needed a clear head, it was now.

Sleep, however, eluded him. He paced and turned the TV on. In no mood for late-night infomercials, he turned it off and tossed and turned. Finally, he drifted off. The gray images he'd successfully deflected during the day invaded his dreams.

Short flashes of turning points in his past, all seen through a child's eyes, kicked him back in time. He might as well have been a six-year-old again.

"Your mother is dead," the social worker said, patting his small, cold hand.

He tasted the metallic flavor of fear and terror and felt his thin body begin to shake.

"Do you have any other family?" she'd asked.

Unable to speak, he shook his head.

"Don't worry, Michael. We'll find someone to take care of you."

The suffocating aloneness and loss of control wrapped around his throat like a vise. He couldn't breathe. His mother couldn't be dead. She was all he had. He ran from the social worker.

"Michael!"

He heard her voice calling after him, but he kept running. His hand connected with something hard. Glass shattered. Pain shot through him and he bolted upright in bed, his chest heaving for breath.

Disoriented by the darkness, he reached for the bedside lamp, but it wasn't there. He groped for a flashlight in the drawer. The lamp lay on the floor in pieces. Perspiration dampened his skin and his heart pounded as if he had indeed been running.

The images of his childhood continued while he was awake. He'd always felt like an unnecessary visitor. For various reasons, three foster families had been unable to keep him longer than a year or so at a time. Too old for adoption, he'd made a home of sorts at the Granger Home for Boys. There was little possibility for forming any emotional connections. That suited Michael fine. But it was a place that fostered dreams. At night in a room with three sets of bunk beds, a boy could sleep. A boy could dream.

He'd dreamed of being a man in control of his life and destiny, a man of wealth and power. But he'd never dreamed of being a father.

Kate's alarm rang at the regular time, waking her just before 6:00 a.m. She slapped the snooze button to quiet the morning deejay who sounded as if he mainlined coffee. She gently eased herself toward the edge of the bed for a shower to clear her head for work when it occurred to her that she no longer worked at CG Enterprises. She still wasn't accustomed to the change in routine. At the thought of being unemployed, her heart raced. Then she remembered her stock options and breathed normally.

Her brain began to whirl like a scratched CD. Thoughts of Michael slid into her mind with the insidious ease of smoke, and the pain of her last encounter with him returned full force. Every time she thought of him, she felt like a fool. Although she'd had strong feelings for him, it hadn't been love on either end. Thinking of him reminded her how much she'd fooled herself. She squeezed her eyes tight and told herself she had more important considerations now. Like the baby.

For the hundredth time Kate wondered how she would tell her parents. Kate had been what her mother called a change-of-life baby. As the long-awaited only child of a woman over forty, she knew she embodied all her parents' hopes and dreams. She winced, picturing her mother fainting and her father's face full of disappointment. *Stall,* she thought and wondered how she might stall for a year. She had a temporary respite since her parents had taken an extended RV trip to Branson, but that wouldn't last forever.

Pushing back her worries, she rose from bed determined to forge ahead. After a shower and a breakfast of tea and toast, she heard a knock at her door. *Neighbor,* she thought, and opened it to Michael.

Her heart jolted at the sight of him. His grim expression etched a sharp contrast from the morning sunshine and spring flowers on the porch of her duplex townhouse. Kate read a lack of sleep on his face, but he still managed to emanate rock-hard strength. It was part of the reason she'd fallen for him. Something about him said he might fall, but he wouldn't break and he would always get back up. He studied her for a long, uncomfortable moment before meeting her gaze head-on, and Kate felt the full power of Michael Hawkins's undivided attention.

"Are you pregnant?"

Kate's breath stalled. She felt as if she'd been

hit by a train. His gravelly voiced question scraped over raw nerve endings. Off-guard, unprepared and rattled, she worked her mouth, but nothing came out. She eyed the door and thought about shutting it against him.

He must have read her mind because he planted his foot in the doorway. "Are you pregnant?"

Unaccustomed to having his undiluted intensity solely focused on her, Kate continued to struggle for balance. He stood too close to her. When she forced herself to take a breath, she inhaled his scent and her body softened in the same way it had the night they'd shared together. "Yes," she said, more whisper than voice.

"We need to talk," he said and entered her house.

Struggling to clear her head, she crossed her arms over her chest, hugging herself, and left the door open. Heaven help her, she wished she was better prepared. "I'm not sure I agree."

He lifted a dark eyebrow of inquiry.

"You pretty much covered everything during our last discussion. You said you would be a rotten father and I shouldn't count on you."

He rested his hands on his hips. "That was before I had all the facts."

"And how does having the facts change things?" she asked, refusing to give into her weakness for him. Her weakness for him had gotten her into enough trouble already. "Do you suddenly have the ability to be a good father now?"

He narrowed his eyes. "No. I may not be able to do much for this baby, but I can be financially responsible." He paused a half-beat. "I can give this baby a name."

"How?"

"We can get married," he said with the same emotion with which he could have proposed buying a car.

Kate forced her brain to work. "Let me get this straight. You don't love me, you don't want to be a husband or a father, but you think it's a good idea for us to get married so the baby will have a name and financial security?"

"I can provide well for this child," he said with a steely resolve that surprised and unnerved her.

"Financially," Kate said, holding fast to her resolve. "But children need more than money from moms and dads. A child needs security, attention, love, affection, instruction, laughter. A child needs to see that love is possible, and you don't believe in love. Why should I marry you, Michael? You don't—" Out of the corner of her eye a familiar vehicle caught her attention. "Oh no!" Kate watched in horror as her parents' RV pulled into her driveway.

She glanced back at Michael. "You have to leave," she told him. "We'll talk later. Go away."

He looked at her as if she'd sprouted another head. "Why?"

"It's my parents. You have to leave," she said, fighting panic and a return of nausea.

"You haven't told them," he concluded.

"I haven't told anyone."

"When were you planning to tell them?"

Kate watched her father climb out of the vehicle and wave. "Oh, four years sounded good," she said in a voice that sounded thin to her own ears. She pasted a smile on her face for her dad. "My mother has this minor heart condition. It's not really dangerous, but I don't want to tempt it. You need to leave," she whispered emphatically.

"I can't. They've blocked me in," he said, and his logical statement made her want to cry.

"Katie," her mother called with a smile as she climbed the steps to Kate's porch. "Surprise! I hope you don't mind. I promise we won't stay long. Just the day. I needed to see you to make sure you're okay." She studied Kate with a mother's knowing eye. "You look a little pale, sweetheart."

Kate felt her stomach twist and turn with the familiar nausea, but continued to smile as she embraced her mother. "I'm fine. It's good to see you too. I thought you two were in Branson."

Her father gave her a quick squeeze and chuckled. "You know your mother. She's not happy if she hasn't seen her little chick in a while. Who's this?" he asked, looking at Michael.

More than anything Kate wished for a magic wand. She would make both Michael Hawkins and her nausea disappear.

Two

"This is my boss," Kate said. "I'm taking some time off and he wanted to go over a few minor details on a special project. Michael Hawkins, Tom and Betty Adams," she said, making speedy introductions. "We're done," she added cheerfully. "You can leave now."

"Oh, there's no need to rush on our account," Kate's mother said. "Katie sent us a newspaper article about your company. Very impressive. She's always had high praise for you."

"Thank you," Michael said, giving Kate a speculative glance. "Kate's been invaluable. Irreplaceable."

Irreplaceable as his secretary, Kate firmly reminded herself.

"That's our Katie," her father said beaming with pride. "She's always been special to us."

Kate's stomach twisted viciously at how quickly her father's pride and joy would disintegrate if he knew the truth. She might be a grown woman, but the thought of hurting her parents made her ill. She felt herself go light-headed and blinked. "Come in and make yourselves at home. I'll be right back," she said, and dashed for the bathroom.

She sat down on the brass stool beside the pedestal sink for a moment to regain her equilibrium, then splashed her face and took several deep breaths. She wasn't given to anxiety attacks, but Kate couldn't imagine a more nerve-wracking situation. Michael Hawkins pressing marriage when he didn't love her and sitting in her living room with her parents. Biting back a moan, she sank back down on the stool.

The door opened, and Michael appeared.

"What are you doing here?" she whispered. "You're supposed to be gone."

He stepped in front of her, crowding her with his body and unhinging her with his intense stare. "Do you do this often?" he asked, crouching in front of her.

"Do what?"

"Pass out."

"I'm not passing out," she retorted, irritated

with his proximity and her continuing lightheadedness. "I was making sure I didn't pass out by coming in here. I'm sure I'll feel much better when you leave. We need to get back out there or my parents—"

"Your mother already suspects something," Michael said. "She said you looked pale."

Kate squeezed her forehead. "Oh, no. I knew this would happen," she wailed, then lowered her voice. "I can't hide anything from her. I always suspected she had X-ray vision when it came to me. I can't tell them. It will hurt them terribly."

"You'll have to tell them sometime," he said with a shrug that indicated he truly didn't comprehend her situation.

"Sometime doesn't have to be now."

"What if you were married?" he asked in a tone entirely too intuitive.

"Oh, don't even go there." Kate knew her mother had been planning her wedding since before she was born. If Betty Adams could have done things her way, she would have arranged a marriage between Kate and the boy down the street who'd become a dentist, had them move next door and start a family right away. Kate shook her head and stood. "I refuse to compound my bad judgment by making another decision with long-term consequences."

"Bad judgment?" he said, slowly rising to tower over her.

"By falling for—" She broke off. "By falling into bed with you. You need to leave."

"Kate," Michael said, taking her arm.

Her heart tripped, unsettling her, confusing her. She pulled her arm away. "You've barely looked me in the eye for two months. Why are you touching me now?"

He paused a half beat, his gaze trapping hers with a power that rocked her. "Circumstances are different now."

Not different enough, she thought, remembering how he had shattered her hopes to smithereens just weeks ago.

"Kate, you know me better than just about anyone."

She licked her dry lips and feigned a careless shrug. "So?"

"So you know I get what I want," he told her, and his eyes might as well have nailed her to the bathroom wall.

Her stomach sank. Kate had seen that look of determination on Michael's face before, but it had always been about business. Now it was about her, yet not about her. It was about the baby. Hearing footsteps, she felt another sliver of panic and it gave her an urge to argue a rain check. She flung open the door and raced out to greet her mother in the hallway. "Mom, Michael was just leaving and wanted to say good-bye," she continued without breathing. Maybe if she talked fast, no one would ask questions. "Do you think Dad would mind moving the motor home?"

Kate tossed a quick glance at Michael and saw him watching her the same way a very clever tiger watches his prey. Her pulse picked up.

"It was nice meeting you, Mrs. Adams. I look forward to seeing you again," he continued, letting Kate know her reprieve was temporary. "We'll talk soon, Kate."

"Bye," she said, biting her lip as she watched him leave.

"I think he might like you, Katie," her mother said, ever hopeful.

Kate shook her head.

"He couldn't take his eyes off you," her mother said. "A man like that, he might make a good husband."

Kate bit back a dozen corrections and squeezed her mother instead. "Mother, you say every man can't take his eyes off me. You just want me married," she teased lightly, but her heart felt heavy.

Michael allowed the evening spring breeze to wash over him as he sat parked in his Lexus down the street from Kate's duplex. Her parents' RV had just pulled out of the driveway. Glancing at his watch, he decided to give Kate a five-minute respite before he rang her doorbell.

Despite his reputation as Tin Man, Michael had been unable to dismiss Kate's pregnancy. The whole situation made him nuts, and he couldn't recall being more driven about anything than he was now to protect his child from every bad thing that had happened to him during his childhood. Long-buried bitterness roiled in his gut at the thought of his child being deprived or feeling abandoned and trapped.

If that weren't enough, his protective urge extended to Kate. The idea of her being alone and pregnant with his child was untenable to him. His blood pressure rose just thinking about it and he was determined to convince her to agree to his plan. Checking his watch again, he pulled into her driveway.

Grabbing a sheet of paper from the passenger seat, Michael got out of the car and climbed the steps to Kate's porch. He rang the doorbell and a calico cat mewed up at him. The outside of her cozy home echoed the warmth of her personality.

Kate answered the door, rubbing her eyes as if she'd been crying. "I didn't expect you."

He would be back every day until they got this settled, he thought grimly, wishing she would smile again. "I drove by and noticed your parents had left." She didn't invite him in, but that didn't stop him from entering. "Why are you crying?"

Kate picked up the cat and cradled it in her arms. She shrugged. "I feel very stupid for getting myself in this situation."

"It took two," he pointed out, thinking that her

home might have had a calming effect on him if he hadn't felt like climbing the walls. He remembered when Kate used to have a calming effect on him. That time was long gone, he thought with irritation. "We didn't finish our conversation this morning."

She shot him a wary glance. "Yes we did."

"No we didn't," he said, fighting a tightening cord of impatience. "There's only one thing for us to do. We need to get married. There's no other choice."

Kate blinked. "That's not true. We're not living in the dark ages. Many single women give birth to children."

"Is that what you want for our child?"

"No, but—"

"Exactly. Kate, I won't take no for an answer."

"You seem to forget that marriage takes two. You also seem to forget that you told me in no uncertain terms that you are neither husband nor father material."

Michael narrowed his eyes, knowing the essence of what she'd said hadn't changed. "I didn't have all the facts during that conversation. You hid a very important fact from me. Why?"

"I didn't want you to marry me because I was pregnant," she returned heatedly. "Which is exactly what you're trying to do."

He ground his teeth. Reasoning with her had been so much easier when she'd been his employee. "People marry for lesser reasons. For the well-being of this child, you and I must marry. Dammit, I won't have a child of mine born illegitimate and without the financial security I can easily afford. I knew too many kids who suffered under those circumstances and this will not happen to my child."

She stared at him for a long moment. "You never talk about your family," she finally said.

He hated like hell to discuss his childhood, but he was determined to make her see the only right course. "I don't have a family. My father left my mother soon after she became pregnant with me, and my mother died when I was six. I spent time in foster care and at the Granger Home for Boys. I can give you a first-hand account of what it's like to grow up without a father and it's not pretty. But you wouldn't know about that, would you?"

Kate put the cat down and turned away from Michael. She'd always wondered about his family, but had never asked. Michael had seemed to be a man with no personal attachments. Now she understood why. With a sinking feeling she also understood why he would be adamantly opposed to putting his child through an illegitimate upbringing. His disclosure took the wind out of her sails. "So what kind of arrangement are you proposing?" she asked in a low voice.

She felt him step closer to her. He gave her a

sheet of paper. She scanned it, but the numbers were a blur. "What is this?"

"My financial statement. I've had my accountant put aside—"

Kate's stomach roiled. "Oh my God," she said, tossing the offending paper to the floor and walking to the other side of the room.

Michael stepped in front of her, his hands on her arms, male frustration emanating from every pore. "I want you to know that I can and will take care of you and the baby. I want you to see it in black and white. I don't want you to ever worry about it."

In some corner of her mind, she suspected his intentions were good. She could see it was vital to him to protect her and the baby, but the timing couldn't be worse. This was a far cry from the sweet, sentimental tale her mother had often repeated to her about her father's proposal on bended knee in an ice-cream parlor. "So this is a business arrangement. You sign over part of your money to me and the baby, you and I get married, we live separately, and I raise our child."

"No," he said firmly, immediately. "You and the baby will live with me."

"Why?" she demanded. "You don't want me."

His gaze traveled over her, and Kate felt a surprising flicker of the forbidden but mutual attraction she'd thought he'd killed. "I never said I didn't want you. I may not have much of a heart, but I am a man. I wanted to take you to bed from the beginning. Every day I saw you, I thought how it would be to touch you and feel you hot and wet. But you were too valuable to me as an assistant to muddy the waters with sex."

"And now?"

"Now you're no longer my assistant," he said. "You're fair game."

Confused, rattled and, embarrassingly, a little turned on, Kate backed away. She took a careful breath and shook her head. "This is just a little too primitive for me. Your protectiveness, the money, the—" she groped for a benign description and came up empty "—the sex." She shook her head again. "I don't know what to say. I don't feel like I know you at all, yet you're insisting we marry."

"Do you remember what it was like between us before that night we spent together?"

She nodded, remembering that underneath the forbidden wanting, there'd always been an ease, occasional laughter, and respect. Everything had felt so dreadfully tense between them, however, ever since that night. "We laughed a lot more."

"You were a friend."

Kate felt the push and pull of loss and confusion. He called her friend, and she felt elated, yet she knew he wasn't offering her a lifetime of love and devotion. She crossed her arms over her chest, then lifted a hand to rub her forehead. "I don't—" She bit her lip. "I don't know. I need time to think."

"You said you cared for me as more than a boss," he reminded her.

She felt the sting of humiliation at how she'd laid her emotions bare for him to see. "That was before you told me you didn't believe in love."

"So you prove my point. You can't count on emotions. Yours have changed."

"I think it would be more fair to say I didn't have all the facts. I didn't know everything about you."

"When do you ever know everything about someone else?" he asked. "You don't." He took her left hand in his and rubbed her ring finger, then met her gaze. "It's right for us to be married." He closed his hand around hers and drew her to him. "Right in a lot of ways."

He lowered his head and took her mouth in a gentle, but firm caress, and she felt the coil of sensual tension inside her tighten. She felt his fingers splay through her hair, tilting her head for better access. He was a heady combination of masculine control and passion, and Kate struggled with overwhelming seductive and forbidden wishes.

He slid his leg between hers and she felt the evidence of his hard arousal against her. Kate remembered how easy it had been to fall into his arms before. Was she ready for that again? The thought cut through the haze of passion, and she pulled back and ducked her head. Her lips and mind were buzzing.

"I need to think," she said, staring at the open collar of his shirt. She knew his chest was strong. She knew how his bare chest felt against her hands and cheek. Kate closed her eyes. "This isn't helping."

She heard him exhale deeply; his impatience shimmered between them. She knew that sound. She'd seen it and heard it a hundred times, but it had always been business-related.

"I don't remember you being this stubborn," he said in a wry voice.

Kate glanced up at him. "Different circumstances," she said.

He tilted his head to one side. "How's that?"

"You used to be my boss," she said. "Now, you're not."

He nodded, taking her measure. "Works both ways."

"What do you mean?"

"Like I said before, now that you're not my assistant, you're fair game." He lifted her hand to his mouth and brushed his lips over her fingers. "We'll talk soon."

Her fingers burned as she watched him walk out the door. She felt as if she'd walked into a cyclone, or perhaps one had walked into her. She rubbed her hand over her face and sagged against the wall. She hadn't counted on Michael's insistence. She hadn't counted on him pursuing her with the same fervor and intensity with which she'd watched him pursue his business interests.

Her chest tightened when she remembered the you-can-fight-but-you-won't-win look in his eyes. Her emotions were all over the place. She felt exhilarated, seduced…. She spied his financial statement on the floor and scowled in disgust. She scooped it up and crumpled it into a tight little ball.

The man was a mass of contradictions. He wanted to protect her, seduce her and marry her.

But not love her.

Kate didn't know what to do. This was definitely not a sentimental story of a proposal on bended knee in the ice cream parlor. She tried to imagine repeating this story to her child. "Yes, a lot of men propose with words of love and devotion and diamond rings, but your Daddy brought me his financial statement instead."

Kate groaned and tossed the paper across the room.

The next morning Kate left before Michael could call or visit. She invited her close friend, Donna, to meet her at a park in downtown St. Albans for lunch. Kate had known Donna since they'd both entered Virginia Tech's computer science program as freshmen, and she valued the longevity and comfort of their friendship. Donna's wide-eyed baby face belied her worldly-wise mind.

"I'm surprised you were able to get away from work," Donna said as they shared a small table overlooking the pond. "It seems like your lunch hours are always used for special projects for the mighty Michael."

"I'm not working for the mighty Michael anymore," she said. "I quit."

Donna's brown eyes rounded. "You're joking!"

"No. I'm pregnant," she said, and Kate told her the whole story to the accompaniment of Donna's repeated gasps.

"His financial statement," Donna said and tried unsuccessfully to swallow a chuckle. "I'm curious. What did it say?"

Kate threw her a sideways glance. "I didn't look. I already know he's got a lot in the bank. I just don't know how terrible it would be to marry him knowing he doesn't even believe in love." She tossed some breadcrumbs toward the geese that begged from the luncheon crowd.

Donna made a face and sighed. "It's admirable that he wants to take care of you and the baby. I hate to say it, but he may be too damaged from his upbringing to really be able to love someone. This won't be a marriage like your parents have."

Donna was voicing all of Kate's concerns. "I know," she said glumly. "It's not that he's a bad person, but since he didn't have an example of how to live in a family, I'm afraid he really won't know how."

"You can't tell me you didn't see this coming like a freight train," Donna said. "You've worked with him for three years."

Kate felt a rush of embarrassment at her foolishness. "That's part of the problem. The only way I know him is through work, and even though that might have consumed a lot of hours, there are things Michael never mentioned about himself. I know it sounds silly, but I just thought I had a terrible, terrible crush. Since we spent that night together, I've been on an emotional seesaw."

Donna groaned. "How hard is he pushing?"

"Very hard," Kate said, feeling the beginning of a headache.

Donna reached over and squeezed her arm. "You could always move to France."

Kate gave a half-hearted smile. Throughout their friendship, they'd taken turns offering the fantasy of moving to France as a way to escape the crisis du jour.

"Whatever you do, don't fall in love with him until he falls in love with you," Donna said.

Kate frowned. "What do you mean don't fall for him? I thought I already had."

"You fell into lust, infatuation. Both of those are temporary. Real love is terminal," Donna said cheerfully. "My mother always told me never to marry anyone who didn't love me more than I loved him. So if you decide to marry him, you just need to make him fall in love with you. Or make sure you don't fall in love with him."

"Great," Kate said wryly. "Do any of these pearls of wisdom come with a magic wand?"

Three

"Michael, if you don't stop talking about the financial arrangements pertaining to this marriage, I'm going to throw up."

Michael blinked. "Okay," he said, setting his papers on the end table beside her sofa.

His unswerving focus on her never failed to unnerve her. She would have to find a way to get over that if she was actually going to go through with this. She'd been unable to sleep thinking about it. It seemed so terribly wrong not to marry for love, but in the stillness of the middle of the night when it was just her heartbeat and her baby's, Kate asked herself if she'd be able to live with herself if she didn't try. Looking at Michael, she prayed she was making the right choice. "I have other concerns."

"Such as?"

"Where we will live, how we will relate to each other, the wedding," she said, thinking that those barely scratched the surface.

"That's easy," he said, waving his hand. "You can choose a house where you'd like us to live. We'll relate to each other the way we always have. And we can get blood tests and be married by a justice of the peace within three days."

Kate bit back a sigh. She agreed with one out of three. They had nowhere to go but up. "I don't mind finding a house for us, but I'd like to know some of your likes and dislikes. I don't think we will be able to relate to each other the way we always have."

"Why?"

"Because you are no longer my boss."

"That means I'll negotiate instead of giving orders."

"Okay. I need you to do something that has nothing to do with stocks and trust funds."

"Name it," he said with such strength and assurance that her heart flipped over.

"I want you to discuss our wedding arrangements with my mother. But I still don't want you to tell her I'm pregnant."

"When?"

"Later," she said, her stomach dipping at the thought. "One thing at a time. Will you talk with my parents?"

"Done," he said. "Your parents seemed like very nice, reasonable people. I negotiate with cannibals all the time. This should be cake."

That night, Michael pulled into Kate's driveway beside an unfamiliar car, a vintage Corvette at that. Curious, he climbed the steps of her porch and rang the doorbell. She answered the door wearing an uneasy expression. "Trent Cavoli is here," she whispered.

Michael immediately recognized the name of the man who'd tried, unsuccessfully, to seduce much of CG Enterprises' talent to Cavoli's company. "What is he doing here?" he demanded.

"I don't know," she said. "He stops by every couple of months to offer me a job or ask me out for dinner."

"Did you go?"

She gave him a dark glare. "I'm sure he wants CG secrets. I can't imagine him being truly interested in me. He's just as hung up on business as you are."

He felt the slightest sting from her words as she turned away from him. She might be partly right in her assessment, but Michael knew Trent had a reputation with the ladies. If he'd known Trent was sniffing around Kate, he would have…. Michael told himself his territorial feelings were related to the company. Stepping inside, he glanced at Trent's smoothly polished appearance and wondered if the man appealed to Kate at all.

Trent's eyes widened when he caught sight of Michael. "Michael Hawkins, I never expected to see you here." Trent extended his hand. "You look a little hassled. How's business?"

"Great," Michael said, barely touching the man's hand. "Kate tells me you've visited her more than once."

Trent smiled. "You can't blame me. She's a smart, beautiful woman. I'd be glad to have her as an employee or a dinner companion. Word is she's no longer working for you, so I thought I'd take my chances."

Michael felt the surprising, yet overwhelming urge to knock a few bleached teeth from Trent's smile. He moved next to Kate. "You're out of luck again. Kate's not available. She's not my assistant anymore because she's going to be my wife."

Trent's eyebrows flew upward. "Damn. I was sure she was your most underrated natural resource. Congratulations and best wishes," he said and gave a little salute.

"Thank you," Kate said politely, as if she sensed Michael's hostility.

Trent walked toward the door and glanced back at Kate. "If anything changes, give me a call."

Kate closed the door behind him and Michael

scowled. "Son of a bitch," he said. "Why didn't you tell me he was making offers?"

Kate shrugged. "It was more a minor nuisance than anything else."

"If he ever comes around you again—"

She waved her hand in a dismissing gesture. "He won't. Think about it. A baby would really cramp his style." She gave him a long glance that almost made him feel as if she could see his entire hellish day written on his brain. "Rough day?"

With her big blue eyes and pink cheeks and lips, she looked so innocent. But Michael knew the truth. Kate had sent him into the lion's den. "I talked to your parents."

Her eyes rounded. "Oh. How'd it go?" she asked in a tone entirely too casual.

He followed her around the couch. "How do you think it went?"

She bit the inside of her lip. "I can only imagine."

He put his hands on either side of her, trapping her and forcing her to meet his gaze. "I want her on my negotiations team for my next merger."

Kate laughed breathlessly. "Piece of cake?"

"Why didn't you warn me?"

"You seemed so confident. So when's the wedding? Next year?"

"Two weeks," he corrected and watched her eyes widen in surprise. He lifted his hand to touch her jaw. "She wanted six months. You weren't using this as a ploy to procrastinate about marrying me, were you?"

Kate wiggled slightly beneath his hands and glanced away. "Not really," she said.

"Good," he said, nuzzling her cheek. "My feelings would be terribly hurt," he told her in a mocking voice.

She shot him a look of disbelief. "Yeah, right," she said. "As if feelings would affect you at all once you've decided to do something."

"I'm glad you understand that about me," he said. "Because you could put ten of your mother in a room with me by myself and it still wouldn't stop me from marrying you." He brushed his lips over hers in a lingering kiss. Damn if he didn't feel like he'd earned it. "So if this wasn't a procrastination ploy, what was it? A test?"

Kate seemed to have trouble removing her gaze from his mouth. "Uh, no." She forced her gaze to his chin. "It wasn't really a test."

"Then what was it? Really?"

"I just thought you should know part of what you're getting into," she said, her eyelashes forming a sexy shield over her eyes and reminding Michael of all the times he'd wanted to lay her down and take her.

"Did you honestly think she would scare me off?" he growled.

"No." She looked up at him. "I know there isn't much that scares you."

The almost hidden come-hither look in her eyes grabbed at his gut, combining with his frustration over the negotiations with her mother and running into a competitor he detested. Drinking in her scent, he slid his fingers through her silky hair and took her mouth with his. She tasted sweet and forbidden, and kissing her only made him want more of her. Sucking at her bottom lip, he consumed her mouth the way he planned to consume her body.

He skimmed his hands down her sides and pulled the hem of her skirt up her legs. Cupping her bottom, he rolled his hips against her.

"What are we doing?" she asked against his mouth.

"Making love," he told her. "Every time I think about how good it was between us that night..." He slid his hands beneath her silk panties and swallowed her gasp with his mouth.

Kate pulled her mouth away, turning her cheek to him. "I—uh—" Her cheeks blooming with color, she seemed to struggle for breath. "This feels kind of fast to me."

"This isn't the first time."

"I know, but—" She broke off and raked a hand through her hair. "That was before."

"Before what?"

"Before I knew about your anti-love policy." She sighed. "You won't understand this."

"Try me."

She stepped to the side, putting a little distance

between them. "Too many hairpin turns. First, I'm your assistant, then we're lovers for a night, then I'm your assistant again, then I'm pregnant, and I'm not your assistant, then you want to marry me." She met his gaze. "I need to catch my breath. It all feels a little unreal to me."

Michael looked at her and saw the conflicting emotions spilling from her. She was a complex creature. Knowing her as a woman, he thought, would be far different than having her as his assistant. She was a seductive mystery to him. The urge to possess her raged through him, but he reined it in. "Okay," he said, and told himself things would be different in two weeks. She would be his wife.

The following morning, Kate greeted the day with a trip to the bathroom for her regular bout of morning sickness. Her hands trembled as she turned on the water faucet to splash her face and drink water. She would be so glad when she got through this stage of pregnancy. Patting her hand over her flat tummy, she could almost think the baby was her imagination if not for her telltale nausea.

The night she'd shared with Michael could have been a dream. Her wedding, however, was coming at her with the speed of an oncoming train. Her mother had already called to chat about plans. Kate scowled into the mirror. Perhaps that had contributed to her nausea.

She opened the bathroom door to Michael. Surprised, she muffled a squeak. "When did you come in?"

"Long enough ago to know you're sick," he said, concern darkening his eyes. "I'll take you to the doctor."

She shook her head. "No. It's just morning sickness."

"Can't the doctor give you something?"

She shook her head more emphatically. "A lot of medicines aren't good for the baby. I don't want to risk it."

"How often does this happen?"

"This is how Cupcake wakes me up every morning," she said with a weak chuckle and headed for the kitchen.

His frown deepened. "How long will it last?"

"The doctor didn't offer any guarantees." She lifted crossed fingers. "But it could be gone in four weeks."

"Four weeks," he said appalled. "Are you sure you shouldn't see the doctor? I don't like the way you look."

She fought a wave of self-consciousness. "I could take offense at that, but since you helped get me into this state, you are partly responsible." She opened her cabinet and pulled out a half-empty box of soda crackers. "Besides, you could have called first or knocked. How did you get in anyway?"

"I picked your lock," he said. When she stared at him in inquiry, he added, "When you didn't answer, I thought I should check on you in case anything was wrong."

She felt him watch her set crackers, a glass of club soda, and a prenatal vitamin on the counter. "What is this?"

"Breakfast," she said and sat down on a bar stool to nibble at a cracker.

"This is no breakfast for a woman who's pregnant. You should be eating fruit or cereal, pancakes, eggs."

Kate blanched. "My objective is to eat something that will stay down," she said, then switched focus. "What brings you here so early?"

"Oh yeah," he said as if she'd reminded him. "I got something for you yesterday and forgot to give it to you last night."

Wary, she looked at him. "This isn't another financial recap or trust fund or—" She gulped when he placed a jeweler's box on the counter in front of her.

"No," he said. "You may need to get it sized, but the jeweler assured me he'd be happy to do it while you wait."

She stared at the box and struggled with a myriad of emotions. If she opened it, then her engagement to Michael would be more real, even though in her heart it still felt like a farce.

"Open it," he said.

Kate felt a lump rise in her throat.

"Kate, it won't bite. Okay, I'll open it," he said, flipping the box open.

Kate gasped at the size. "Omigod. It's so—" she blinked "—big." She looked up at him. "Why did you get such a big one?"

"I'm told that no matter what women say, size matters," he said, his gaze falling over her intimately. "With diamonds and other things."

Kate felt her cheeks heat. She would never forget that Michael had been an incredible lover. He had left her with the sensation of being thoroughly taken, yet incredibly satisfied. She resisted the urge to fan her cheeks and cleared her throat. "I was talking about the diamond in the ring."

"Do you think it's pretty?"

She moved her head in a circle. "In a big way."

"There are larger diamonds," Michael assured her.

"Yes, I saw the Hope Diamond at an exhibit once. I didn't think it looked that much bigger than this one."

"Kate, I can afford this. It's about the same as buying a forty-foot cabin cruiser. Let's put it on your finger and see if it fits."

Kate pulled her hands to her chest. "No."

"Why?" he asked, impatience edging into his tone.

"It's too big," she said. As if remembering her upbringing, she quickly added, "I mean I appreciate the thought and it's lovely, but I can't imagine wearing it."

He spun her stool around so she was nose to nose with him. "Why not?" he demanded.

She bit her lip and appeared so nervous he almost felt sorry for her. "I'm sorry, Michael, but I just can't imagine wearing a cabin cruiser on my finger."

He counted to ten. He couldn't explain why it was so important for Kate to wear his ring. He just knew it was. "If you don't like this, then what would you like?"

She slid her gaze to the ring, then back at him and lifted her shoulders. "I don't know. Something that doesn't scream *rich guy's wife*. Something more like me," she said in an unsteady voice. Her eyes turned sad. "Something that doesn't make me feel like a fraud."

That night Michael didn't visit Kate. Instead he called and they shared a muted, brief conversation. After such an inauspicious beginning to his day, he buried himself in his work and fell asleep when his head hit the pillow. The phone awakened him.

Rubbing the sleep from his eyes, he reached blindly for the receiver. "Yes," he murmured.

"Michael?"

The unsteady voice bore a vague resemblance to Kate's. "Kate?"

"I'm sorry to bother you so late," she said. "I would have called Donna, but she just went out of town on a business trip."

Michael's gut gave an uneasy twist. She sounded as if she were holding back tears. "Stop apologizing and tell me what's wrong."

"Well, I need a ride," she said. "I—uh—don't have my car."

He sat upright in bed. "Where are you?"

"The duplex beside me had a little gas problem."

Michael felt the cord of tension inside him knot. "Where are you?" he asked again, rising from bed and grabbing his jeans.

"There was a fire and there was a lot of smoke—"

"Kate, where are you?"

"At St. Albans General Hospital." Her voice cracked, and he felt something inside him crack too. "Could you come and get me?"

Four

Michael jerked on his clothes and defied the speed limit. He'd barely cut the engine before he stepped out of his car and raced into the emergency room. He approached the receptionist's desk, and Kate walked straight into his arms.

Unprepared for an action that demonstrated such pure trust, he stood still, stunned. It was a totally new sensation. She smelled of smoke. Instinct kicked in and he tightened his arms around her, wanting to make sure she was okay. "What happened?"

"There was a fire," she said, her face pressed into his shirt as if she wanted to absorb him. "Some of us suffered from smoke inhalation."

Alarm clanged through him like a discordant bell, and he urged her head from his chest. *"Us?"*

"They gave me oxygen," she said. She looked as if she were struggling to remain composed. "I was worried about the baby," she whispered, her face crumpling, the expression grabbing at something deep inside him.

Michael held his breath. "What did the doctor say?"

"The baby and I are fine."

Michael breathed a sigh of relief at the same time as he battled frustration. "Why didn't you call me?" he demanded.

"Everything happened so fast when the ambulance arrived, and then I had to wait. I was so scared," she said, her voice quivering. "I wasn't that worried about me. I just didn't want anything to happen to the baby. I tried to call Donna, but she was gone. I didn't want to bother you."

Michael tightened his arms around her again. "You should have called me. For Pete's sake, I'm going to be your husband," he scolded, thinking he could have prevented this if he'd been with her. He should have prevented this.

She pushed her hair from her face. "I know, but we don't really have a normal engagement."

"You're going to have to get used to calling me," he told her. "I may not know much about what husbands do, but I damn well know you call them in an emergency."

Staring at him as if some of his words were sinking in, she slowly nodded.

"I don't think they want me to go back to my house yet."

"Damn straight you're not going back to your house. You're coming to my apartment," he said emphatically.

"But I don't know where Parkay is and—"

"Parkay?" Michael struggled to follow her, wondering if, perhaps, the lack of oxygen had affected her brain.

"My cat. Parkay. She's not much of an outside cat, so I need to go look for her."

Michael shook his head. "It's the middle of the night. You can't go looking for a cat in your condition." His mind clicked through possibilities. "I'll take you home, then go look for her," he said, although how in hell he would find a cat at night was beyond him.

He took her home and settled her into his apartment. "Take my bed," he ordered, and when she started to protest, he cut her off. "You need the sleep. I'll take the couch after I get your cat."

So, at three o'clock in the morning, armed with an open can of tuna, Michael conducted a search-and-retrieval mission for Kate's cat. By three-thirty, he had seven feline friends trailing after him, mewing. But none was a calico. He sneaked past the yellow caution tape and in through the back door. Using his flashlight, he searched through two rooms until he caught sight of green eyes under Kate's bed. Parkay clawed him until he gave her a bite of the tuna.

After he returned home, he allowed the cat to finish the tuna while he washed his scratches. Unable to sleep after the events of the night, he quietly pushed open the bedroom door and looked at Kate.

Crossing his arms over his chest, he watched her for several moments. She could have been hurt much worse tonight, he thought, and the prospect disturbed the hell out of him. At the office, Kate had always been capable and strong. He knew she still was, but he had never seen her more vulnerable than tonight. Sure, she had a strong stubborn chin, a young, fit and wholly sensual body and an intelligent mind. But she also had a tender heart and at times she pushed herself too far and too hard. She believed the best of people, sometimes when she shouldn't. She'd believed the best of him.

His chest tightened.

She was too important to him. Too important to him to lose. Even if he didn't deserve her.

He had the crazy urge to build a wall of protection around her, but knew it was impossible. Still she had to be protected, and he was the man to do it.

Kate awakened the next morning to the sound of a cat purring. She opened her eyes to find Parkay curled in a ball next to her stomach. She smiled. Michael had found her. Stretching, she glanced around the sparsely furnished room and her gaze stopped on the nightstand. Salted crackers and soda. Her chest squeezed tight.

He had come for her last night. He had come through for her last night. She felt a softening inside her, a glimmer of hope. Then his words echoed through her mind, snuffing it out. *I don't believe in love.*

She sighed and sat up. She was in his bed, she realized, rubbing her fingers over the sheets. She had dreamed of sharing his life, sharing his bed. But not this way.

She tugged the sheet up to her nose and sneaked in a quick breath of his scent, then pushed crazy dreams aside and got out of bed. Glancing around the room, she looked for pictures on the wall and saw none. She looked for books. Still none.

Frowning, she pushed open the door and walked down the hall to the kitchen. The complete absence of Michael's personal expression throughout the house surprised her.

"Good morning," he said from behind her, making her jump. She whipped around to find him looking down at her. His gaze swept over her. "I like my shirt on you."

She tugged at the collar and crossed her arms over her chest, then dropped them to her sides. She rubbed her thighs together, all too aware of her bareness beneath his shirt. There was something just a little different about the way he was looking at her. His gaze held a tinge of possessiveness edged with tenderness. Kate blinked and the expression was gone.

"Thank you for coming for me last night and for giving up your bed. I was just looking around your apartment. Why aren't you at work?" she blurted out, unable to stifle her curiosity.

He waved his hand toward another room which held a desk, a raft of papers and a laptop. "I'm working from the laptop this morning. How are you?" he asked, and his gaze turned assessing.

"Fine. I'm great compared to last night. I'm sorry I was a little weepy." She smiled. "My stiff upper lip is back this morning."

"It's okay. I didn't break out in hives from your tears."

"True," she said, remembering how he had held her. She glanced at his hands and saw scratch marks. Wincing, she reached for one. "Parkay?"

He nodded. "She was under your bed and didn't want to come out."

"Ingrate," she said.

"Tuna helped, but I almost had to bring home a lot of her friends."

"Oh I bet you were popular with all the kitties." She released his hand and sighed. "How long have you been here? Did you move in recently?"

"Three years ago," he said with a shrug. "I've been busy."

"But there are no pictures, no plants. Do you have a CD player?"

"I think my alarm clock has a radio, but I kill plants."

She bit back a moan. "Michael, there's nothing of you here."

"Almost all of me has been at the office." He glanced at his watch. "Which is where I'm going now that I know you're okay." He backed away to turn off his computer and load it in his attaché. "Call me if you need anything."

Wondering if she'd made him uncomfortable with her questions, she joined him at the door. "Michael," she said, drawing his attention back to her.

He looked down at her, and she acted on an impulse. Standing on her toes, she kissed him lightly. "Thank you."

He slid his arm around her waist and gave her a deeper, hungry kiss. "Tonight."

He left and she leaned against the door, touching her lips as they buzzed. Her entire body buzzed. She covered her eyes and shook her head. "Get a grip."

She looked up, her gaze taking in her barren surroundings, and decided to make a few changes. By the time Michael arrived home tonight, his apartment would at least be more comfortable. It was the least she could do. The man had rescued her cat and been there when she called him.

Michael arrived home late that night to the sound of Santana gently playing on a boom box and the kitchen table set with new china and flatware. A pitcher in the center of the table held a small bunch of spring flowers. Candles had been lit and snuffed out, and he inhaled the mouthwatering scent of something Italian. He glanced in the refrigerator and spotted lasagne.

Michael blinked. His refrigerator usually only held stuff like beer and soda, occasionally juice and a few leftovers that resembled chemistry experiments gone bad. Lasagne.

Closing the door, he tugged at his tie and walked through the apartment in search of Kate. He found her asleep in his bed with a book folded over her stomach. Parkay lay at her feet.

She had waited for him, he realized. It was an odd feeling. He couldn't remember anyone waiting for him. A whispery sweet feeling snuck under his skin. Damn strange thing. He liked it and felt uncomfortable with it at the same time. Frowning, he dismissed the sensations and turned his attention back to Kate.

He carefully lifted the book from her stomach and set it on the nightstand. She rolled over onto her side, causing her nightshirt to gap slightly. The sight of her dusky nipple reminded him how she had felt in his hands, how she had tasted in his mouth. So incredibly responsive. He remembered how soft her inner thighs had felt when he'd coaxed them apart, and her femininity softer still as he'd slid inside her.

He wasn't exactly sure how she did it, but her combination of head and heart reminded him he was a man instead of a machine. She reminded him of needs and desires he'd made a habit of turning off like a faucet. He liked the way she looked in his bed, he thought, but he'd like it better still when they would share it. Soon.

The following morning, Kate rose early with the intention of getting back to her duplex. She'd spent the entire day yesterday trying to add small touches of comfort to Michael's apartment. She had so wanted to surprise and please him. Although he hadn't known she'd prepared a meal for him, she wished she had known he would be late so her feelings weren't so squashed.

As she nibbled a cracker and dressed, she told herself her feelings should not be hurt. If she kept repeating it, maybe she would believe it.

She took a deep breath as she left the bedroom and smelled coffee brewing. Michael was up and dressed already. No surprise, there, she thought with true envy. The man required far less sleep than normal humans, especially this pregnant human.

"I'm sorry I missed dinner," he said, glancing up from his coffee.

"No big deal. It was just a thank you for giving me and Parkay a place to land."

"You went to a lot of trouble. I think my refrigerator is in shock from having something other than beer and soda in it."

She felt a sliver of amusement. "I think both of you may be in shock. I hope you'll get a chance to enjoy it. You can reheat small portions of it in the microwave here or at the office. I appreciate you sharing your apartment, but I'll get out of your hair now. I'm going back to the duplex today to air it out, and I'm hoping it will be livable by tonight."

Michael frowned. "I don't think you should go back."

"The gas problem is repaired and I've been given the all-clear sign."

"Move in here," he said. "We're going to be married in less than two weeks."

Butterflies danced in her stomach at the thought. "My parents will be here in a few days, and my mother will want to be a part of the wedding planning. In fact I'm going to let her plan most of it. I still can't believe I'm doing this," she murmured.

"Why?"

"It's just not what I envisioned for myself."

"You didn't envision getting pregnant," he said.

"Not before the wedding," she said. "And not by my boss."

"What did you envision?"

Uncomfortable beneath his scrutiny, Kate glanced away. "I don't know. In my mind, I guess I thought I would date someone for a while, and there would be a courtship, and then he would propose." She shook her head. "You and I have it backwards. We haven't even been on a date. There's so much we don't know about each other. What if we get married and don't like each other?"

Hearing the frantic edge to her voice, Michael took her arms and looked into her eyes. "That's not going to happen. You're panicking, but you believe it's the right thing to do."

She moved her head in a circle. "Kinda."

"Kate..." he said, searching for a way to reason with her.

"I'm not sure how to explain this, but it's like a merger. Usually you learn everything about the company you're merging with, you court them and negotiate differences. But you and I, we're signing the contract first," Kate mused.

As far as Michael was concerned, the sooner they married, the better. "I know the best way to solve this."

"How?"

"You need to be sleeping with me."

Kate groaned. "That's what got me in trouble in the first place."

"So you can't get into any worse trouble now."

She shot him a dark look that alternated between sexy and wary. "That's a matter of opinion," she said and flounced toward the door. She stopped when she put her hand on the knob. "There is one other thing," she said, not turning to face him.

Her reluctance to look at him piqued his curiosity. "Yes?"

"I realize it will be a challenge, but when we're around my parents, you need to act like you're crazy about me. It will be hard, but if you use one-tenth of the energy and creativity you've used for your business, you might be able to pull it off."

Then she whisked out of the door, treating him to a tempting view of her curvy backside. Michael couldn't decide if he'd just been complimented or insulted. Perhaps both.

After work, he drove to her duplex and found her on a stepladder armed with a screwdriver while she worked on a curtain-rod bracket. Anyone else looking at her wouldn't have a clue that she was pregnant. Slim and curvy in shorts and tank top, she was barefoot, but her legs caught and held his attention. Until he thought about the nasty combination of the ladder and her pregnancy.

"Have you lost your mind?" he asked as calmly as he could.

He must have startled her because she let out a little shriek, then jumped and struggled for balance.

His heart hammering, he ran toward the ladder and wrapped his hands around her waist.

"Why did you do that?" she asked, scowling down at him. "You scared the living daylights out of me."

"Did you forget you're pregnant?"

"No," she said. "But as long as no one comes up behind me and disturbs me, I should be fine on the ladder."

"Let me finish," he insisted.

"It's not necessary," she protested.

"If you won't do it for yourself, then do it for Cupcake," he said, using her term of endearment.

She thought about it for a moment, then handed over the screwdriver. "Okay."

Michael swung her off the ladder to the ground, and climbed it. "Nice screwdriver. I'm surprised."

"Why?"

"Because you're a woman."

"That's sexist," she said. "Besides, there's an unwritten rule. Every woman should have a good screwdriver, a drill, and a black bra."

The screwdriver slipped in his hand, but he caught it. "And do you?" he asked. "Have all three?"

"Yes."

Michael was struck with the wicked wanton image of Kate in a black bra and not much else. He sucked in a quick breath and frowned at the odor. "Still smells like smoke."

"It was strong when I first got here, so I ran two fans on high and went out for a while. I must've gotten used to it this afternoon."

"You know I can't leave you here, don't you?" he asked, finishing the screws and descending the ladder.

"Why not?"

"Because if you got hurt, I couldn't live with myself."

Her eyes widened. She folded her arms over her chest. "I'll be fine."

"I would have thought you'd be fine two nights ago," he pointed out. "But you weren't. Any other climbing you planned tonight?"

"No," she said reluctantly. "If you keep acting nice and attentive, you're going to confuse me."

"If you get confused, does that mean you'll show me the big three?"

"Big three?" she echoed.

"Your screwdriver, your drill and your black bra."

Five

Surprised, Kate gave a double take. Her heart skipped a beat. "Are you serious?"

"Yes," he said, moving closer to her. "I'd like you to show me your big three."

Was he flirting with her? Michael didn't flirt with her. "The drill is in my toolbox."

"And the black bra?"

"Bottom dresser drawer," she said, wondering how far he was going to take this.

"I want to see it on you," he told her, sending a wicked rush through her.

"Maybe another time," she said.

He took her hand when she started to turn. "Is that a promise?"

She studied him. "What is with you?"

"It's time we left the boss-assistant relationship totally behind."

"And how do we do that?" she asked.

"I have some ideas," he said and pulled her into his arms.

He took her mouth in sensual exploration, quickly warming her from the inside out. "Every time I looked at you during the last three years, I said no. I'm not saying no to myself anymore."

His words surprised and aroused her. He felt solid, strong and distinctly masculine against her. He took her mouth again, this time with his tongue, seeking and seducing her, sipping at her as if she were his favorite drink, and he'd been thirsty for a long time.

"You smell like sex," he whispered.

Kate felt her knees lose their starch. His desire for her was intoxicating. She slid her fingers through his hair and rubbed her chest against his, craving a closer touch. The atmosphere in the room turned steamy. He slid his hands down to her bottom, guiding her against his hardened masculinity. Long denied needs rushed to the surface, and Kate fought against letting go. "I'm not sure about this," she asked.

"I'm just practicing," he said, skimming one of his hands over the side of her breasts. The movement teased and taunted.

Kate bit back a moan. "Practicing what?"

"Practicing for when we're married." He skimmed his hand over her breast again, this time closer to, but not touching her tight nipple.

Kate's moan escaped her throat.

"Do you like that?" he asked, rubbing his thumb over her nipple.

She pressed her breast into his hand, an unspoken confession.

"I'm going to find out what else you like," he said, and pulled her with him down onto the sofa. Pulling her onto his lap, he lifted her shirt and flicked his tongue over the tip of her breast.

Kate couldn't suppress another moan. When he unfastened the top button of her jeans, she put her hand on his. He was making her dizzy. "This feels fast."

"It could be faster," he said.

She shook her head and swallowed over her dry throat. She lifted her hand and was surprised to find it trembling.

Michael looked down at her hand and took it in his.

"It's going to sound crazy," she said, searching his gaze, "but when you said those things in your office the day I quit, a big part of me gave up on you."

"What are you afraid of?" he asked. "That I'll abandon you or stop supporting you? Because I won't. I—"

She shook her head. She couldn't tell him what

she feared. She had too many fears, and, unfortunately, she had every reason to believe they would come true. "I think I need some time. I think we need to take this slowly."

His gaze held hers for a heart-pounding moment. "Okay, we'll trade," he said. "We go slow, and you come back with me tonight."

Kate started to shake her head.

"This isn't negotiable," he told her. "You can pack or I'll pack for you."

"Why? I'll be fine."

"I'm here to make damn sure of it," he said. "You can either walk out of here or I'll carry you out to my car and let the neighbors stare when you scream. But I'm not leaving you here until your parents arrive."

She didn't like having her wings clipped. "I thought you said we were leaving the boss-assistant relationship behind."

"I'm just practicing to be your husband," he said in a maddeningly calm voice.

"I wish you would practice differently," she retorted.

"I will," he said, his tone dark with sensual promise.

"You're getting what?" Justin nearly shrieked as he slammed his mug of beer down.

"I'm getting married in less than two weeks, and you two are invited," Michael calmly said.

Dylan just stared at him for a long moment, then cleared his throat. "Isn't this a bit sudden?"

"Yes," Michael said, although he still preferred the idea of chartering an airplane to Las Vegas and taking care of the vows instantly. "It would have been sooner, but Kate's mother wants a church wedding."

"Why the speed?" Dylan asked, his eyes narrowed as if he sensed there was more to the story.

"Because there are no doubts," Michael said. Except on Kate's part. Michael was damned sure of what he was doing; he just wanted it done as quickly as possible.

"Kate?" Justin said in disapproval. "The only Kate you've ever mentioned is your assistant."

"She's no longer my assistant. She'll be my wife."

"Something about this doesn't smell right," Justin said with a frown. "I could have sworn you were just as anti-marriage as I am."

"Don't dig," Michael said in a level tone. "I just wanted to invite you to the ceremony. Kate's mother asked me to invite my family and I have none. You're the next best sorry thing, so if you want to come, great. If you don't, that's okay, too."

Justin exchanged an uncomfortable glance with Dylan. He shrugged. "Well, sure, I'll come. I just think you're making a big mistake. Marriage is a messy, expensive business. It sucks the life force out of your wallet like nothing else. Of course, kids are next in line for expensive, but—" Justin broke off as realization hit him. "Kids," he said, shaking his head. "You didn't—" He made a grimace. "Oh, damn. She's not—"

"Don't dig," Dylan cut in, correctly reading the closed expression Michael knew he was wearing. "What have you learned about the home for unwed teenage mothers?"

"It's a good cause. We should donate."

Justin took a swig of his beer and shook his head. "The irony is just too sweet."

A short while later, Michael entered his apartment. His conversation with his partners in philanthropy had left him irritated. The knowing expressions combined with the skepticism in their voices made something inside him twist. Michael wanted the marriage done. "Kate," he called, ready to complete the next step. "Kate, I have something for you."

Poking her head out the bedroom door, she regarded him warily. "What?"

"I brought you—" His phone rang, surprising him. It rarely rang unless someone was calling him from work. He picked up the receiver. "Hello."

A pause followed. "Kate Adams?" a male voice enquired.

Irritated at the intrusion, he frowned. "She's here," he said. "Who's calling?"

"Jeremy," the man said. "Jeremy Ridgway. We dated in college."

Michael thrust the phone at Kate. "Jeremy Ridgway. You've got thirty seconds to break his heart, or I'll help."

Kate's eyes widened. "Thirty seconds!"

"How did he get this number?" Michael asked with a scowl.

"Since I'm captive in your cave, I had my calls forwarded."

"Twenty seconds," Michael said.

Kate glared at him and turned her back to him. "Jeremy, it's been a long time. Yes, my living arrangements have changed," she said and paused. "Yes, you're right, I always enjoyed sailing, but—"

"Ten seconds," Michael murmured behind her.

"I can't. My significant other," she said, rolling her eyes at the term, "would object. Thanks anyway. Tell your sister I said hi. Take care. Bye now," she said and hung up the phone. She shot him a chilling glance. "Was that necessary?"

"Significant other?" he echoed, and ground his teeth.

Kate shifted from one foot to the other. "I was rushed. Nothing else seemed right."

Michael counted to ten. He couldn't remember a deal that had exasperated him more. Pulling the jeweler's box from his pocket, he flipped it open and took the phone from her hand at the same time he handed her the box.

Kate looked at the ring in complete silence. This time, however, he didn't see horror on her face. She took a deep breath and finally met his gaze. "It's beautiful."

He pulled the diamond solitaire surrounded by tiny pearls ring from the box. "Then you'll wear it."

She nibbled her lip. "I—uh—" She cocked her head to one side. "There's no rush. There's really no rush for the wedding. I mean, it's not as if I'm even showing."

His patience shot, Michael cut to the chase. "How do you plan to explain the baby's premature birth date to your parents?"

She sighed in resignation. "Okay. How did you know I would like pearls?"

"You used to wear pearl earrings to the office. You touched them a lot," he said, "as if you liked the way they felt."

Surprise, followed by a dark wary sensuality deepened her blue eyes. "I didn't know you noticed."

"I notice a lot of things," Michael told her and pushed the ring onto her finger. "It fits." He tugged her closer. "Seal it with a kiss," he said and took her mouth.

He inhaled her sexy scent and struggled with the craving to seal the moment with something far more than a kiss. Her lips were soft, lush and addicting. "Husband," he said against her mouth. "Say it."

"Fiancé," she corrected, pulling back slightly, but holding his gaze. Her reticence alternately aroused and frustrated him. "One step at a time."

Michael swallowed his impatience. It was better than *significant other*. "You can tell your mother two of my friends are coming to the wedding."

Her eyes widened. "Pardon?"

"Two of my—"

"—I didn't know you had any friends," she blurted out, then seemed to catch herself. "I mean you've always been so busy with work that you never seemed to have time for much in the way of personal relationships."

"We go way back. These two guys stayed at the Granger Home for Boys."

"Oh, well, can I meet them?"

"Sure," Michael said. "I told you they were coming to the wedding."

Kate's lips twitched. "I meant before the wedding."

"We'll see. Anything happen today that I should know about?"

"Not today," she said.

He lifted an eyebrow at her choice of words. "Tomorrow then?"

"I have an appointment with the obstetrician."

"Something wrong?"

She shook her head. "It's routine." She waved her hand. "It's a long shot, but last time the nurse told me I might be able to hear the baby's heartbeat at this appointment."

"What time?"

"Two o'clock at the Robinson Medical Center. Dr. Dent."

"I have a conference call with the new manager of R and D on the west coast."

"No problem," she said a little too casually. "You really don't need to be there."

Michael almost didn't make it. Although he rescheduled his teleconference, traffic and his latest clueless assistant conspired against him. He strode into the doctor's office at 2:20 and wangled his way into Kate's examination room.

Lying on the table with the doctor's stethoscope on her abdomen, Kate looked at Michael in surprise. "I thought you had a meeting."

"Rescheduled."

The doctor glanced up. "Dr. Dent," she said, introducing herself. "Are you the father?"

Michael felt a clench in his stomach at the question, but nodded. "Michael Hawkins."

"I'm trying to find your baby's heartbeat. It may be too early, but…" She moved the stethoscope and smiled, then turned up the volume on a small magnification device. "There it is."

Michael listened to the fast swishing sound and

his gaze met Kate's. Her eyes were filled with wonder.

"It's so fast," she whispered.

"It's in the normal range," the doctor said. "Sounds good and strong. Just one," she added with a smile.

Transfixed, Michael listened to the sound of the tiny heartbeat and felt something inside him click. Their child, he thought. Although he'd known it was real before, the only outward evidence Kate had exhibited had been morning sickness. The swishing heartbeat made it undeniable. A small somebody was totally dependent on him and Kate. He felt a velvet bond wrap around him.

The doctor removed the stethoscope, gave a few perfunctory instructions, and left. After Kate rearranged her clothing, she looked up at Michael and he saw the same awe-stricken sense of wonder and responsibility he felt mirrored in her eyes.

He pulled her into his arms and put his hand on her abdomen and kissed her. The emotion he felt was electric and too big, too powerful to be contained in a single moment. Kate covered his hand with hers and passionately responded to him. Michael felt a wholly primitive need to claim her as his again. "Doctor's office," he muttered to himself and pulled back.

"We could really mess this up if we're not careful," she said.

"We won't," he said, and he was deadly determined.

"How can you be sure?"

"I've got the money. You've got the heart."

Her eyebrows furrowed in concern. "If anything should ever happen to me..." she began.

"It won't," Michael said immediately, violently rejecting the notion. "I won't let it."

She smiled gently. "I didn't know you had final say over those things. Life and death happen, Michael," she told him. "If something happens to me, your money won't be enough. You'll have to grow a heart."

The very thought of it made Michael break into a sweat.

Time was ticking, and Kate felt her wedding date rushing toward her. Unable to bear the tension in Michael's apartment any longer, she decided to pay a visit to the home for unwed teenage mothers. She must have stuffed the paper describing the charity in her purse. Despite the fact that she wasn't a teenager and a marriage was in her near future, Kate felt a strong affinity for the group.

The home, which had been a small bed and breakfast hotel in the early 1900s, was located in the west end of town. The building reminded her of a genteel elderly lady, a bit worn, but clean and, in a way, elegant. The receptionist, Tina, who greeted her was six months pregnant and sixteen years old. "I'm sorry the director was called away. One of the girls went into labor. I can tell you a little about the place though."

"Please do," Kate said, seeing in Tina a maturity beyond her fresh-faced years.

"Everyone who comes here is drug-free and has pretty much been kicked out of home with no financial help. The home offers free counseling and medical care. An instructor comes five days a week and teaches us the basics. Everyone pitches in with cooking, cleaning and managing the office. We have a curfew, but since most of the fathers have disappeared, most of us aren't interested in dating right now," she said wryly.

"What happens to the babies?"

"Some girls put them up for adoption. Most don't, which is part of what our director, Ms. Lambert, is working on right now. A lot of girls don't want to give up the babies, but we don't have good job skills. Ms. Lambert has been looking for someone to teach us computer stuff, but volunteers are tough to find because those people really rake in the bucks."

It was strange, but Kate felt more at home here than she did in Michael's apartment. She would be bored out of her gourd if all she did was spend her days shopping and house-hunting. "I think I may know someone who can help," she said. "What kind of computers do you have?"

Tina wrinkled her nose. "One computer," she

said, pointing to an ancient machine in the back office.

Kate glanced at it and sighed. "A little younger than the house, huh?"

Tina laughed.

"Well, we have no place to go but up."

Kate left the home, stopped by a computer discount store, and purchased two machines. She spent the afternoon and evening setting them up at her old duplex. She craved the familiarity and since her lease wasn't up, there was technically no reason she couldn't visit the place every now and then.

A knock sounded at the door just before it opened. She glanced up to see Michael. He looked at the two computers. "What are you doing?"

"Setting up two computers I bought today."

"But you already have a computer and a laptop." He walked closer. "This doesn't have the best name-brand processor."

"Don't be snooty," she warned him. "This processor may not be a designer brand, but it'll do the job. It's fast. I'm donating Claire and Delores to the home for unwed teenage mothers because the one computer they have must have been donated by the pilgrims. I visited the home today; they need a computer teacher, and I am now it."

"Claire and Delores," he muttered. "I never understood your propensity for naming machines."

"It keeps me from smashing them to pieces when they crash."

"Why didn't you bring them to my apartment?"

"I don't like your apartment," she said and felt him staring from behind her. The tension which had drained from her began to seep in again.

"Why?"

"It's bare," she said. "There are no plants or pictures. No memorabilia. It doesn't tell anything about you."

"I wasn't aware that was a requirement," he said dryly. "I don't have a lot of cute pictures of me from my childhood."

Kate felt a pang at the thought of Michael's lost childhood, but the hour was late and his proximity made her itchy. "Why is that?" she asked. "Were you an ugly child?"

He gave a double take, then chuckled. "I'm sure that's a matter of opinion. Redecorate it?"

"No. Because then it would be my apartment instead of our apartment," she said as she installed the last program on the computer. "I need to know your preferences, your favorite colors, what kind of art you like, what things make you feel good and comfortable—besides chocolate chip cookies," she said remembering his penchant for stealing them when she'd brought a few to the office.

He gently guided her chin around. "I like blue. I don't like art that I can't figure out. I like lots of windows and I don't like heavy draperies. I like comfortable furniture. I like plants and flowers that I can't kill. And I like you," he told her with topaz eyes that made seductive promises she knew he could deliver, "in my bed."

Six

Kate delivered Delores and Claire to the home for unwed teenage mothers the following day and was impressed with the director. Unable to bear the terminal beige decor of Michael's apartment, she picked up a few more things to add some color. She kept herself busy for fear of a flat-out panic attack as the wedding date drew nearer.

Although Kate had never thought of herself as helpless, she couldn't help feeling like a mouse with Michael as the sleek, savvy cat. She'd watched him negotiate mergers and while he'd always made the companies he acquired feel good, they still ended up being eaten. His forceful masculinity drew her in at the same time she felt the need to protect herself from it. It was enough to interrupt her sleep knowing he was nearby and wanted her.

Another day passed, and Kate's parents called to remind her they would be coming tomorrow. On edge, she received a curious call that afternoon from the home for unwed teenage mothers. Just when she'd thought Michael's blood ran green for dollars instead of red, he proved her wrong.

Michael arrived home at close to eight o'clock. He'd buried himself in work. Knowing Kate was in his bed filled him with visions that left him in a state of permanent arousal. Michael had a strong understanding of timing and negotiations, and he knew he'd pushed Kate into the marriage. Pushing her into making love with him before the ceremony might put his ultimate goal of marriage at risk. This situation reminded him of nitroglycerin and he refused to upset the precarious balance. Rocking her already emotional boat by pushing her into bed with him could make her run in the wrong direction—away from him. He mentally understood and believed all of this, but his libido and need to possess her taunted him relentlessly.

The scent of a delicious home-cooked meal and chocolate chip cookies greeted him when he opened the door. "Oh, God," he said. "I've died and gone to heaven."

"Welcome," she said and regarded him with a smile that made him wonder what inspired it. She wore a little skirt that captured and held his attention. Kate had great legs, he thought again. Slim ankles, curvy calves, and silky thighs, and in between them, he remembered, her femininity forming a wet, snug, velvet welcome to him.

Michael grew hard and stifled a sigh. He loosened his collar. "What's the occasion?"

"Farewell dinner," she said.

Everything inside him stopped. "What?"

"My parents are descending tomorrow," she said with a lopsided smile.

Michael relaxed slightly.

"Do you like beef stew?"

"Yes." Michael watched the mind-bending swing of her hips as she walked toward the counter. The scent of delicious food and the sight of her delicious backside combined to form the opposing sensations of complete satisfaction and complete frustration. Soon, he promised himself, he would be consuming more than Kate's food.

After they shared the meal, he sat back replete. Kate shooed away his offer to help remove the dishes. She took care of them quickly, then leveled a gaze on him.

He felt an odd sensation in his gut at the intent expression in her eyes. She looked like a woman with a mission as she walked toward him.

"I think I need to pass on a thank you."

He frowned. "What do you mean?"

"I mean the home for unwed teenage mothers called to thank me for the twenty computers that arrived today along with a quarter-million-dollar donation."

Michael shrugged. "What does that have to do with me?"

"I believe you," she said, pointing her index finger at his chest, "are responsible."

Her blue eyes searched his. "I had just told you about the home's needs and the following day the computers and funds arrive. Too much of a coincidence."

"I'm sure the home's been begging for help from everyone. Any number of people could have chosen them for a tax write-off."

Impatience flashed in her eyes. "I'm not going to let you reduce this to a tax write-off."

"I can't take responsibility for this," Michael said, thinking of the oath of secrecy he and his friends had taken.

Confusion furrowed her brow. "Are you saying you had nothing to do with the recent donations?"

"I'm not personally responsible," he said carefully.

"And if you were somehow involved, your complete motivation would have been for the tax write-off," she said, clearly frustrated with his reticence. "Okay, well just in case you know someone who was partly responsible, I'd like you to give them a message.'' She leaned her slim sexy body into his and pressed her lips to his mouth. ''Tell him I said it was very nice.'' She brushed her lips back and forth over his. ''Tell him I said thank you.''

Kate opened her mouth and Michael felt as if she'd set his clothes on fire. She rubbed her wicked open mouth over his, darting her tongue out to taste him until his brain went into complete meltdown.

Michael took over the kiss, devouring her mouth the way he wanted to consume all of her. She tasted like chocolate chip cookies and her body held the promise of pure satisfaction. His blood racing through his bloodstream, he ran his hands down her sides to her bottom and drew her into the cradle of his thighs.

She wriggled slightly against him and a groan escaped his throat. Sliding his fingertips beneath her panties, he touched her silky bare skin.

She pulled his tie loose and tugged at his shirt buttons, and it dimly occurred to him that if this was how Kate reacted to a charitable donation, he might become the biggest philanthropist in St. Albans.

He pulled her shirt loose, then backed down onto the sofa and urged her down on his lap. The sight of her breasts swelling over the cups of her lace bra reminded him how responsive she'd been the night they'd shared together, how she'd held back nothing.

Needs denied roared through him like a freight train. He lowered his mouth to her breasts and nuzzled her bra down to taste her nipple. He heard her swift intake of breath as she grew taut in his mouth. He slid his hand upward between her thighs and felt her damp and swollen. The sensation only made him more hungry for her.

He wanted all barriers removed between them. He wanted her naked and straddling him. He wanted to fill her as she pumped him into oblivion. Michael ripped her panties and rubbed his thumb over her tender engorged bead of sensation. Her breath came in short gasps. He could feel her nearing the precipice, and the sound was excruciatingly arousing to him. Closer. Closer.

The phone rang. Once, twice, penetrating the thick, steamy intimacy surrounding them. Kate pulled back slightly, her cheeks flushed, the pupils of her eyes large with arousal, her lips swollen. She stared at him while the phone rang as if she knew one of them should be answering it, but she couldn't coordinate her mind and body. "Can you get that?" she finally asked in a husky whisper.

His body still clamoring for release, he gently put her to the side and rose to answer the phone. "Hello," he said, and struggled to take in the words accompanying the voice of Kate's mother. He handed the receiver to Kate.

She met his gaze with a woman's need in her eyes so powerful it made him want to toss the phone out the window. But she bit her lip, and looked away, covering her eyes with her hand. He heard her make a few soft comments, but she kept the call blessedly short. She pushed the Off button and looked up at him, her expression a mixture of too many emotions for him to read. "My parents are here early. They're waiting at my house."

Although her legs felt like butter, she forced them to move. She stood and her partially ripped panties slid to the floor. Her head spun. They had been so close. Kate swallowed over a strange lump of emotion in her throat and tried to walk forward. Her knees buckled.

Michael caught her and pulled her against him. "Are you okay?"

Tears threatened, followed by a curtain of embarrassment. "I will be. I just—" She took a quick breath. "I was really—"

"So was I," he said in a rough voice that did serious damage to her already shattered nerve endings. "It's only a week," he said, but sounded as if he were reminding himself. "I'll take you home."

"I can take myself."

"If you're having a tough time walking, I sure as hell don't want you driving," he said bluntly, leaving her with no argument.

On trembling legs, she made her way to the bathroom and pulled herself together. Since most of her things were still at her house, she only needed to pack a few toiletries. They left the apartment and Kate sat beside Michael with her eyes closed.

Drinking in the heady scent of his aftershave, she felt a visceral response to him. She could have abandoned herself to him. She could have given herself to him again and again, and she had no clue how to hold back her heart and keep it safe. She knew she could give herself to Michael in a way that would change her forever. She also knew, however, that Michael would never give himself to her in the same way.

When Michael pulled into her driveway, Kate's parents rushed out of their motor home to greet them. Her mom swept her into her arms. "I'm so happy, darling," she said, her voice swollen with threatening tears. "I've been dreaming of your wedding since you were born."

Kate's heart constricted. "I know you have, Mom."

Her father pumped Michael's hand. "Congratulations, son. You've got a jewel, but I'm sure you already know that."

The pretense of the situation turned her stomach. How was she going to survive a week of this? Kate closed her eyes and gave her mother an extra squeeze.

"I'll let the three of you visit awhile. I'm sure you're tired from traveling and Kate's been working on moving, so she's beat too."

"You don't have to leave," Kate's mother protested.

Michael shook his head. "I don't want to keep you up." He met Kate's gaze and reached for her hand. "You need some rest," he told her, pulling her toward him. He lowered his head and kissed her, sending her heart into a staccato rhythm.

"What are you doing?" she whispered in his ear as he held her.

He nuzzled her neck. "You asked me to act like I'm crazy for you in front of your parents. How am I doing?"

The next few days were a whirlwind of pre-wedding activity driven by the indomitable force of her mother. Kate's waking hours held the quality of a circus carnival. During the days, she was so busy trying to convince her parents that everything was peachy that she didn't have time to think until night. Alone in her bed, she thought about what would happen after the wedding. Would she and Michael be able to build something lasting when only one of them believed in love?

Shoving the thought aside, she joined her mother

on a mission to collect childhood pictures of Michael.

"It wouldn't look right for us to have pictures of you when you were a child at the reception and not have any of Michael," her mother insisted. "I know he was a foster child, but somebody somewhere must have some pictures of him."

The two of them paid a visit to the Granger Home for Boys. Kate took in the large dark foyer and tried to imagine what Michael's life had been like. The windows, she noticed, were shrouded in heavy draperies, and the floors were dark wood. It looked like the kind of place that would be drafty in the winter, and despite the cleanliness and strength of the surroundings, she could almost smell the scent of hopelessness and desperation.

Wrinkling her brow, she peeked into the office. "Hello? Can you help us?"

A young blond woman with startlingly green eyes standing in front of a desk glanced up. She looked from Kate to her mother. "I don't know. I think everyone's gone to lunch. I don't work here, but I guess you could say I'm familiar with the lay of the land. My mother used to manage the cafeteria, so I spent many of my growing-up years here."

"We'd like some pictures," Kate's mother said. "My daughter is marrying one of the former residents, Michael Hawkins—"

"Michael!" the woman exclaimed, and her face

broke into a smile. "Michael is getting married? I'm stunned."

No more than Kate was.

"Congratulations," she said. "He was a fine person when I knew him." She extended her hand. "I'm Alisa Jennings. I just moved back to the area and was taking a little visit down memory lane."

Kate shook her hand, liking the young woman immediately. "Kate Adams, and this is my mother Betty."

"You want pictures. Try this," she said, walking behind the desk to a file room. "I bet they still keep them in the same place. Yes," she muttered, as she surveyed the tall cabinets. "They haven't changed the labels."

"Should we be in here?" Betty asked.

"Probably not, but we can claim special dispensation if anyone fusses." Alisa pulled open a drawer and grabbed a file. "Here's Michael," she said, peeking inside the file, then handing it to Kate. "They're mostly black and white."

Kate opened the file and looked into a pair of grown-up eyes in a very young boy. Her heart wrenched. He looked thin, but sturdy, with hair a tad too long, clothes that didn't fit exactly right, but the set of his chin showed pride and determination.

"How serious," her mother murmured, looking over Kate's shoulder.

Kate flipped through the pictures, seeing signs

of the man she knew in the growing boy. The last picture was out of order. It showed Michael around five years old, dressed in Sunday clothes and his hair painstakingly combed. He stood in the circle of his mother's arms. Dark shadows rimmed her eyes, but she and her son wore matching smiles.

He had lost so much at such a young age. A tear slid down Kate's cheek, surprising her. Quickly swiping it aside, she glanced up. "Is there somewhere we could make copies?"

Alisa slid a glance toward the door. "There used to be a copy shop just down the street."

Kate didn't pause. "Thank you," she said, and her mother joined her. Betty filled the silence with chatter about the wedding plans as they located the shop and waited. Kate nodded, but couldn't have repeated a word. She was steeped in thoughts of Michael and what his childhood had been like. She would have had to have been made of stone not to be moved by the pictures. Every time she looked at a picture, she bit her lip at the sharp emotions that stabbed at her.

When the clerk finished the job, Betty reached for the copies, but Kate intercepted them. "I choose," Kate said.

Betty frowned. "But—"

"I choose or none of them is displayed," Kate said.

Betty appeared to take in Kate's determined expression. "You've got the same look in your eye you had when you told your dad and me you were moving to St. Albans.'' She sighed. ''There's no fighting you when you're like this. Will you consider the baby picture at least?''

Kate smiled. Tucked between some papers, they'd found a baby picture of Michael. ''Yes, but the rest is my choice.'' She felt as if she'd stepped into a secret part of Michael's life, a part filled with pain and vulnerability, and Kate was compelled to protect him. It was incredibly odd because if ever a man indicated that he didn't need protection, it was Michael.

They encountered Alisa Jennings just outside the main hall. ''Oops, there you are. The secretary is back, so maybe you should let me return those for you.''

''Thank you,'' Kate said and meant it.

''No problem,'' she said and turned, then stopped and turned back around. ''The thing I remember about Michael was what he did with his cookies.'' She smiled. ''My mom made the best chocolate chip cookies. Unfortunately, there never seemed to be enough to go around. Whenever she made them, the boys could smell them and they'd race because the ones at the front of the line were more likely to get cookies. There was a boy named Harold Grimley who wore braces on his legs and he never made it to the front of the line. But Harold always got cookies because Michael gave his to Harold. I bet Michael's a tough nut to crack, but he's a special guy." She pulled a business card from her pocket. "Here's my card if you ever need a liaison with the Granger Home again."

Kate watched Alisa leave. Another tear slid down her cheek. She brushed it aside and heard her mother sniff. "C'mon Mom," she said, pulling herself together and telling herself she would sort all this out later. "You've managed the impossible again. You got the pictures."

Despite Kate's protests, Betty insisted on a brief rehearsal at the chapel. This was the first time she'd been with Michael for more than a few moments, and seeing his pictures had shaken something inside her.

"You look pale," he said, brushing her lips with a kiss. Her heart sped up. This was for the benefit of her parents, she reminded herself.

"I'm fine. The last few days have been challenging," she said, wanting more than ever to sink into his strength.

"You're taking care of yourself," he said, more as an order than a question.

She nodded.

"Your father is angry with me," he told her.

"Why?"

"I wouldn't let him pay for the rehearsal party."

Kate smiled. "Ah, you attacked his masculinity."

Michael scowled. "I was trying to protect his

wallet." He glanced across the room and nodded. "Here are the friends I mentioned to you."

Kate took in the two men as they stepped closer. Both wore guarded, assessing expressions. "Kate Adams, meet two of the most successful alumni of the Granger Home for Boys, Justin Langdon and Dylan Barrow."

Justin and Dylan gave Michael sideways glances, then turned their attention to Kate. Justin extended his hand. "Michael's a catch since he hit the big time. Best wishes."

It took a moment for his message to sink in. Justin clearly felt protective of Michael. He probably thought she was a gold digger. Kate smiled broadly. "You mean since he hit eight figures."

Justin watched her carefully. "That's the bottom line, isn't it?"

Kate sighed. Now she understood why Michael had harped on the money angle. "Just between you and me, I'm not marrying Michael for his millions," she whispered. "I'm marrying him for his potential."

Justin wrinkled his brow in confusion. "Financial potential?"

Kate shook her head. "No. This is related to cookies."

He looked at her as if she were crazy and she decided that was okay. She turned to Dylan. "It's a pleasure to meet you. It means a lot for you to be here for him."

Dylan shook her hand and kissed her cheek. "Our honor," he said and won her heart.

"I ran into someone the three of you might know. I happened to be over near the Granger Home and met a woman named Alisa Jennings."

"Alisa," Dylan said, his expression growing intense. "What was she doing?"

"Just paying a little visit to the home. She told me she grew up there. Her mother was the cafeteria manager."

"The cookie girl," Justin said. "She used to sneak cookies to us when we had to shovel snow."

"What were you doing at Granger?" Michael asked quietly.

Too quietly, Kate thought and felt her nerves shake. "Showing Mom the town. Alisa was lovely. She said she'd just moved back here."

"I thought she was engaged to a politician in Connecticut," Justin said, then glanced at Dylan. "Didn't she have a crush on you?"

"Long time ago," Dylan said, but Kate got the distinct impression there was more beneath the surface.

Kate's mother clapped her hands together. "Time for the rehearsal. Kate, you go to the back of the chapel, and Michael, come up front. Where's your bridesmaid, Donna?"

"Right here," Donna said, rushing in the door. "Sorry I'm late." She stood beside Kate while Betty issued instructions. "I kept thinking you would come to your senses and cancel," she whispered.

"Get thee behind me, Satan," Kate muttered, unable to dodge the enormity of what she was about to do.

"Are you sure you want to do this?" Donna asked, concern shadowing her baby face. "You can still back out."

"It's not a matter of being sure in the traditional sense. It's more a matter of trying to make the best choice in an imperfect situation."

"What a practical attitude. I wonder if the wives of Henry VIII said the same kind of thing," Donna said slyly.

Kate frowned at her friend. "Michael may be arrogant, but he doesn't have a guillotine in the basement. Besides, you're my maid of honor, so you're supposed to be supporting me, not encouraging me to run away."

"I'll encourage you," she promised. "I'm taking you out on the town after the rehearsal party."

"You know I can't drink."

"You can't drink, but you can dance," she said with a sweet smile that brought to mind discarded halos.

"Time for the maid of honor," her mother said.

Kate swallowed a strangled sound of panic as her father approached her. Donna gave her arm a squeeze and silently mouthed the words, *You can still escape.*

"Here you go, baby," Tom Adams said, offering his arm.

It's still just practice, Kate repeated to herself as she slowly walked up the aisle. She looked into Michael's eyes and took a deep breath. It would be okay, she told herself. It had to be.

"Dearly beloved," the minister began, but Kate was too aware of Michael by her side to hear anything else. Her father kissed her cheek and left, then Michael enveloped her hand in his.

"After you repeat your vows, I'll say you may now kiss the bride and present you—"

Michael swooped down and kissed her. Chuckles followed. "You looked like you were about to faint," he told her, concern darkening his eyes. "We should have gone to Vegas."

After the small rehearsal party at a local hotel where Kate faked drinking the champagne and smiled through the toasts, Donna whisked her away to a noisy, crowded nightspot.

"Refresh my memory," Kate said. "Why are we here?"

"This is your last night as a single woman. We're here to tear the house down. Your assignment is to dance with at least twenty-five men."

"Twenty-five!"

Ignoring Kate's protests, Donna glanced around and crooked her finger at a man across the room.

"It will make you forget what a huge mistake you're making. Here's number one."

So Kate took to the dance floor and shook and shimmied to everything from disco to rap. Donna was right about one thing. The whole exercise was wonderfully mind-numbing. Around number twenty-one however, physical reality began to intrude. Pregnancy had not made her more energetic, and what Kate really wanted was a cot.

She'd successfully avoided the slow dances, but when a romantic song by Savage Garden began to play, she was tugged into a familiar pair of arms. Kate glanced up at Michael. Her heart leaped. "What are you doing here?"

"Looking out for your welfare," Michael said in a dark voice. "Will Donna have you dancing on tabletops soon?"

"She's trying to cheer me up."

Michael dipped his forehead against hers and slid his hand dangerously low on her hip. "Are you saying you're not ecstatic to be marrying me tomorrow?" he asked in a velvet voice that indicated his ego wasn't suffering in the least.

"Your friend thinks I'm marrying you for your money," she said, annoyed with her attraction to him. She had always been drawn to him when he looked like this, shirt collar unbuttoned, tie loosened, and hair slightly mussed. Too touchable.

"Justin," Michael said. "He believes marriage

is the giant sucking sound in many men's bank accounts. He'll never get married."

"That's what you said," Kate reminded him.

"I had other reasons," he said, backing her into a corner and skimming his lips over her neck. "You don't look pregnant," he murmured. "There's something about me knowing it while no other man in the room has a clue that makes me want you. It's our little secret," he said, nudging her mouth up to his and sucking at her lips while his lower body undulated against hers.

Despite her weariness, Kate felt a shot of pure heat. The tips of her breasts grew sensitive to the brush of his chest against her. "Why are you trying to seduce me?"

"It feels a helluva lot better than that blasted wedding rehearsal did. I'm taking you out of here," he growled and she was too tired to protest when he led her to his car. Kate waved to Donna on her way out the door.

Michael helped her into the car, then slid into the driver's side and closed the door. He immediately backed his seat away from the steering wheel and pulled her onto his lap.

Surprised, Kate blinked at him. "What is this?"

His eyes looked dark and dangerous. He lifted his hand to her head and slipped his fingers through her hair. "I know what's been running through your mind since the rehearsal."

Kate fought a rush of nerves. The man could not

read her mind, she told herself. "What do you mean?"

"You've been reviewing all the reasons not to marry me." He released her hair and slid his hand down to cup her chin and rub his finger over her mouth. "Over and over, you've been thinking of all the things that make you nervous about me."

"You don't make me nervous," she denied, disliking him for nailing her feelings so accurately.

He leaned close enough to kiss her, close enough to rattle her nerves even further. He found her pulse in her neck with his index finger, then spoke against her lips, "You're lying. If you keep thinking that way, there's no way you'll make it through the wedding tomorrow. You've been wallowing in all the bad stuff. Now it's time for you to think about the good stuff."

"What good stuff?" she asked, still peeved that he'd cornered her.

"There must be something you like about me, or you wouldn't have continued to work as my assistant."

"You pay well."

He widened the gap between his legs and leaned back slightly, reminding her of his sexuality. "Correction. There must be something you like about me or you wouldn't have made love to me like a firestorm two and a half months ago. You said you cared about me, remember?"

Weary and edgy, she looked away and remained

mute. She didn't want to contemplate the things about Michael that she found so compelling. She wanted to keep a clear head, and that wasn't easy sitting on his lap.

"Okay," he said, leaning his head back against the head rest. "I can wait all night."

"This is ridiculous," she said. "We both need to get our sleep. Tomorrow is going to be a big day."

"So give me your list," he said in a patient tone that grated on her because her insides were the exact polar opposite of patience.

Kate sighed. "This is crazy."

"Call me crazy, then tell me ten things about me that make you want me."

"Ten!"

"Twenty," he said, ever the negotiator.

"You haven't given me a list of ten things you like about me. Why should I give you a list of ten things I like about you?"

"Because you have cold feet. I don't."

"You are a major pain."

"That doesn't count," he said, the corner of his mouth lifting in an almost-grin that was entirely too sexy.

"Okay," she said. "I like your eyelashes. I like it when you unbutton your shirt and loosen your tie. I like how protective you are of the company. I like it that you made a donation to the unwed teenage mother's home even though you don't want to admit it to me. I like it and don't like it when you look at me like I'm the only other person in the world. You overdo it,'' she warned him, ''but I like it that you're protective of Cupcake. I like it when you whisper in my ear and tell me secrets about you. I like it when you stop using your mouth to tell me about your financial statement and kiss me.''

His eyes were dark, intent and seductive. He sat there projecting cool, but his gaze was watchful. ''That's only eight.''

Kate looked into his topaz eyes and felt as if she were taking a free fall. Having Michael's intently undivided attention for these moments was more potent than three triple margaritas.

Unable to resist a chance to get under his skin, she leaned closer to him. ''Most of all though, what I really like is your great big sexy—''

Seven

Michael's eyes watched her the same way a tiger's would just before he pounced. "Yes?" he prompted.

"Your great big sexy brain," she told him boldly.

His lips twitched. "I wasn't expecting that," he said.

"I'm sure you weren't," she said wryly. "Even though I don't agree with all your thoughts," she quickly added, lest his head grow too large to fit in the car, "I have always been fascinated by the way you think."

He rubbed his index finger over her ring finger,

over the ring he'd bought her, then twined his fingers through hers. The gesture was oddly sensual and made her feel warm all over.

"And number ten?" he prompted.

Kate thought about the other big reason that made her want Michael and decided to keep that stored in her heart. "Number ten is a secret."

He pulled her mouth to his and took her lips in a kiss that knocked the breath out of her. "That's not satisfactory."

She shook her head to clear it. "Sorry, Mr. Boss, you have a bunch of secrets. Number ten is my little secret."

"I'm going to know all your secrets, Kate," he told her pressing his mouth to her throat. "But tomorrow when you're walking down the aisle, and you're starting to wonder and doubt, think about reason number nine. Think about reason number ten."

She shuddered at the sensation he aroused in her. He slid one of his hands above her knee and traced the skin of her thigh with his fingers.

"I'll know what makes you so hot you burn," he said, kissing her jaw while his hand drew dangerously close to the tops of her thighs. "Do you have any idea what it does to me to watch you dance?" he asked. "To have you on my lap and feel your skin?"

"What?" she asked, needing to know that she

affected him at least half as much as he affected her.

But Michael didn't use words. He used his mouth on hers. Taking her lips in a sensual, yet carnal kiss, he sent a thousand yearnings through her body. He made love to her mouth with his, tasting her, taking her. She could feel his heat, his rising excitement, and an edgy wanting clamored inside her.

He skimmed his hand beneath her blouse to the outer edge of her breast, tempting, but not taking. His thumb glanced near her nipple. His other hand edged beneath the silk of her panties. His fingers stroked her where she was swollen for him.

He swore under his breath. "I want you," he said. "I want to take you right now in the car."

The urgency in his voice sent an echo of need slamming through her bloodstream. "If you weren't pregnant, I would," he told her, and took her mouth again.

He stroked her femininity as if it were the petals of a rose, and Kate had the wicked urge to strip off her clothes and do her own share of taking. But Michael was turning her to pure liquid beneath his hands and mouth. It was as if since he couldn't take her one way, he would claim her in another. Gently, he slid his finger inside her.

Kate moaned, feeling the urgency inside her turn into a coil of frenzy.

"Tomorrow will be different," he promised.

"Tomorrow I will touch and taste every part of you. Tomorrow," he said, his voice dark with desire and something more, "you won't wonder anymore."

Kate felt the ripple of release rip through her, leaving her breathless.

Michael swore under his breath. "You have no idea how sexy you are, no idea how much I want you. And tomorrow," he promised, his eyes shining with topaz determination, "you'll be mine."

In a small room off to the side of the chapel's sanctuary, Michael adjusted his tie. The dark wooden room held a wall of reference books, a small table and chairs, a kneeling bench and a window. The kneeling bench was obviously for people who prayed, and Michael hadn't ever been big on praying. Instead, he stared out at the late spring morning. Although he was calm, he felt the faintest edge of discomfort. It wasn't nerves, more a feeling a claustrophobia. Accustomed to being alone, he took his privacy for granted, but lately his solitude had been breached. Between Kate's well-intentioned but ever-present parents, her cat, her friends and calls from ex-boyfriends, his privacy had been invaded.

In an odd way, his aloneness had grown reassuring to Michael. It meant he could make it alone, that he didn't need anyone else to survive. That was vital to him. He wasn't sure how he would keep himself centered in his solitude once he married Kate, but it was a requirement.

The door behind him opened.

"Michael...?"

Michael turned to face his prospective father-in-law, also dressed in a black tux. Tom Adams was a big, barrel-chested man with an affable air and shrewd eyes. "If this is about the bar bill from last night, I've already covered it and don't want to be reimbursed."

Tom chuckled and shook his head. "No." He gave Michael a measuring glance and his expression sobered. "There are some things a father discusses with his son on his wedding day. Since your father isn't around, I thought I'd step in."

A tinge of the bitterness he'd avoided his entire life sneaked through his blood. "I've done fine without my father's presence in my life."

Tom raised his eyebrows and nodded slowly as if he knew some secret that Michael didn't. "Maybe," he said. "But you're taking a big step today, and you're taking it with my daughter. If you mistreat her, I don't care how many millions you have, there'll be hell to pay."

"I won't mistreat Kate. I'll take care of her."

Tom shot him a wry look. "Good luck. She's got an independent streak a mile wide. But that's another subject. What I want to tell you is something very basic. The common belief about marriage is that it's a fifty-fifty proposition. I'm here to tell you that's a myth. If you go into this with the idea that you'll give fifty percent and Kate will give fifty percent, you'll fall far short of one hundred. I've been married for a lot of years to a fine woman, but I'm telling you, Michael, when it comes to giving in a marriage, it takes one hundred and ten percent.''

Michael often thought in terms of negotiation, so he balked at the idea of giving up that much of anything right off the bat. ''I don't doubt your experience, Mr. Adams, but if you add fifty and fifty, you get one hundred. That would seem more than enough for me.''

Mr. Adams gave him a pitying glance. ''It's a strange rule, son, but anything under a hundred will get you in the doghouse. You give a hundred and ten and your return will double.''

A knock sounded on the door and Justin Langdon rushed in pulling at his collar. ''The preacher said it's about time to roll.'' He nodded toward Kate's father. ''Mr. Adams.''

Tom gave Michael one last hard look. ''Remember what I said.''

''One hundred and ten percent,'' Michael said, out of respect.

Tom shook his head. ''No, remember…there'll be hell to pay,'' he said and left the room.

Justin glanced at Michael. ''Daddy didn't look happy. Does he know you knocked up his little girl?''

"No," Michael said, "and he's not going to know either because that would be unconfirmed information. Right, Justin?"

Justin sighed. "Yeah. You sure you don't want to back out? There's still time."

"I'm not backing out."

"Nagging wife, screaming kid," Justin said.

"Regular sex and saving a kid from my childhood."

Justin grew thoughtful. "Okay, but you did get her to sign a pre-nup, didn't you?"

Silence followed. Alarm crossed Justin's face. "Man, tell me you got her to sign a pre-nup."

"Justin, I'm going into this with my head and instincts, and both of those have served me well."

Justin made a moaning sound as the minister poked his head in the door. "Would you join me for a word of prayer before the ceremony?"

"Better make that prayer without ceasing," Justin whispered. "You're gonna need it. You might as well be playing the Super Bowl without a cup."

"I don't know how much more of your support I can stand," Michael muttered, and shook hands with the minister.

In a room behind the foyer of the chapel, Betty Adams adjusted Kate's veil for the sixth time. "Mom," Kate said, fighting her own nerves, "the veil is fine."

Betty dabbed at her nose with her tissue. "Oh,

you're just so beautiful. I've been planning this day since you were born."

Not exactly this way, Kate thought, but smiled instead. "You've done a terrific job in such a short time. Thank you, Mom."

Betty, dressed in a filmy aqua mother-of-the-bride dress, waved the praise aside. "It was nothing, but there is something else I must tell you."

Kate felt the knot in her stomach tighten. She hoped her mother couldn't tell that Michael didn't love her.

Her mother patted her hand. "Now I know you're all grown up, but I've been married to your father a very long time. Katie, when it comes to marriage, giving anything less than one hundred and ten percent just won't do. If you want to have a happy marriage, you can't hold back. You have to give it your all. Remember that because I want you to be happy." Betty sniffed, then her eyes gleamed. "And if Michael Hawkins ever hurts you or mistreats you, he will have to answer to me."

Kate glanced down at her five-foot mother and felt a combination of amusement and tenderness. She smiled. "I'm sure he'd rather face down a lion."

"Darn straight."

A knock sounded at the door and Donna peeked inside. "Show time," she said.

Kate felt a riot of butterflies in her stomach. Betty gave her a hug, then quickly scooted away.

"You can still back out," Donna told her.

"I'm not going to back out. I'm getting married."

"I know that's what's on the schedule, but I just want to remind you that you can still change things. Nothing's irrevocable right now."

Kate slid her hand over her abdomen. "That's not quite true."

"Point taken, but I still think Paris is a terrific alternative."

"Donna," Kate said as she moved toward the door.

"What?"

"Shut up and hold my bouquet." Kate watched her father walk toward her and she felt a jolt of terror. She lifted her lips in what she hoped was a smile. "Hi Daddy."

"Hi darlin'. Here's your big moment," he said in a choked-up voice, and Kate felt like a fraud. She thought of her parents' loving marriage. In comparison, this was a sham. Her stomach turned. She was doing this for Cupcake, she reminded herself, and slid her hand through the crook of her father's arm.

As she walked through the entryway of the chapel, she immediately saw Michael. He looked sure, but distant, she thought and felt another tremor of nerves. What if this didn't work? What if she ended up loving him and he never loved her? Kate's heart wrenched. "Number ten," she said to herself. "Cookies," she said, remembering the generosity of the boy Michael had once been.

"Are you okay, sweetheart?" her father whispered.

Kate nodded. *Cookies.*

She finally reached Michael's side and her father placed her hand in Michael's. After that, the ceremony turned surreal. The minister spoke briefly, she and Michael repeated their vows, and suddenly the minister announced, "I now pronounce you man and wife."

Michael kissed her long enough for her to feel the impact of him, then said in a tone intended for her ears only, "It's almost over."

Hugs and best wishes from family and friends followed at the reception. Kate felt like a windup doll that was running down. Michael must have sensed when her composure began to fray. Under the guise of an eager groom, he whisked her away from the reception to their hotel suite.

As soon as he shut the door, she began to tremble from the events of the day. Embarrassed, she sank down on a chair before her knees gave out. She alternated between the overwhelming urge to cry and numbness.

Michael silently looked at her, disappeared into the bathroom for a second and she heard the jets of a shower. Michael returned and headed straight for her. "You look whiter than that dress," he said, kneeling down to tug off her shoes. "Stand," he instructed.

"What are you—?"

"Just do what I say," he said, and, as soon as she stood, he unzipped the back of her dress.

Shock raced through her. "What—"

In one sweeping movement, he pushed down the dress and slip, then tugged down her stockings. Her face flaming from her sudden partial nudity, she stuttered. "I—I—"

Before she knew it, he'd unsnapped her bra and lifted her off the floor. He carried her to the double shower and gently nudged her inside.

Kate stood in front of the water too stunned to move. Seconds passed and Michael, naked, joined her. Sliding his hands over her shoulders, he pushed her under the spray.

She shook her head. "What are you doing?" she demanded.

"You were locking up," he told her.

"I hate the pretending," she said, slowly taking in the strength and warmth of his body. Something real and warm on a day that had felt unreal and cold. Rivulets of water turned his muscular arms shiny and plastered the spray of chest hair downward. Her gaze traveled to his abdomen and further—to his hard thighs and potent masculinity. He was now her husband.

"No more pretending." He dipped his head to

her chest and slid his tongue over the top of her breast.

Kate shuddered and lifted her hands, needing to hold on to his shoulders. He looked down at her, water droplets clinging to his dark eyelashes. "Let's seal the deal," he said, his sensual tone at odds with the businesslike words. He took her mouth in an endless claiming kiss as the water showered down on them.

Her nipples glanced his chest and she was all too aware of the swollen bulge against her abdomen. Kate's temperature suddenly shot up. She needed the end of pretending. She wanted to feel.

He continued to eat at her mouth while his fingers traveled with abandon over her slippery skin. He touched her shoulders, then her breasts. He plucked at her tender nipples and skimmed his hands down to her abdomen, rubbing as if her pregnancy was already showing. Then he moved his hands lower between her thighs, caressing and pleasuring her with his fingers.

A flush of heat stole over her body at the sensations he created. He made her want so much, ache so powerfully. She kissed him with the same urgency he created inside her. Her hands grew restless and she savored the sensation of the wet skin of his chest and abdomen, and lower.

He gave a rough growl of approval that rippled throughout her nerve endings. "I want you in every way," he said and moved his mouth down her body. As if he'd been denied too long, he consumed her. He took her breast in his mouth, suckled her hardened nipple, and she sensed he couldn't get enough. He treated her other breast to the same carnal pleasure, then skimmed his tongue down her abdomen.

Kate held her breath in suspended anticipation as she felt his seductive tongue trace a path of liquid fire over her skin. Dropping to a knee, he rubbed his cheek against her tummy and thigh, and took her intimately with his mouth. He stroked her sensitive, swollen femininity with his wicked tongue, taking her over the edge until her knees began to buckle.

Michael caught her before she fell, slowly rising up her body at the same time that he moved his hands up her legs to her waist. His eyes dark with primitive need, he pressed her back against the cool tile of the shower wall. "Hang on," he said and urged her legs around his waist.

His gaze holding her and claiming her with the same insistence as his body, he eased her down on his hardness with a slow, sure thrust.

Everything about him, his body, his gaze, said *you are mine*. "Oh, Kate," he muttered. "You feel so good."

Sucking in a deep breath, he pumped inside her, erotically massaging her femininity with each stroke. Kate felt the rush of her climax like a landslide roaring through her. She stiffened, clenching around him.

He swore and through the haze of her own peak, she watched his pleasure roll through him. Still holding her tightly, he dipped his head against her shoulder and glanced her bare skin with a kiss.

"Does it feel more real now?" he whispered.

Kate curled her arms around him, inhaling his essence. "Yes."

Two hours later, Kate awakened to the sight of Michael sleeping beside her. She knew it was an unusual sight, because he found the need for sleep a nuisance more than anything else.

Her *husband,* she thought, and felt her heart race. Waking up to Michael Hawkins was like waking up to a powerful, wild animal in her bed. The dark fringe of eyelashes softened a picture of chiseled angles on his face and a hard, muscular body built for endurance.

Kate wondered what he dreamed. She tentatively lifted her hand toward him to touch his hair.

His eyes flashed open and his hand snaked out to catch her wrist. Her breath caught and she stared into his tiger's eyes.

"What are you doing?" he asked.

"Watching you while you sleep," she said and smiled. "It's so rare."

"You weren't just watching," he pointed out, drawing her closer.

"I thought about touching your hair," she said. "Next time I'll stick to thinking so I don't wake you up."

He shook his head slowly, his gaze fastened on hers. "You're invited to touch," he said, lifting her hand to his hair.

Her heart turned a flip at the simple gesture. "I also wondered what you dream."

"Nothing," he said. "I don't spend much time sleeping, so I don't dream much."

"Maybe," she said skeptically. Kate had a tough time believing a man who was such a visionary didn't have dreams. "But you have secrets, and I plan to learn those."

His gaze turned remote. "Nothing interesting. You don't need to trouble yourself with my secrets," he said, then lowered his head. "Besides, this is the night of our marriage. I've got plans for you."

She struggled with a vague feeling of disappointment, but he kissed her and her body grew warm, her bones turned to liquid, and her head began to swim.

They shared one night of lovemaking and left the suite the following morning after a champagne brunch conducted primarily in the nude. Kate had to pass on the champagne because it wasn't good for Cupcake, so Michael served her orange juice in a flute.

She still felt odd in his apartment and added touches from her place to provide some comfort. She looked at a few houses, then nixed the idea when Michael couldn't join her. She simply didn't feel ready to make such a big decision without his input. In the meantime, her adjustment to wifedom was rocky. Michael made love to her nearly every night, but he missed dinner with her as often as he joined her. More than one night she'd prepared a meal and he hadn't arrived home until after nine o'clock. It occurred to her that she'd known his schedule when he'd been her boss, but it hadn't bothered her too much then. "I didn't prepare the food, then," she muttered to herself as she glanced at the clock. "It wasn't my meal that got cold."

Michael breezed in the door. "Smells great, but I can't stay. I've got to meet the guys at O'Malley's."

"Guys? Excuse me?" She glanced at the chicken parmesan and wondered how he could possibly prefer O'Malley's.

He brushed a lingering kiss to her lips and pulled his tie loose. "I promised Justin and Dylan I'd meet them two nights ago and forgot. If I don't show tonight, they might come knocking here, and I don't want them scaring my new bride."

"But dinner—"

"—looks great," he told her. "I'll eat when I get home. I shouldn't be long."

"Okay," she said, but it didn't feel okay when

he walked out the door and she looked at the uneaten meal on the table. Sighing, she shrugged and put the meal into the refrigerator. She heard a ringing noise, but couldn't place it. It stopped, then started again. Kate followed the noise to the bedroom and found Michael's cell phone on the bed.

"Must've forgotten it," she said and picked up. "Hello?"

A pause followed. "I think I have the wrong number."

"You probably don't," she said quickly. "This is Kate Adams—uh—Hawkins. Michael's wife," she said, the reality still foreign to her.

"Bill Reynolds from Legal. I've got some urgent news. Could Michael return my call as soon as possible?"

"Yes," she said, wondering at the worried tone in Bill's voice. She promptly called O'Malley's, but there was a baseball game on the bar TV and the noise was so loud neither she nor the bartender could hear each other. Giving up, Kate got in her car and drove to the bar. It took her a few moments to spot Michael and his two friends at the far end of the room. She walked up behind them and overheard Dylan.

"I have to say I'm surprised you've lasted this long," he said. "Your bride was as pale as a sheet and you looked like you were gearing yourself for a marathon."

"This guy is stuck in the worst way. He didn't get her to sign a pre-nup," Justin said.

Dylan looked at Michael as if he'd lost his mind. "Where was your head?"

"That's obvious," Justin said. "Michael explained it to me. He said he married her for regular sex and because he'd knocked her up."

Kate's stomach gave a vicious twist. She blinked. Justin's words reverberated in her brain. *Regular sex, knocked her up.* A dozen emotions raced through her, all of them painful. She thought of the nights they'd shared in Michael's bed and the nights she'd prepared a meal for her *husband* and he hadn't bothered to show. Humiliation crowded her throat. She felt like a fool.

"Hey lady, you're standing in the middle of the walkway," a man loudly said.

Kate blinked and stumbled to the side. As if in slow motion, she saw Michael turn around and spot her.

"Kate," he said, surprise on his face. "What—?"

She wanted to be anywhere but here, anyone but his wife. She thrust his cell phone at him. "You left your cell phone at home. Bill Reynolds from Legal called. He said it's urgent. Bye," she said, and raced away, headed anywhere except to Michael Hawkins's apartment.

Eight

Michael slowed his car as he neared the home for unwed teenage mothers. He spotted Kate's Volkswagen in the small parking lot and something inside him eased. He'd found her and she was at least physically okay.

Parking his car, he grabbed the flowers from the passenger seat, stepped out and slammed the car door behind him. He adjusted his tie and strode toward the building.

Kate hadn't returned to his apartment last night. Nor had she gone to her old duplex or to Donna's. Michael had almost called her parents, but Kate's protectiveness of them had given him pause. He suspected he knew what had made her run. She'd clearly overheard Justin shooting off his mouth.

Seeing her ashen face had caused something inside him to shift. He knew her open affection for him was something precious, and in one moment, he'd lost it. More evidence of the capriciousness of human emotion, he thought cynically.

Although Michael couldn't blame Kate for her response, he refused to let her go. In his mind and gut, her leaving was not an option. Now he had to convince her.

He climbed the front porch steps and rang the doorbell to the old house. A young, very pregnant woman answered the door. She glanced at the roses in his hand then looked at him quizzically. "Yes?"

"I'm here for my wife," Michael said. "Kate Hawkins."

The teen nodded in recognition. "Oh, Kate Adams," she said, then smiled. "You'll have to get in line. She's in the back finishing a tutoring session. This way."

Michael followed the young woman down a long hallway and saw Kate working with another young, very pregnant woman in front of a computer. He drank in the sight of her, surprised by how much the tension inside him eased. She appeared incredibly focused, yet vulnerable. At first glance, she looked as if she were completely composed. Dressed in a black skirt and blouse, she exuded competence. That was a big part of the reason he'd hired her. Michael looked closer, however, and saw hints of shadows under her eyes, and her smile was strained.

"I like your idea of sending résumés from the home to local companies for the residents to perform off-site computer work. After you complete your list, you can just use mail merge to—"

"You have a visitor, Kate," Michael's guide said.

Confusion crossed Kate's face. "Visitor?"

Her glance fell on him and Michael felt an arctic blast. His stomach sank. This was not going to be easy. "I brought you roses," he said, stepping forward to offer them to her.

"They're beautiful," her student said with a trace of envy.

"Yes, they are," Kate murmured and set them down. "Would you excuse me for a moment while I talk with—" She broke off as if she were reluctant to call him her husband. "I'll be right back," she said, then turned to him. "Outside."

Coming from a man, those words may have led Michael to expect a bloody brawl. His sense of unease tightened in the back of his throat. But he forced the words out anyway. "I'm sorry," he said as they stepped out onto the front porch.

Surprise flickered across her face. "For what?"

"For Justin shooting off his mouth and hurting you last night."

She crossed her arms over her chest. "According to Justin, he was just repeating your words."

Frustration bucked through him. "Justin was giving me a hard time the day we got married. He's got even more of a bottom-line mentality than I do. I just gave him some facts about marriage on his level to get him off my back."

"He was giving you a hard time?" she repeated.

"He thought I shouldn't marry you and that we should do a pre-nup."

"Perhaps you should have followed his advice."

Michael tamped down his anger at her words. "No. I knew marrying you was the right choice, and I sure as hell didn't need a pre-nup because you've made it clear you're not after my money. Where in hell did you go last night? I checked everywhere, everyone except your parents."

"I went to a hotel. I needed some time to think."

"And?"

"And I'm not sure us being married is going to work."

"I didn't take you for a quitter."

Her eyes shot sparks. "You didn't have your role as a wife reduced to sex and pregnancy. I don't think you and I share the same ideas about marriage. To put it in your terms, the synergy may not be there. You've said that during a merger the policies, purpose and sociology of the two companies need to complement each other and respect each other's value. I'm afraid we may be way apart.''

Michael felt a trickle of perspiration run down his back. He told himself it was the summer heat, but the injured expression in Kate's eyes told him he'd lost a lot of ground with her. ''Then we'll negotiate.''

She looked at him askance. ''You forget that I've seen you negotiate, Michael. For every concession you make, you demand three.''

''We're going to make this work,'' he told her.

''That will take two.''

''What do you want?''

''The impossible,'' she muttered under her breath and turned away.

He moved closer to her. ''Kate,'' he began.

She rounded on him. ''You have no idea how humiliating it was for me to hear that. I've been knocking myself out trying to fix dinner for you nights when you don't bother to come home and make a home and life for us. How silly for me to try so hard when all you want is sex and to give your baby a name. I feel like such a fool.''

The hurt emanated from her in waves. ''The whole idea of marriage is foreign to me. You're going to have to tell me what you want. This is not my area of expertise.''

''Women don't like to have to say everything they want. They want men to—''

''—guess,'' Michael interjected. ''Often incorrectly. This is too damn important to be guessing, Kate."

She took a deep breath. "I still don't know."

"Quitting after a month?" he asked, challenging her pride.

Kate glowered at him. "I want to have dinner together five or six nights out of seven. I want us to go house-shopping together. Even though we didn't have anything resembling a courtship, I'd still like to go out on a date. I want you to talk to me. I want you to need—" She broke off and shook her head as if she knew that was impossible. "I want you to let me know you. Really know you."

Michael didn't feel itchy until her last request. He'd almost rather trade his company than let anyone fully know him. One thing at a time. "Dinner tonight. Your choice of restaurant."

"No," she said.

Surprised and put off, he narrowed his eyes. "Why not?"

"The place you choose says something about you. It's another way of letting me know you."

Choosing a restaurant was considerably less painful than spilling his guts. Michael accepted her terms. "Good, I'll pick you up at the apartment at six-thirty."

"I don't know if I'm ready to go back to the apartment," she said.

"Yes, you are," he said, backing her against a

corner post on the porch. "I may not fit your mold of the ideal husband, but there's one very important thing I don't do. I don't bore you, and I'm betting just about every other man you've been involved with has."

Kate gazed at him silently for a long moment. She wore a don't-push-me expression and her black outfit hid what he knew—that her body was just beginning to show the signs of the baby she carried. He inhaled her scent. It amazed him how sexy he found her even in this tense sliver of time.

"Okay," she finally said. "I'll be at the apartment tonight."

Something inside him eased and the urge to make love to her pushed and pulled. Reining it in, he lifted her left hand and caressed her ring finger where she still wore the ring he'd given her. He lifted her hand and kissed it. "Tonight, then."

That night, Kate fought her nerves and her hair. She scowled into the mirror. Why had she agreed to this? She should have stayed at the hotel, or at the very least moved back into her duplex. Michael might be fascinating, but he was difficult too, which meant her life would likely be difficult.

And fascinating, the small voice inside her said.

"Oh, shut up," she muttered. "Listening to you is how I ended up pregnant and married."

She adjusted the black sheath dress and turned to the side. She didn't quite look pregnant yet. Just fat, she thought with another scowl. She heard the kitchen door open and jumped, dropping her lipstick. There was no reason for these nerves, she told herself. This may be a first date, but she was married to the guy, for Pete's sake. She quickly applied the lipstick and left the bathroom.

Michael stood next to the kitchen counter glancing through the mail. He wore a dark sport jacket, white shirt and silk tie, and when he directed his attention from the mail to her, his expression was just this side of predatory. "You look good," he said. "Ready to go?"

"Yes, thank you," she said, fighting her awkwardness. "Where are we going?"

"A surprise," he said with an enigmatic gleam in his eyes and ushered her out the door.

They were quiet during the drive. When he pulled into a parking lot, and she saw the restaurant he'd chosen, she smiled in pleasure. Although she'd never been here, she'd always wanted to come. "The Vineyard," she said. "I didn't know this was one of your favorites."

"It wasn't. This will be my first visit."

"How did you find it?"

He hesitated. "I did some research."

Curious, Kate studied him. "Why do I sense there's a story here?"

Michael sighed. "Do I have to reveal my sources?"

"Yes."

"I sent an e-mail to five employees and one friend asking for their top three favorite restaurants along with descriptions. You'll understand why I chose this one when we get inside."

As soon as they were led to the table and placed their orders, Kate understood his choice. The restaurant boasted a ceiling of skylights, ficus trees with tiny white lights, and a waterfall in the center. "I love the greenery."

"I thought you would. I pulled a few strings to get us next to the waterfall," he said.

"Whose suggestion was this?"

"Dylan's. He has a busy social life. Lots of different women."

"You don't sound envious," she said.

He looked at her meaningfully. "I'm not." He pulled out a handful of change and put it in the middle of the table. "Bet you can't reach that stone on the other side with a coin."

Challenged and charmed, she took three coins. "What do I get if I can?"

"What do you want?"

She thought for a long moment and felt a strange yearning swell inside her. He was such a dichotomy for her, such a challenge. She feared loving him, and at the same time she couldn't stay away from him. "I want a story," she said. "I want you to tell me something about yourself that I don't already know."

"Okay," he said, with the same expression he might wear if she were giving him a tetanus shot.

She took a penny, aimed and missed by inches. She chose a nickel next, aimed and hit it.

"Something tells me there are a few things I don't know about you," he said, lifting his brow.

"I was pitcher for the high-school girls' softball team and played intramurals in college," she said with a smile. "Pay up."

"My favorite ice cream is—"

"—raspberry sherbet. You have to do better."

"I made excellent grades in high school without studying,"

"I could have guessed that," she said.

He frowned at her. "I graduated number three in my high-school class."

"That low?" she teased with a cheeky grin.

"Did anyone ever tell you that you're demanding?"

Remembering what a challenging boss he'd been, she couldn't contain her smile. "Talk about the pot calling the kettle—"

He lifted his hand to cut her off. "Okay. I wanted to learn to play the guitar when I was a teenager, but couldn't afford one."

She paused, trying to imagine Michael as a teenager. She suspected he'd grown up quickly after his mother died. "Very good. Acoustic or electric guitar?"

"Electric," he said.

"You wanted to be a rock star!" she said, the realization delighting her.

"I did not," he quickly denied. "Okay, I might have worn an Eric Clapton T-shirt for most of a year, but that was just a stage."

"Did you play any sports?"

"Basketball in the gym at Granger's. I kept a part-time job, so I didn't have time for school team sports."

"Always a working man," she said, wondering if some of the same things that had driven him as a teen still drove him now.

"Dinner," he said, closing the discussion as the waiter delivered the meal.

Kate saw a flicker of relief cross his face. Why, she wondered, did he find it so hard to talk about himself?

After dinner, Michael drove them to his apartment. It had been a long meal and the hour was late. A darkened kitchen and her cat greeted them. She reached for the light switch, but he covered her hand. "Leave it dark."

Her heart flipped at the hint of sensuality in his tone. She allowed her hand to drop from the switch.

"I haven't dated much in the last few years," he said. "But I recall a tradition."

"What's that?" she asked, his nearness doing crazy things to her pulse. The darkness blocked everything out of her senses except him, the sound of his voice and his clean, musk scent.

"A good-night kiss," he said, sliding his arm to her waist and drawing her to him. His lips, firm, yet full, brushed over hers. Side to side, he moved his mouth as if savoring the sensation of her. He was slow, seductive and so gentle it made her chest tighten up with tenderness and longing. He stood so close Kate wondered if he could hear her heart beat.

His tongue slid past her lips, still slowly, inviting her to taste him. He tilted her chin for better access and she couldn't hold back a soft moan at the sweet richness of the moment.

He continued the kiss as if her mouth absorbed and fascinated him. Spreading his legs, he drew her lower body against his. She felt his swollen arousal, but his mouth was her focus.

With each seductive stroke of his tongue, she felt her breasts grow heavy and a yearning tighten between her thighs. Instinctively, she rubbed against him.

Giving a groan of approval and pleasure, he gently ground her against him. Kate felt her breath slip away. It was so easy for her to want him, to want to feel the power of his arousal, to allow him to take her at the same time she took him. It would be so easy to make love with him now, here in the kitchen, against the wall, or in the bed she shared with him.

Justin's taunt rang through her mind like an ill-tuned key on a piano. The hurt sliced through her again. She pulled back and dipped her forehead. The sounds of their fast breaths were mingled in the darkness. She felt the tug of unspent passion in her pulse and his.

"You're remembering what Justin said," Michael said in a low voice. "Forget it."

Her heart twisted. "I can't," she said. "Not yet. Too soon."

He gave a ragged sigh.

"You've given up your bed enough for me. I'll take the couch."

"No," he said. "We'll sleep in the same bed."

"But—"

"It's where you belong. I'll wait for you."

Kate searched the planes of his face in the darkness. "Wait for me to do what?"

He looked at her and his gaze had the impact of a sexual loaded pistol. "For you to want me again."

As if by mutual consent, Kate and Michael stayed busy every night. The following week they took a whirlwind tour of homes for sale and found *the* house on the seventh night. The two-story brick colonial boasted four bedrooms, a study, a den, formal living and dining room, kitchen with a nook and a surprise sunroom. Kate was pleased to see several young children playing in the neighborhood and Michael had no complaints about the twenty-minute commute.

True to form, Michael didn't waste time. He signed a contract for the house the same night they found it, then left for the west coast the next morning. Out of consideration for Cupcake, Kate stayed in St. Albans. She'd read that flying and early pregnancy might not be a great combination, so she made a few purchases for the new house.

Every night as she went to sleep, she looked at the pillow beside her and remembered how it had felt to share the bed with Michael. She tried to deny it to herself, but every night she missed him more.

The evening Michael was scheduled to arrive she went to the airport even though they'd agreed he would catch a cab. She watched him disembark and immediately sensed something was wrong. His face was lined with strain and his gaze was focused somewhere out there. She had to call his name twice to get his attention.

"Michael," she said for the third time, stepping in front of him. "Hello," she said with a laugh.

He blinked, then glanced from side to side. "Hello," he murmured. "What are you doing here? Was there an emergency call from the office?"

"No," she said, growing concerned with his strange attitude. "I wanted to surprise you."

Then he looked at her and really saw her. He

dropped his carry-on and took her in his arms. Kate could have sworn he was seeking some kind of solace. She returned the embrace. "What's going on?" she asked.

"Not much," he said, but his tone didn't echo his words.

She pulled back and searched his face. "I think you're not telling me something."

His eyes were hard. "I think this is none of your business."

Kate stared at him in shock. He was so far from her he might as well still be in California.

Nine

"Is that everything?" Kate asked, after Michael had loaded the trunk.

The weight of her concerned gaze and determined cheerfulness grated on him. After this trip, however, everything on the planet would grate on him. "Yeah. I'll drive," he said, wondering how he could be so damn glad to see her at the same time that he didn't want to see her at all.

"Oh, no. I'll drive. You're tired," she said, letting herself into the driver's side of the vehicle. "And cranky." She smiled a little too brightly. "It's always been my belief that cranky people don't belong on the road."

"That could cover half the population at one time or another," he said, sliding into the passenger seat and closing the door.

"My point exactly." She pulled away from the metropolitan airport and pushed a CD into the player. The familiar guitar strains filled the car. Eric Clapton.

Michael took a deep breath and tried to relax.

"Y'know," she said calmly as she pulled onto a main thoroughfare, "if I weren't so happy to see you, I'd club you for talking to me that way in the airport."

Michael did a double take. "What way?" he asked, even though he knew. He was chomping at the bit for a fight.

She shot him a quick glance. "None of my business," she quoted him.

"It is," he said grimly, "none of your business."

Kate's cheeks turned pink. She jerked the steering wheel to the side and pulled into a gas-station parking lot. She turned on him. "I'm your wife, bozo brain. If something's bothering you, it sure as hell is my business too."

She rarely swore, Michael thought, taking in the glorious sight of her anger. Pink cheeks, sparks shooting from her eyes, and tongue primed to rip him to shreds. "Bozo brain?"

"If the shoe fits," she said, over-emphasizing her consonants. He would have to remember that sign for the future. "Only a bozo wouldn't tell his wife if something was bothering him."

"I don't want you worrying."

"Cut the bull, Michael. You know as well as I do that you didn't marry any fragile flower. If I could take three years as your assistant, I can handle whatever happened to you in California."

"Takeover," he said, amazed at the instant relief telling her provided. "Only I'm not doing the taking this time. Another company is prepared to make a hostile takeover of CG Enterprises."

She stared at him silently for a long moment.

He rushed to reassure her. "You don't need to worry about money. We're set if I don't work another day. You and the baby will be—"

She covered his busy mouth with her fingertips. "At this moment, I am much more concerned about you."

Michael felt his chest swell with the oddest, most disconcerting emotion. He didn't know what to make of it. He just knew it wasn't all bad. "I'm okay," he said. "I have to get together a strategy for how to fight this. It will involve some long hours," he warned her.

"But not tonight," she said, and leaned forward to kiss him. "I'm glad you're home."

Michael settled back in his seat as she drove toward the apartment. He was ironically uneasy with the ease he felt with her. He trusted her, but he always had. There was something else. After a cross-country flight, he couldn't quite put his finger on it, but he wasn't totally comfortable with the situation.

He carried his luggage inside and Parkay greeted him with her customary snarl. He wondered if that cat would ever accept him. He inhaled a heavenly aroma. "What do I smell?"

Kate smiled. "Chocolate chip cookies. I made them this afternoon. Milk or beer?"

"Beer," he said.

He stowed his luggage in the bedroom, then returned to the den and sank down on the sofa. He started to go through the mail, but she took it from him and handed him a beer and two cookies.

Kate sat down beside him. The silence between them was easy. He wolfed down the cookies, swallowed the beer, and drank in the sight of her. Her blue eyes held secrets he wanted to know. Her hair looked like rich silk, her cheeks glowed, and her mouth looked inviting. It felt as if it had been forever since they'd made love. His gaze traveled down her body. Everything about her seemed more ripe, including her belly.

"You look pregnant."

"Thank you," she said, beaming. "Wanna see my belly?" She poked it out at him.

Charmed, he nodded. "Do I get to touch?"

"Yes. Cupcake is moving."

He felt his gut tighten. He slid his hands up under her blouse. "You felt the baby move?"

She nodded, clearly delighted. "At first I thought it was gas, but it's the baby. It might be a few more weeks before you can feel the movement."

Losing his company, knowing his baby was moving. He was hitting both ends of the scale at once. Michael closed his eyes at the dichotomy of emotion. He felt Kate's fingers on his forehead and wanted more. But he'd made a promise, he reminded himself.

Unwilling to test his ragged control tonight, he stood. "I'm beat. I'll take the sofa tonight."

Her eyes met his, seeing possibilities in him he hadn't known existed. She stood too. "No. You belong in our bed."

He felt a knot in his stomach. Knowing he could probably persuade her to give him ease in the most sensual sense didn't mean it would be best in the long run. "Kate, I want you tonight, and I'm fresh out of any Boy Scout chivalry."

She laced her fingers through his, and even that sensation affected him. "I think you should get ready for bed. There's something I want to tell you."

Too tired to argue, he headed for the bathroom and washed the day off himself. When he finished, he looped a towel around his waist and walked through the open door.

With the bedside lamp's gentle illumination, she sat in the middle of his bed wrapped in a short white filmy nightie that revealed the hint of her dusky nipples and the slight swell of her belly. She reminded him of all the Christmas presents he'd ever wanted and not received. She crooked her finger at him and patted the bed beside her.

He took the dare in her eyes and dropped the towel before he joined her on the bed. "What do you want to tell me?"

"Number ten," she said, touching his face with one hand, skimming her other palm down his shoulders and chest.

Michael would have traded his soul for her touch. He wasn't sure his soul was worth much, but it was all he had, save his millions. And Kate, being Kate, wasn't interested in his millions.

"What is number ten?" he asked, closing his eyes and giving into the pleasure of her slow touch.

"The tenth reason I want you," she said.

He grinned slightly. "Ah, the secret reason. The one you wouldn't tell me the night before our wedding."

"Right," she said. "The reason that kept me from running."

"What is it?" he asked, opening his eyes.

"Chocolate chip cookies."

Confused, he wrinkled his brow. "Chocolate chip cookies," he echoed, wondering if she was missing a few cookies herself.

"You used to race to the front of the cafeteria

line and you always got cookies. But you always gave your cookies to Harold Grimley."

Stunned, he stared at her. "How did you know that?"

"That's for another time," she told him, waving her hand in a dismissing gesture. "Now is the time for me to show you what happens to the man who gave his cookies to Harold Grimley," she said and kissed him.

She flowed over his body like a soft, sensual shower. She lingered with her mouth on his, then dragged her lips down his throat to his chest. Her combination of tenderness and passion nearly undid him.

She nuzzled his chest and he felt her chiffon-covered breasts against his crotch. Each movement of her body taunted his burgeoning hardness. Michael felt his blood soar through his veins.

Continuing her trail of sensual destruction, she drew her sensitive lips down his abdomen. Now he felt the stiffened peaks of her breasts on his thighs. He was achingly swollen.

"Kate," he said, trying to warn her. Before he could form another word, she kissed him intimately. All air left his lungs.

She took him into her mouth with mind-blowing strokes from her tongue. Each caress from her tongue pushed him nearer the edge. But it had been too long since he'd had her. He didn't want to go this way.

He urged her head from him and pulled her upward.

Her eyes dark with passion, she looked at him with sensual confusion. "Why did you stop me?"

"Because I want more of you," he said and kissed her mouth. The fact that she tasted of his essence made him wild. He quickly discarded her filmy nightie and groaned at the sensation of her naked silky skin against his.

He touched her full breasts, then slid one hand between her thighs. She was already wet and swollen. The knowledge was too much for him. Holding her with an endless kiss, he gently rolled her on her back and plunged inside her.

She gasped, and a sliver of concern raced through him.

"Too rough?" he asked.

She shook her head and rocked her hips so she enclosed him more deeply. "Don't stop."

Her openness did something to him emotionally, physically. His restraint ripped in two and he pumped inside her wet, tight femininity. Her ripple of climax sent him into blissful oblivion.

It took a few moments for Michael to regain his faculties. He pulled her against him.

"Are you okay?" she asked.

"That's supposed to be my line."

Her eyelids lowered, giving her a mysterious look. "Not necessarily."

"If I ever see Harold Grimley again, I'll have to thank him."

Kate laughed and the sound made everything inside him feel lighter. How did she have such a powerful effect on him? Uneasy with the strength of his emotions, he silently held her.

She snuggled closer to him and it occurred to Michael that he could get used to this. He could grow to count on her. Michael knew that would be a mistake. Nothing was forever.

Michael turned his attention to the company with a vengeance. Kate understood that the company was like a child to him, but she missed him. Their finest moments seemed to come at night after they made love.

Summer turned to fall and she kept busy managing the move from the apartment to their new home and tutoring the girls at the home for unwed teenage mothers. She told herself that Michael's business crisis wouldn't last forever, but she feared another would take its place and she would essentially have an absentee husband. The possibility hurt, but she buried it as best she could.

Her doctor scheduled an appointment for her ultrasound and she invited Michael. She even went so far as to write a note on the refrigerator so he wouldn't forget.

When she reclined on the examination table and the doctor put cold goop and the ultrasound device on her growing belly, she was by herself. As she watched the screen in fascination, she counted the fingers and toes of her baby. The joy she felt was so great that she almost didn't need Michael, she told herself.

That night, she followed an impulse and met Donna for dinner at a trendy downtown bistro. "You look glorious," her friend said with the slightest trace of envy. "If I knew any men who'd make a decent father, I'd be tempted to follow in your footsteps."

Kate winced and took a sip of herbal tea. "You might not want to do it exactly the same way I did."

Donna gave Kate a searching glance. "How's your husband?"

"Busy with the company right now," she said. "Very busy."

The waiter delivered their salads and Donna lifted her eyebrows. "How busy?"

"Home late almost every night. He works most weekends." She pushed a broccoli floret around her plate and confessed, "He missed the ultrasound today."

"Ah," Donna said with cool eyes. "The unhusband."

The unusual term gave Kate pause. "I hadn't really thought of him that way."

"But it's true."

Kate didn't want to be disloyal. "He does have a legitimate crisis at work."

"How long are you going to give him to figure things out?"

Kate's stomach tightened. "What do you mean how long?"

"I mean if this is impossible, you don't have to be miserable with him the rest of your life."

"I'm not miserable," Kate said, feeling tears threaten. "I just wish he didn't always seem so far away."

Donna took a bite of salad and swallowed, then leaned forward. "You haven't fallen in love with him, have you?"

Kate sat there silently, that small voice inside her screaming *yes*. Her heart sank. When had it happened? she wondered. Or perhaps, she always had. Not like this, however, she thought. She had not cared for Michael as if he were a part of her before. But now she did. Now, his happiness meant nearly everything to her.

Donna looked at her with sympathy. "Oh, Kate."

Unwilling to wallow in self-pity, she shook off her sadness and took a deep breath. "I'm okay. This is temporary," she said firmly, as much for herself as for Donna. She just hoped it was true.

Michael was drowning in a sea of paperwork. The VP of Wayland Inc., the company that wanted to acquire CG Enterprises, was known as "the shark." He devoured the companies Wayland acquired until they bore little resemblance to their original state.

Michael and his legal department were working overtime scrutinizing every word of the offer in order to protect CG and Michael's staff. One of many bones of contention was a vague clause suggesting the whole company be moved to the west coast.

Michael knew he probably couldn't stop the takeover. Wayland was too large, with deep pockets, but he'd negotiated enough of these from the other side to know the company being acquired often possessed more leverage than they believed.

The idea of giving up his company turned his stomach, but Michael was determined to look at it from a business angle. It was the only way he could keep a clear head, and too many people were depending on him for him to lose his perspective now.

A knock sounded on his door and he frowned. He'd told the latest assistant to turn away all visitors and callers. Irritated, he turned back to his work. The door opened and he didn't look up. "I'm busy," he said.

A long silence followed. "I thought you might like some cookies."

Michael glanced up to see his wife in the doorway. His chest tightened, and he was filled with a dozen opposing emotions. Lord, what a sight for sore eyes. He tossed his pencil on his desk and stood. "Come in. I thought you were Legal. Those guys are doing a bang-up job, but I've had it up to the gills with them today."

"Getting close?" she asked, walking toward him with a small bag in her hand.

Michael rubbed the back of his neck and shook his head. "Don't ask. Did I hear you say something about cookies? What have you got in that bag?"

"I'm assuming lunch was coffee."

"You assume correctly," he said and looked her over from head to toe. She looked all shiny and polished in a black dress and stockings, yet very pregnant. He felt a strange yearning sensation. Looking at her reminded him how much he'd missed her. They hadn't made love as often because he'd been gone so much. There was a strained quality between them caused, he knew, by his absence, but he couldn't change it. Not now, anyway. "You look beautiful," he told her. "You look more pregnant every day."

"Which brings me to the bag," she said, giving it a gentle shake.

"Cookies?"

"And Cupcake," she said with a lopsided smile.

Curious, he took the bag and looked inside. Beside the cookies something was nestled in tissue paper. He pulled it out and looked at a black-and-white photo in a picture frame. The photo was an ultrasound. The ultrasound he'd missed. Michael swore. "I missed it." He swore again. "It was a week ago, wasn't it?"

"Yes," Kate said.

"Why didn't you tell me?"

"I did," she said. "I used several different modalities, including a note on the refrigerator."

He looked at her calm expression and didn't know how to respond. "I would have expected anger."

She glanced away and thought for a moment. "If anything, I was more hurt than angry. But to be brutally honest, I feel pretty lucky. I got to see Cupcake move, and suck on a thumb. I got to count fingers and toes. You're the one who missed out. I brought you the picture on the off-chance that sometime you'll look up from your paperwork, and it might make you smile."

Her words were soft and the gesture sweet, but her honesty ripped at him. It wasn't his goal to hurt her. "I apologize."

She gave a slight wince. "Apologize to yourself."

His chest tightened. She hadn't seemed so distant from him in a very long time. "Why did you bring the cookies and the photo to the office?"

"To remind you that you are more than CG Enterprises." She bit her lip and hesitated. "I can't make you share yourself with me, although God knows I wish I could. I can't make you want to be with me. For that matter, I can't make you want me." She placed her hand over her full abdomen and chuckled. "Especially now. The only thing I can do is remind you every now and then that life is more than work and so are you…and I hope someday you'll see it too."

Again her calmness bothered him. He almost preferred her in-your-face demands. She had retreated from him. He moved toward her. "You have this all wrong. I still want you as much as I—"

She shook her head as if she were embarrassed. "I understand," she said. "I'm *big* now."

Michael pulled her into his arms. "Dammit Kate, don't put words in my mouth. I know what I want and I want you. You being pregnant with my baby just multiplies the feeling. Do you have any clue how sexy it is knowing I helped put that baby in you? If I weren't afraid of hurting you, I'd show you on that desk right now."

He kissed her at the same time he deliberately placed his hand on her belly. Roiling with too many emotions, he took her mouth, hard. A moment passed and he felt a trace of wetness on his cheek, then tasted a salty tear. He pulled back and saw the tears on her cheeks, and he had the sinking godawful sense that he was going to lose her.

Ten

Three weeks later Michael sat in his office at six o'clock at night. He was nearing the end of negotiations, he could feel it. He just hadn't quite figured out how to get a little more leverage for CG in this deal. The shark had already made surprising concessions.

The phone rang and he narrowed his eyes at it. He almost chose not to answer it, but thought of Kate. She only had three weeks until her due date and he damn well wasn't going to miss the birth of their child.

"Hawkins here," he said.

"Hawkins is supposed to be *here*," Kate said.

The pseudo-snooty tone in her voice made him smile. Since the day she'd visited him in his office, there was still a slight uneasiness between them, but it hadn't stopped him from making love to her. Michael was determined to remind her frequently that she belonged with him.

"I'm nearing the end of this," he told her.

"Yes, but the end is not going to happen tonight. I need you to come home now," she said.

His chest tightened. "Is anything wrong?"

"We discussed this. You told me if I need you to come home for any reason all I have to do is ask. I'm asking."

"I want to know the reason," Michael said, wondering if he would be making a trip to the hospital tonight.

"You will when you get home," she told him, and hung up on him.

Michael pulled the receiver away from his ear and stared at it in surprise. The woman had hung up on him. She'd never done that before. Pique warred with worry. He replaced the receiver in the cradle, grabbed his jacket and headed out the door. Providing his wife wasn't ready to give birth, he planned to have a little discussion about phone etiquette with her as soon as he arrived home.

As he pulled into the driveway of their new home, he noticed the lights on the Christmas tree were illuminated. It gave him a warm feeling knowing Kate was waiting for him, but at the same time he told himself not to count on her. He secretly wondered if she might leave him if he lost the company. He rejected the notion, but a doubt remained, bothering him like a sore tooth.

Pulling into the garage, he stopped and got out. He frowned when he looked through the kitchen door and saw darkness. His trickle of worry turned to a stream. He pushed open the door. "Kate?"

"Surprise!" a group of voices chorused. The light flashed on and Michael gaped at the small group before him. He saw the head of personnel and his wife, two guys from the legal department, Dylan and a redhead, Justin and Kate. It took him a full moment before he remembered it was his birthday. After his mother died, he hadn't celebrated it much because it fell so close to Christmas.

Kate smiled and stepped forward. "Happy Birthday, Michael."

"How did you—?"

"You forgot it was your birthday, didn't you?" Kate asked, shaking her head. "This makes me feel a little better about the ultrasound," she murmured under her breath.

Justin walked up to join in. "Your wife here looks like she's about to pop."

Michael slid his arm around Kate. "Yeah, she looks beautiful."

Out of the corner of his eye, he saw Kate's lips twitch. "I'm providing my husband with a tax exemption," she said, speaking Justin's language.

"By the way, Michael and I have been discussing names and we're thinking of using yours if it's a boy."

Justin's expression was a mixture of surprise and bewilderment. "Is that so?"

"Yes, we're also considering you as a candidate for godfather."

Justin's eyes grew wide. "Godfather!"

"Yes. Michael said you might be reluctant, but I told him I have this feeling you secretly love children."

Justin looked like he'd been poleaxed. The sight was so comical Michael couldn't prevent a chuckle.

Kate glanced up at Michael with a secret gleam in her eye. "Excuse me while I get you something to drink."

"Godfather," Justin repeated after she left and cleared his throat. "I may not be the right guy for the job. No offense, Michael, but I don't like kids. I didn't even like being a kid when I was one. Maybe Dylan—"

Dylan walked into the conversation, eyeing Justin with suspicion. "Maybe Dylan what?" he interjected.

Justin tugged at his collar. "I was just suggesting some alternatives for the godfather of Kate and Dylan's baby."

"Me?" Dylan asked.

"Hey, I took a turn with the best-man thing. It's your turn now."

"It can only be my turn to be best man if you get married."

Justin shook his head adamantly. "Absolutely—"

"Sorry I'm late," a blond woman said as she entered the room and laid eyes on the three men and the redhead standing next to Justin. Her gaze lingered an extra second on Justin before she looked back at Michael. "Happy birthday."

Michael frowned, unable to recognize her instantly. There was something familiar about her.

"The cookie girl," Justin said.

"Alisa Jennings," Michael said, feeling a pang of nostalgia. "How did—?"

Alisa reached forward and gave him a quick, warm hug. "Your wonderful wife. We met just before your wedding. We performed a little mission impossible work to get some photos of you copied."

"Photos?" he echoed.

"For the wedding reception," she said, then laughed. "Just like a guy. You must not even have noticed."

For the life of him, Michael couldn't remember seeing pictures at the brief wedding reception. He'd been too busy keeping an eye on Kate to make sure she didn't run.

Dylan stepped forward and kissed Alisa's cheek. "I heard you were engaged," he said smoothly.

She turned cool. "I was," she said. "I'm not now." She appeared to glance over his shoulder at the redhead behind him. "Alisa Jennings," she said. "Lovely dress."

"Thank you. I'm Vanessa."

"And you," Alisa said, turning to Justin. "I hear you're spinning straw into gold with the stock market."

"Slight exaggeration," he assured her in a rare humble moment. "Did you bring any cookies?"

She lifted her hands. "Fresh out."

"What are you doing in St. Albans?" Michael asked.

"I'm a translator for a company performing a merger with a French company."

"And your art?" Dylan asked.

She hesitated. "In my spare time," she said, and Michael noticed she didn't meet Dylan's gaze. "I need to thank your wife for inviting me," she told Michael.

"She's probably at the bar fixing me a drink."

Alisa smiled. "You got lucky," she said and headed for the bar.

"I think I'll get a drink, too," Vanessa said.

"Great legs," Justin said with a sigh after the women left. "I have to say the cookie girl has grown up very nicely."

Dylan stared after her.

Justin nudged him. "Hey, didn't you two have a puppy-love thing?"

Dylan nodded. "Teenage crush. We met again briefly while we were in college."

"Oh really?" Justin said, his tone full of innuendo.

"Can it, stock stud," Dylan said in a rough voice, surprising Michael.

"Here are the photos," Alisa called from the other side of the room. "On the buffet."

Curious, Michael made his way to the buffet. Arranged on top stood a collection of photos of him as a child. An odd assortment of emotions hit him as he studied them. In most of them, he looked lost. He remembered feeling lost and trapped. He remembered how helpless he'd felt when other people made life-changing decisions for him without his consent.

"Cute guy, huh?" Kate said from behind him.

Frowning, he shrugged and turned away. "I guess."

He felt her studying him. "You surprised me with this," he said.

"That was the idea," she said with a mock-solemn nod. "A *surprise* party."

"I've never done much celebrating on my birthday," he told her.

"Then I guess we have a lot of making up to do. We can start with the cake. Think about your wish." She guided him over to the table where the cake was lit with candles. "Wish fast, the candles are melting on the cake." She turned to the small crowd. "Time to sing."

Surrounded by friends singing a slightly off-key rendition of the birthday song, Michael stood in front of a cake decorated with white frosting that said Happy Birthday Michael.

He felt incredibly silly. And heaven help him, he felt special. He couldn't remember the last time he'd felt this way. He felt almost like that kid he'd seen in those photos on the buffet. Funny how a little surprise birthday party could throw a grown CEO for a loop.

Later, after the guests left and he and Kate had gone to bed, he watched Kate as she slept. Although she was uncomfortable, she tended to fall asleep quickly these days. She just didn't stay asleep. Restless and unwilling to wake her, he carefully rose from the bed and wandered into the den. He turned on the Christmas tree lights.

Seeing them warmed him. Most everything Kate did to the house seemed to warm him. Everything except the photos. He walked back to the buffet and looked at each of the photos again. They disturbed him. He opened a drawer in the buffet and began to put them away.

"Why don't you like them?" Kate asked from behind him, catching him by surprise.

He slowly turned. "You walk quietly considering your—"

"—girth?" she supplied wryly.

"I was going to say your stage of pregnancy."

She walked to his side with a slight waddle that amused him, but he kept that to himself.

"Why don't you like the photos?"

"I remember how I felt then," he said, looking at another picture. "Helpless, hopeless, trapped. I hated it."

"Every minute?"

He shrugged. "A lot of minutes." He walked toward the Christmas tree and picked up a sprig of mistletoe from an end table. Kate had put it all over the place. She'd said Christmas was for kissing.

He saw her gather the pictures and again walk/waddle toward him. "Not every minute. Look," she said, lifting up a photo of him shooting a foul shot. "What do you see?"

He glanced at it. "A gangly teenager passing the time in a drafty gym."

She shook her head. "I see something else. What are you looking at?"

He glanced again, still idly messing with the mistletoe in his hand. "The basket. What else would I be looking at?"

"Look at your eyes, how focused they are. You look like you could shine a laser beam between you and that basket. I bet you made it."

"Yeah. So?"

"So even then you had incredible focus. That

focus is part of the reason you're so successful today.''

He conceded her point. "Okay."

"What about this one?" she asked, showing a picture of him holding a certificate for winning the high math award in fourth grade. "Too tough for a smile, but you can still see the pride." She pulled out the lone picture with his mother. "This is my favorite. See how her arms form a circle of love around you?"

It was strange, but it hurt to look at that picture. "She died and the circle of her arms couldn't protect me."

"No, but she gave you something that helped make you the guy who gave Harold Grimley chocolate chip cookies, and the man who donates computers and hires the home for unwed teenage mothers for off-site contract computer work."

His chest grew tight and achy. Her eyes searched his like that laser she'd mentioned earlier, and he felt it shining a light on his dark soul.

"The reason I like these pictures is they show the makings of the man you've become, but I don't have to leave them out if they bother you. Putting them away won't take those parts away from you. They just show a few of the reasons I love the boy you were and the man you are."

Michael felt as if a bomb was going off inside him. He swallowed hard over a lump in his throat.

He hadn't expected a declaration of love from her. He felt unworthy of it.

"Why do you love me? I'm the Tin Man. No heart, remember?"

"I may have had a choice at one time, but I can't not love you now. When I look at you, I see much more than the Tin Man." Her eyes grew shiny with unshed tears. "I just hope that someday you'll feel safe enough with me that you can share all of you with me."

His chest clenched so tight he could hardly breathe. He pulled her against him and swore. "Kate, I don't deserve you. But I sure as hell am not giving you up." Remembering the mistletoe he'd nearly crushed in his hand, he lifted the greenery above her head and kissed her.

The following day, Kate felt distracted as she conducted a tutoring session at the home for unwed teenage mothers. She was worried about Michael. His identity was so tied up with the company that she feared what might happen if he lost it. She wasn't worried about money or him having a job. She was worried about how the takeover was affecting his heart because try as he might to believe he didn't possess a heart, Kate knew he did.

"Okay, that's enough," Kate said to Tina, who was now the mother of a baby boy. "Let's decorate the tree."

Tina nodded in agreement. "I brought the ladder

and lights down from the attic this morning. Let me go get the ornaments. I'll be right back."

Kate walked into the formal living area and approved the tall Fraser fir. Rubbing her lower back, she walked around it, deciding which side should face the window. She carefully got down on her hands and knees and adjusted the tree stand, then slowly rose. She felt the baby move and touched her stomach. The movements always made her smile.

Humming "O Little Town of Bethlehem" she unraveled a string of lights from one of the boxes and laid it out on the floor. She unraveled a second and eyed the ladder. Michael would kill her if she climbed it, but she felt perfectly balanced. A few steps up wouldn't hurt, she told herself.

Taking one of the strings of lights, she climbed two steps and paused. "Seems sturdy," she murmured, and climbed two more. Leaning to the side, she looped the strand around the top branches. The sticky branches didn't immediately cooperate, so she learned a smidge further.

She heard a gasp behind her. "Mrs. Hawkins!" Tina cried.

Kate whipped her head around at the sound of Tina's distress and lost her perfect balance. She shifted her feet to try to regain her equilibrium, but she slipped and felt her feet fall out from under her. She crashed downward on her side.

Pain immediately seared her.

"Oh, Mrs. Hawkins!" Tina dropped the boxes and rushed to her side. "Are you okay?"

Beads of nervous perspiration formed between her breasts and unbidden fear throbbed in her pulse. Another pain sliced through her. "I don't know," she said, trying to gather her composure. "I think I am." She tried to stand, but the pain kept her on the floor.

"Oh, no," Tina said, wringing her hands. "I could slap myself for startling you."

Panic trickled in, but Kate took a careful breath. She felt wet on the back of her dress. "My water broke," she said, feeling a mixture of relief and anticipation. "It's my water," she said, but when she glanced at the back of her dress, it wasn't water. It was blood.

Eleven

Wayland's VP of Acquisitions continued to refuse Michael the autonomy he demanded for CG Enterprises. An assortment of lawyers from both companies and Michael and his own VP were attending the meeting, which had been going for four hours straight.

"We have more resources. We can provide the backing necessary for you to expand at triple the rate you've projected," Stone Davidson, "the shark," said. "But we can't give you carte blanche. We have requirements for how the backing is monitored."

"What you're saying is that there are strings,"

Michael said. "I understand. There are always strings, but if you're not careful the strings can tangle up a process that's already working. Strings can also choke the life from a company that's already profitable."

Michael looked into Stone Davidson's hard face and had a revelation. He'd been searching for the leverage and he realized that *he* was the leverage. Irony flashed through him. "If you want me to remain at CG, you will have to provide greater autonomy. Otherwise you can color me gone."

The room sat in stunned silence. Stone's jaw twitched. "I have difficulty believing you would abandon your own company."

"It wouldn't be my company anymore."

Unbelievably, Michael's assistant du jour chose that very moment to enter the room. He had instructed her not to interrupt him for any reason. He glared at her.

Clearly cowed by him, she darted over to him and handed him a piece of paper, then ran out the door. Michael scanned the note and felt his blood drain from his head. Kate was at the hospital. His heart pounded in his chest and he broke into a sweat. "I have an emergency," he said, standing. "I have to leave."

Stone stood, the picture of indignation. "Mr. Hawkins, nobody walks out on negotiations with Wayland."

Michael didn't bother to answer; he let his actions do his talking for him. In his mind, he was already at the hospital with Kate.

Driving with grim determination and speed, he made it to the hospital in less than ten minutes. He had no details except that there'd been an accident at the home for unwed teenage mothers. What kind of accident? he wondered. How bad was it? If anything happened to her, he didn't know what he would do.

He found a nurse familiar with Kate's situation. Scanning a chart, she wore a guarded expression. "Mrs. Hawkins lost consciousness soon after she arrived. She'd apparently fallen and lost a lot of blood. She was taken into surgery. That's where she is now. You might prefer to wait in the surgery waiting area upstairs."

Lost a lot of blood. Michael's heart stopped. He could barely form the words, "Is she going to be okay?"

"The doctors are doing everything they can."

"The baby?" he said, hearing his voice crack.

"Was in distress. The prognoses for your wife and baby are uncertain right now," she reluctantly revealed, her eyes solemn. "I'm sorry we don't know more. There's a phone in the surgery waiting area if you need to make any calls."

Michael blindly walked toward the waiting area. What if he lost Kate? What if he lost Kate and the baby? He'd worked himself into the ground the last six months to protect their future, and what if there was no future?

A wave of hopelessness he'd thought he'd left behind consumed him. This was why he never wanted to count on another human being. This was why he didn't believe in love. If he truly didn't possess a heart, though, why did he feel as if he'd been gutted?

If he lost Kate, he would lose every bit of light in his life. He would lose his reason for living. Sinking down on a plastic chair, he leaned forward with his head in his hands. "She has to live," he whispered.

Raw with fear and grief, Michael called Dylan and left a message on his voice mail. Then, though he'd always been a man with a heavy dose of skepticism about God, he began to pray.

Moments passed like hours, and Michael paced the small waiting room feeling like a caged animal. He had wasted so much time. Now he would give anything for another moment with Kate. In her gentle, persistent way, she'd tried to show him the way she saw him, as a good man. She'd tried to love him, but he hadn't let her.

Hearing footsteps behind him, he quickly swung around to see Dylan and Justin. Both wore expressions of concern. "I came as soon as I picked up your message," Dylan said, patting Michael on the back. "Any news?"

Michael shook his head. "The prognoses for both Kate and the baby are uncertain."

Justin winced. "Sorry, guy. If there's anything we can do—"

The heavy weight in Michael's chest grew heavier. "If you've got a direct connection with the man upstairs, I could use it now."

Justin shifted uncomfortably and popped an antacid. "I'll get you some coffee."

Michael felt Dylan's gaze. "Do you know what happened?" Dylan asked.

"She fell. She was helping decorate a Christmas tree," he said, hearing the catch in his voice and unable to prevent it. He closed his eyes. "Oh, God, I've wasted so much time. I've been so focused on preventing a takeover I may have missed out on the best thing that ever entered this life."

Dylan sighed, squeezing Michael's shoulder again briefly. "You won't be the first of us to let a woman slip through your fingers. I'm still paying for my stupidity in college, but that's another story. You might still have a shot at it," Dylan said with a force that belied his usual casual, careless manner. "If you do, don't mess it up."

A nurse dressed in scrubs appeared in the doorway with a baby bundled in a blanket. "Mr. Hawkins, here is your daughter."

Michael froze. "Daughter?" he repeated.

"Yes," she said, putting the soft weight of the baby in his hands. "She's fine."

Michael stared into his daughter's tiny face and clenched his body to keep from trembling. "Kate?" he said, unable to keep the desperation from his voice. "What about my wife?"

"The doctors are still working on her. The baby was in better shape than we expected, but the baby usually gets the easy end of the deal with a cesarean section. We'll call you as soon as your wife is in recovery."

Almost afraid to hope, he shook his head. "Is she going to be okay?"

The nurse nodded. "It was touch and go when she first arrived, but she must have acted very quickly when she fell." She glanced at the baby and smiled. "She must have been determined to bring her into the world safely."

The relief that rushed through him was so powerful it hurt. He looked down at his daughter and saw Kate in her sweet face. A tear streamed down his cheek, and Michael could have sworn that in that moment, he grew a heart.

Before he had time to catch his breath, another nurse appeared in the doorway. "Would you like to see your wife?"

Baby in hands, Michael plowed into Justin as he entered the doorway, splattering coffee on Justin's shirt. "Sorry," he said. "Kate's okay. The baby's okay. Congratulations," he said impulsively. "You are co-godfathers."

"Co-godfathers!" Justin and Dylan said at the same time.

"Why would I want to be a godfather with you?" Justin demanded.

"Because you're so obsessed with the stock market you probably couldn't do it by yourself," Dylan told him.

Hearing his friends' argument, Michael's heart grew a millimeter lighter as he walked toward recovery. The moment he saw Kate, his breath stopped. "She's so pale," he said to the nurse.

"She lost a lot of blood, but she's going to be okay. Expect her to be groggy."

Kate heard Michael's voice as if it were coming from far away. She struggled to get closer to it.

"I'm giving up the company," he told her. "I walked away from the table. I'll just start another one if Wayland won't accept my conditions. You're too important and I don't want to miss another minute with you."

I must be dreaming, she thought, feeling a dull pain in her abdomen.

"Katie, love," he said, his voice strained. "I wish you would wake up so you could see our little Cupcake."

Cupcake! The baby. Kate remembered her fall and panic hit her. "The baby," she murmured, struggling to open her eyes. Her eyelids felt as if someone had put two-hundred-pound weights on them. She finally succeeded and saw Michael holding a bundle of blanket. Her brain was too scrambled to make sense of the images. Why was he holding a blanket?

"Michael."

He bent toward her. She was astonished to see a tear on his face.

"I love you," he told her. "You and the baby are the most important things in the world to me."

Kate closed her eyes. "I'm dreaming."

Michael gently shook her shoulder. "Don't go back to sleep. Please stay awake."

The pleading note in his voice tore at her, and she struggled to open her eyes again.

"I need you," he said. "I didn't want to, but I think I always have. Before I even met you, I needed you."

She looked into his raw, desperate eyes and lost her heart again. "Am I dreaming?"

He shook his head. "No." He lowered the bundle of blanket, and showed Kate the baby. Their baby.

Her heart soared. "Omigod, it's Cupcake." She reached out her fingers to touch her baby's head.

"She's okay," Michael said. "I've counted her fingers and toes. You got her here in time."

Michael set the baby in the bed beside her and took Kate's hand. "You and the baby are the most important things in the world to me. Never forget it."

Kate looked into his eyes and saw the awesome focus and commitment she'd seen before for other things, but this time she could see what she had always seen. Michael was no Tin Man. He had the biggest heart in the world. He just had hidden it well. No more, she thought. He finally knew it too.

One month later, Kate was giving Michelle Justine Hawkins her bath and telling her a love story. "You're such a lucky girl. You have a great daddy. Your daddy loves us so much he would give up his big company for us."

Michelle blew bubbles.

"He tells me he loved me before he even knew me. He tells me I gave him a heart." Kate sighed and wrapped her precious child in a hooded towel and held her close. "When you grow up, darling, I hope you will find a man who loves you like your daddy loves me."

"She will," Michael said, surprising her from the hallway. "She comes from a long line of lovers."

Kate stood and smiled at him. "What are you doing here?"

Michael kissed her, then took Michelle from her arms. "Since Wayland caved in to my demands, I promoted one of my project directors to VP of Operations. That will free me up a little more." He glanced down at Michelle as she yawned. "A bath makes her sleepy every time. I'll put her down."

He returned in no time and walked with Kate to the couch in the sunroom. He pulled her into his arms and Kate closed her eyes at the sensation of being held by him. It would never get old for her. Since Michelle's birth, he'd taken more time off from work, and he often came home early. The unhusband had turned into the perfect husband. She almost couldn't believe how lucky they were.

"Having a VP of Operations is the best professional move I've made in a long time," he said. "But my best move ever was hiring you." He brushed his lips over hers. "Marrying you." He deepened the kiss and drew back after several moments. "Loving you," he finally said.

Kate felt her heart spill over. "The Granger Home for Boys sent us one of their newsletters today."

"Oh, really?" he said in a disinterested tone that didn't fool her one bit.

"Yes, it seems a mysterious donor has contributed a fund for a ten-year supply of gourmet chocolate chip cookies for the home's cafeteria. Gosh," she said in a mock innocent voice. "I wonder who would make such an eccentric donation."

"I have no idea."

She let him keep his little secret since he shared so many of the important ones with her nowadays. She sighed. "Well I would do some pretty amazing things to a man who would give that kind of donation."

He hesitated. "What amazing things?"

"It would probably involve my mouth," she said and met his extremely interested gaze, "and every other part of my body."

He stared at her, his gaze growing warm. "I thought the doctor said—"

"The doctor released me this morning."

He gave her a look that said come and get me, and her heart turned a flip. "I think you should show me what amazing things you're thinking."

Kate loosened his tie and began to unbutton his shirt. "You do?"

He brushed his lips against hers, and the moment, like their lives, was filled with promise. "I do," he said. "Forever."

* * * * *

Look out for Millionaire Husband, *the next book in Leanne Banks'
exciting mini-series*
MILLION DOLLAR MEN.

On sale March 2002 from Silhouette Desire®.

THE DAKOTA MAN

By
Joan Hohl

JOAN HOHL

is the best-selling author of almost three dozen books. She has received numerous awards for her work, including the Romance Writers of America's Golden Medallion award. In addition to contemporary romance, this prolific author also writes historical and time-travel romances. Joan lives in eastern Pennsylvania with her husband and family.

To my dear Melissa,
the editor from…
heaven.

One

His brow furrowed in a frown, his square jaw clenched and his lips sealed in an anger-tight thin line, Mitch Grainger sat at his desk and stared at the object cradled in the palm of his broad hand. He could only scowl at the brilliant, multi-faceted engagement ring of clustered pink diamonds, encircled by smaller rubies.

Less than an hour ago, Mitch had retrieved the ring from the floor near his desk. Which is where the object had landed after bouncing off his chest, hurled at him in unreasonable fury by Natalie Crane, the beautiful, cool, usually unemotional woman who had been his fiancée mere moments before.

The flawless gemstones caught the afternoon sun rays slanting through the window blinds behind him. Mitch made a soft sound that was part rude snort, part unpleasant laugh.

Women. Would he ever understand them? Had any man ever understood them? More to the point, Mitch mused, closing his fingers around the bauble, did he give a damn anymore?

Not for Natalie Crane, certainly, he thought, answering his own question. Without allowing him the courtesy of offering an explanation for the scene she'd witnessed, she had jumped to the wrong conclusion. Coldly calling him a cheat and telling him their engagement was over, she had thrown the ring at him.

Fortunately, Mitch had never deluded himself into believing he was in love with her; he wasn't and never had been. He had simply decided that, at the age of thirty-five, it was time to choose a wife. Natalie had appeared eminently suitable for the position, being from one of the most wealthy and prestigious families in the Deadwood, South Dakota, area.

But now Natalie was history. With her precipitous accusations, she had impugned his honor, and he forgave no one for that.

Honor, his personal honor, was the one standard Mitch held as absolute. He had believed Natalie knew the depths of his sense of honor. Apparently, he had been mistaken, or she never would have misconstrued the situation she had happened upon, immediately leaping to the erroneous conclusion that he was playing around behind her back with his secretary, Karla Singleton.

Poor Karla, Mitch thought, recalling the stricken look on his secretary's face after the scene. Shaking his head, he slid open the top desk drawer, carelessly tossed the ring inside and slammed it shut again. He had never really liked the token, anyway. The concoction of pink diamonds encircled by clustered rubies had been Natalie's choice; his preference had been a simple, if large, elegant two-and-a-half-carat, marquis-cut solitaire.

Poor, foolish Karla, he amended, heaving a sigh raised by both sympathy and impatience.

Mitch could understand passion, he had experienced it himself...quite often, truth to tell. But what he couldn't understand, would never understand, was why in hell any woman—or man, either, for that matter—would indulge their passions to the point that they'd risk their health as well as pregnancy through unprotected sex.

But believing herself in love, and loved in return, Karla had risked all with a man who had taken his pleasure…then taken off. He had supposedly left to find a job with a future, but nonetheless leaving Karla devastated, pregnant, unwed and ashamed to tell her parents.

Not knowing what else to do, Karla had turned to her employer, sobbing out her miserable tale of woe on Mitch's broad shoulder. Of course, Natalie had picked that moment to pay a visit to his office. She had witnessed him holding the weeping young woman in his comforting arms and heard just enough to erroneously conclude that, not only had he been fooling around with Karla, but that he had impregnated her, as well.

As if he would ever be that stupid.

In retrospect, Mitch figured it was all for the best, since he certainly didn't relish the thought of being married to a woman who didn't trust him implicitly. From all historical indications, marriage could work without depthless love, but in his considered opinion, it couldn't survive without trust.

So had ended his brainstorm of acquiring a wife, setting up house and having a family.

On reflection, Mitch acknowledged the niggling doubts he had been having lately about his choice of Natalie, not as a wife—he felt positive she would make an exemplary wife—but as the mother of his children. And Mitch did want children of his own some day. While he had admired Natalie's cool composure at first, he had recently begun to wonder if her air of detachment would extend to her children...his children.

Having grown up with two brothers and a sister, in a home that more often than not rang with the sound of boisterous kids, controlled by a mother who had always been loving, even when firm, Mitch desired a similar upbringing for his own progeny.

In all honesty, Mitch admitted to himself that he was more relieved than disappointed by the results of Natalie's false assumptions.

But he still had Karla's problem to contend with, for she had asked for his advice and help. Mitch had always been a sucker for a woman's tears, especially a woman he cared about. His own sister could give testimony to that. The sight of a woman he cared for in tears turned him, this supposedly tough, no-nonsense C.E.O.

of a gambling casino in Deadwood, South Dakota, into the stalwart protector, the solver of feminine trials and tribulations...in other words, pure mush.

And Mitch did care about Karla, for her sake, because she was a genuinely nice person, and for his own sake, for she was the best assistant he had ever employed.

He had made some progress with Karla after calming her down following Natalie's dramatic little scene. With some gentle probing—in between dwindling, hiccuping sobs—Mitch had learned that Karla was determined to have and keep her baby. Not for any leftover feelings for the father, because she had none, but simply because it was *her* baby.

A decision Mitch silently applauded.

Still, Karla had maintained that she felt too ashamed to go to her parents, who lived in Rapid City, to ask for their financial or moral support. Karla was an only child, so there were no siblings to apply to for assistance. And, though she had made some friends in the year and a half she had been in Deadwood, she felt none were close enough to dump her problems on.

That left him, Mitch Grainger, the man with the tough exterior, surrounding a core of marshmallow in regards to weeping, defenseless females.

Helluva note, for sure.

An ironic smile of acceptance teased the corners of his sculpted, masculine lips. He'd take on the combined roles of surrogate father, brother and friend to Karla because of his soft spot...and because, if he didn't, and his sister ever found out about it, she'd have his hide.

His humor restored, Mitch reached for the intercom to summon Karla, just as a timid rap sounded on his office door, followed by the subdued sound of Karla's voice.

"May I come in, Mr. Grainger?"

"Yes, of course." He sighed; despite the numerous times he had asked her to call him Mitch, Karla had persisted in the more formal address. Now, after the emotional scene enacted mere minutes before, the formality seemed ludicrous. "Come in and sit down," he instructed as the door opened and she stepped inside. "And, from now on, call me Mitch."

"Yes, sir," she said meekly, crossing to the chair in front of his desk and perching on the edge of the seat.

He threw his hands up in exasperation. "I

give up, call me anything you like. How are you feeling?''

"Better." She managed a tremulous smile. "Thank you...for the use of your shoulder to cry on."

He smiled back. "I've had plenty of practice. Years back, my younger sister went through a period in her teens when she was a regular waterworks." His wry confidence achieved the desired effect.

She laughed and eased back in the chair. But her laughter quickly faded, erased by a frown of consternation. "About Miss Crane...I'd like to go see her, explain..."

"No." Mitch cut her off, his voice sharp.

Karla bit her trembling lip, blinked against a renewed well of tears. "But...it was a misunderstanding," she said, her voice unsteady. "Surely, if I talked to her..."

He silenced her with a slashing movement of his hand. "No, Karla. Natalie didn't ask for, or wait long enough to hear an explanation. She added one and one and came up with three—you, me and your baby. Her mistake." His tone hardened with cold finality. "It's over. Now, let's discuss another matter of business."

She frowned. "What business?"

"Your business."

"Mine?" Karla's expression went blank.

"The baby," he said, nudging her memory. "Your baby. Have you made any plans? Do you want to keep working? Or…"

"Yes, I want to keep working," she interrupted him. "That is, if you don't mind?"

"Why would I mind?" He grinned. "Hell, you're the best assistant I've ever employed."

"Thank you." A pleased glow brightened her brown eyes, and a flush colored her pale cheeks.

"Okay, you want to continue working."

"Oh, yes, please."

"How long?"

"As long as I can." Karla hesitated a moment before quickly adding, "I'd like to work up to the last possible minute."

"Forget it." He shook his head. "I don't think that would be good for you or the baby."

"But the work's not really physical," she insisted. "Having a baby is expensive today, and I'll need every dollar I can earn."

"I provide excellent health insurance coverage for you, Karla," he reminded her. "Including maternity benefits."

"I know, and I appreciate that, but I want to save as much as I can for afterward," she explained. "I'll need enough to tide me over until I can go back to work."

"Don't concern yourself with finances, I'll take care of that. I want you to concentrate on taking care of yourself, and the child you're carrying." He held up a hand when she would have protested. "Five more months, Karla."

"Six," she dared to bargain. "I'll only be seven-and-a-half months by then."

He smiled at her show of temerity. "Okay, six," he conceded. "But you will spend that sixth month training your replacement."

"But it won't take me a whole month to train someone," she exclaimed. "I won't have anything to do!"

"Exactly. Consider it a small victory that I'm allowing that much."

She heaved a sigh of defeat. "You're the boss."

"I know." His grin lasted all of a few seconds before turning into a grimace. "Damn," he muttered. "When the time comes, how in the hell are we ever going to find someone suitable to replace you?"

A little over a month later, and many miles distant to the southeast, an individual ministorm raged beneath a sun-drenched corner of Pennsylvania....

"Rat." The scissors slashed through the voluminous skirt.

"Louse." A seam tore asunder.

"Jerk." The bodice was sheared into small pieces.

"Creep." Tiny buttons went flying.

"There...done." Her chest heaving from her emotion-driven exertions, Maggie Reynolds stepped back and glared down at the ragged shards of white watered taffeta material that had formerly been the most exquisite wedding gown she had ever seen.

With a final burst of furious energy, she gave a vicious kick of one bare foot, scattering the pile of material into large and small pieces that glimmered in the early June sunlight streaming through the bedroom window.

Tears pricked her eyes; Maggie told herself it was the glare of sunlight, and not the fact that she was to have been married in that designer extravagance in two weeks' time.

The sting in her eyes grew sharper. Just two days before, Maggie's intended groom had thrown her a vicious curveball right out of left field. After sharing her apartment and her bed with him for nearly a year, and after all the arrangements for their wedding had been in place for months, she had come home from work to find all of his belongings gone, his clothes closet empty, and a note—a damned note—propped against the napkin holder on the kitchen table. The words he had written were imprinted on her memory.

Maggie, I'm sorry, I really am, he had scrawled on the lined yellow paper she kept for grocery lists. *But I can't go through with our marriage. I have fallen in love with Ellen Bennethan, and we are eloping to Mexico today. Please try not to hate me too much. Todd.*

The thought of his name brought his image front and center in Maggie's mind. Average height, sharp dresser, attractive, with coal-black hair and pale blue eyes. And, evidently, a class-A cheat. A sneer curled her soft lips. Hate him? She didn't hate him. She despised him. So, he had fallen in love with Ellen Bennethan, had he? Bull. He had fallen in love with her money. Ellen, a meek, simpering twit, who had never worked a day in her life, was the only child and heir of Carl Bennethan, owner and head honcho of the Bennethan Furniture Company, and Todd's employer.

Dear Todd had just taken off, leaving Maggie to clean up the mess after him. Which in itself was bad enough. But the thing that bit the deepest was that they had made love the very night before he split.

No, Maggie corrected herself with disgust. They hadn't made love, they had had sex. And it hadn't been great sex, either. Great? Ha! It had never been great. Far from it. From the beginning, Todd had been less than an enthusiastic lover, never mind energetic.

Or was she the less-than-energetic one?

How many times over the previous year had she asked herself that question? Maggie mused, self-doubt raising its nasty little head in her mind. In truth, she acknowledged, she had never become so passionately aroused that she felt swept away by the moment. Perhaps there was something lacking in her….

The hell with that, Maggie thought, anger reasserting itself to overwhelm doubt. And, to hell with Todd, and men in general. In her private opinion, sex was highly overrated, a fictional fantasy.

Outrage restored, Maggie made a low growling sound deep in her throat, and gave the rendered sparkling white pieces another scattering kick.

"Bastard."

"Feel better now?"

Maggie spun around at the sound of the smoky, dryly voiced question, to glare at the young woman leaning with indolent nonchalance against the door frame. The woman, Maggie's best friend, Hannah Deturk, was tall, slim, elegant and almost too beautiful to be tolerated.

Maggie had often thought, and even more often said, that if she didn't like Hannah so much, she could easily and quite happily hate her.

"Not a hell of a lot," Maggie admitted in a near snarl. "But I'm not finished yet, either."

"Indeed?" Hannah raised perfectly arched honey-brown eyebrows. "You're going to take the scissors to your entire trousseau?"

"'Course not," Maggie snapped. "I'm neither that stupid nor that far gone."

"Could'a fooled me," Hannah drawled. "I'd say, any woman who'd tear apart a gorgeous three-thousand-dollar wedding gown in a fit of rampant rage is about as far gone as is possible for a woman to be."

Just as tall as her friend, just as slim, and no

slouch herself in the looks department, with her long mass of flaming-red hair and her creamy complexion, Maggie gave Hannah a superior look and a sugar-sweet smile.

"Indeed?" she mimicked. "Well, there's possible, and then there's possible. Stick around, friend, and I'll demonstrate possibilities that'll blow your mind."

"You almost scare me," Hannah said, a thread of concern woven through her husky voice. "But I will stick around...just to ensure you don't hurt yourself."

"I'm already hurt," Maggie cried, a rush of tears to her eyes threatening to douse the fire of anger in their emerald-green depths.

"I know." Hannah relinquished her pose in the doorway to go to Maggie. "I know," she murmured, drawing her friend into a protective embrace.

"I'm sorry, Hannah," Maggie muttered, sniffing. "I promised myself I wouldn't cry anymore."

"And you shouldn't," Hannah said, her voice made raspy with compassion. "That son of a bitch isn't worth the time of day from you, never mind your tears."

Maggie was so startled by Hannah's curse—

Hannah *never* cursed—she stepped back to stare at her friend in tear-drying amazement.

Hannah shrugged. "Occasionally, when I'm seriously upset or furious, I lose control of my mouth."

"Oh." Maggie blinked away the last of the moisture blurring her vision and swiped her hands over her wet cheeks. "Well, you must be seriously one or the other, because I've known you since soon after you arrived here in Philadelphia from flyover country, and this is the first time I've ever heard a swear word from you."

"Actually, I'm seriously both," Hannah drawled, her tone belying the glitter in her blue eyes. "It just fries me that you're tearing yourself apart over that…that…slimy, two-timing, money-grabbing slug."

"Thanks, friend," Maggie murmured, moved by Hannah's concern for her. "I appreciate your support."

"You're welcome." A smile curved Hannah's full lips. "And it's Nebraska."

"What?"

"The flyover country I come from is the State of Nebraska," she answered.

"Oh, yeah, I knew that," Maggie said, interest sparking in her green eyes. "What's it like there…in Nebraska?"

Hannah frowned, as if confused by both the question and her friend's sudden show of interest on a topic she'd never before evinced any curiosity over. "The section I came from? Mostly rural, kind of placid, and at the time I decided to move to the big city, I thought, pretty dull."

"Sounds like just the ticket," Maggie mused aloud in a contemplative mutter.

"Just the ticket," Hannah repeated in astonishment. "For what? Being bored silly? What are you getting at?"

Maggie's smile could only be described as reckless. "You know those possibilities I mentioned?"

"Ye-e-es..." Hannah eyed her with budding alarm. "But now I'm almost afraid to ask."

Maggie laughed; it felt good, so she laughed again. "I'll tell you, anyway. Come with me, my friend," she invited, turning away from the room and the scattered debris that had once been her wedding gown. "Venting my spleen in here made me thirsty. We'll talk over coffee."

"You can't be serious." Her half-full cup of coffee—her third—in front of her, Hannah stared at Maggie in sheer disbelief.

"I assure you I am. Dead serious," Maggie

said, her features set in lines of determination. "I have already started the ball rolling."

"By slashing your gown to ribbons?" Hannah asked, her tone reflecting the hope that her friend hadn't done something even more drastic.

"Oh, that. That was symbolic." Maggie dismissed the act with a flick of her hand. "I couldn't stand looking at it another minute. No," she said, shaking her head. "What I have done to get the ball rolling was to spend this lovely Sunday morning composing notes to all the guests invited to the wedding, informing them that there would be no wedding, after all, e-mailing those on-line, and preparing the rest for snail-mail delivery."

"If you'd given me a holler, I'd have gladly helped you with that," Hannah said, heaving a sigh of exasperation.

"Thanks, but, well…" Maggie shrugged. "That chore is done."

"You didn't e-mail your parents…." Hannah's eyebrows shot up. "Did you?"

"Well, of course not. I telephoned them." Maggie sighed. "They were understandably upset, insisted I go spend some time with them in Hawaii."

"Good idea."

Maggie gave a quick head shake. "No, it isn't. They both took early retirement and moved to Hawaii to relax after Dad's mild heart attack. If I went there, in the mood I'm in, Mom would probably knock herself out to fuss all over me. Dad would likewise fret, curtail his golf games and try to distract and entertain me. And I'd feel guilty as hell because of it."

Hannah frowned but nodded. "I suppose."

Maggie soldiered on. "I also drafted a letter to my superior at work, giving my one-month notice of my intention to leave the firm."

Hannah's eyes widened with alarm. "Maggie, you didn't."

"I did," Maggie assured her, raising a hand to keep her friend from interrupting. "What's more, I faxed a Realtor I know, asking him if he'd be interested in listing my apartment for sale."

Hannah jumped from her chair. "Maggie, no." She shook her head, setting her sleek, bobbed honey-brown hair swinging. "You can't do that."

"I damn well can," Maggie retorted. "My grandmother left this place to me, I own it free and clear." She rolled her eyes. "And the forever taxes that go with it."

"But..." Her hair swung again, wildly. "Why? Where will you go? Where will you live?"

"Why? Because I'm tired of the treadmill, nose to the grindstone, following the rules." Maggie shrugged. "Who knows, maybe I'll join the circus."

"I don't believe I'm hearing this." As if unable to remain still, Hannah began to pace back and forth in front of the table. "To give up your job, sell your apartment..." Hannah threw up her hands. "That's crazy."

"Hannah—" Maggie came close to shouting "—I feel crazy."

"So you're just going to take off?"

"Yes."

"For how long, for Pete's sake?"

Maggie hesitated, shrugged, then answered, "Until I'm broke, or no longer feel crazy enough to break things and hurt people...Todd what's-his-name in particular."

"Oh, Maggie," Hannah murmured in commiseration, dropping onto her chair. "He's not worth all this anguish."

"I know that," Maggie agreed. "But knowing it doesn't help. So I'm cutting out, cutting loose."

"But, Maggie..." Hannah actually wailed.

Maggie shook her head, hard. "You can't change my mind, Hannah. I've got the itch to run free for a while and I'm going to scratch it."

"But you must have some idea where you're going," Hannah persisted, always the one for detail.

"No." Maggie shrugged. "Who knows, maybe I'll wind up in Nebraska."

Two

Three months later

The redhead knocked the breath out of him. A jolt of energy, physical and sexual in nature, made the body-blow a double whammy.

Mitch was both shocked and confused by his reaction to the woman Karla ushered into his office. It certainly wasn't that she was a stunning beauty; she wasn't. Oh, it wasn't that she was not attractive; she most definitely was, very attractive. But he knew many attractive and even a few stunning women, and yet he had never experienced such a strong and immediate response to any one of them.

Strange.

Baffled, yet careful not to reveal his condition, Mitch studied the woman as she crossed the room to his desk. On closer inspection, one might even concede she possessed a particular beauty...if one had a weakness for tall, slender women with creamy skin, a wide mouth with full lips, slightly slanted forest-glen-green eyes and long, thick hair of a deep shade of flaming red.

Apparently, Mitch wryly concluded, he did have such a previously unrecognized weakness.

At least, his knees felt a little weak; he felt the tremor in them when she drew closer.

Up close, she looked even better...damn the luck.

But, one thing was for certain, Mitch mused, she sure as hell hadn't dressed to make an impression. Her casual attire made a silent declaration of her utter disregard for conventional, or his personal, opinion.

She came to a stop next to a chair in front of his desk.

Mitch came to his senses.

Cursing his uncharacteristic distraction, he made a show of perusing her application.

"Ms. Reynolds?" Raising his gaze from the papers in his hand, he offered her a faint smile.

"Yes." Her attractive voice was soft, modulated, neutral, her return smile a pale reflection of his own.

He leaned forward over his desk and extended his right hand. "Mitch Grainger," he said, amazed by the tingling sensation caused by the touch of her palm to his in the brief handshake. "Have a seat." He flicked the still-tingling hand at the chair beside her.

"Thank you." With what appeared to be relaxed and effortless grace, she stepped in front of the chair and lowered herself into it. Settled, she met his direct stare with calm patience.

Watch it, Grainger, Mitch advised himself. *This is one woman determined not to be intimidated.*

He arched a brow. "If you'll excuse me a moment, while I give your application a quick once-over?"

She deigned to nod her permission.

Cool? Mitch speculated, unlocking his gaze from the brilliant green of hers to skim the application. Or was she, like Natalie Crane, just plain glacier-cold, through and through?

To his astonishment, after the fiasco of his engagement, Mitch found himself anticipating the opportunity to discover the answers to his questions about this particular woman.

Speed-reading the forms, Mitch quickly concurred with Karla's enthusiastic opinion; Maggie Reynolds's credentials were very impressive. A fact that had been pleasing to them both as Karla had been thus far unsuccessful in finding a suitable replacement.

Lifting his head, Mitch tested her with a piercing stare and his most forbidding tones. "You can produce references to confirm the information provided?"

"Not at hand," she said, her voice as cool and unruffled as her demeanor. "But I can obtain them."

He nodded; he had expected no less. "You appear to be well qualified for this position," he admitted, unfamiliar excitement quickening inside him at the idea of her working for him, at his beck and call, five days a week. But his hidebound sense of honor insisted he be completely honest. "In fact, you are overqualified. A bigger city would offer you much better opportunities for corporate advancement.''

She smiled.

His blood pressure rose a notch.

"I'm aware of that," she said. "But, while I appreciate your candor, and advice, I'll pass on it."

Too cool, Mitch reiterated...and just a hint of condescension. The woman had guts to spare; not many dared to condescend to him.

"Why?" He shot the question at her.

She didn't shoot back. Then again, maybe she did, only she fired with a flashing, mind-bending smile.

Mitch felt the hit...and rather enjoyed it.

"As I explained to your assistant, and as my application attests, I've been there, done that," she said. "I'm tired of the struggle." She shrugged. "I suppose you might say my edge got dull."

Mitch wouldn't have said there was a damn thing dull about her. At any rate, he wasn't prepared to say it to her, not at this point of their association. And, for some reason, or quirk in his own nature, he was determined on their having an association.

"I see" was all he would say.

"Besides," she continued, "I like the look of this town, the Old West ambience. It's quaint."

Quaint. Mitch nodded. It was that. "When did you arrive? Have you seen much of the town?" He had to smile. "Not that there's much to see."

"I...er, strolled around this morning," she answered, her hesitancy and obvious reluctance revealing her first signs of uncertainty.

Mitch decided to probe for the reason for her reticence. "You didn't take a ride on the Deadwood Trolley?"

She shook her head, setting her hair swaying around her shoulders like living flames...and kicking his imagination into high gear.

"No." Her full, tempting lips curved into a faint smile; his imagination soared off the gauge. "My father always said that shoe-leather express was the best way to see any city," she explained. "I can ride the trolley another day."

As fascinated as Mitch surely was by her mouth, he didn't miss the fact that she had answered only part of his two-part question. Naturally, he wondered why.

"And when did you say you arrived?" he asked, with gentle persistence.

A spark flared to life in the depths of her fabulous green eyes. Annoyance, anger? Mitch mused.

"I didn't say." Her voice held an edge.

Good, Mitch thought. He wanted her on edge, off balance, her cool composure rattled. In his experience, he had found he learned more that way.

"I know." He smiled...and waited.

She sighed, clearly losing patience with his persistence. "I arrived yesterday," she finally admitted.

Mitch wasn't through yet. "From where? Philadelphia?"

She gave him a level look, as if taking his measure. Mitch felt that tingly sensation again, this time throughout his entire system. He liked it. Once more, he merely smiled and waited, returning her measuring look.

"No." She didn't smile; she met his look with green fire. "I left Philly months ago, on an extended vacation tour of the country. I arrived here via a small town in Nebraska, where I had stopped for lunch."

"But you were originally headed for Deadwood?" Mitch thought it a reasonable question. Evidently, Ms. Maggie Reynolds did not, if her fleeting expression of exasperation was anything to go by.

"No." She shook her head, setting the red strands swirling once more.

Mitch's fingers itched to delve into the fiery mass, just to see if it burned him. When she didn't continue on with an explanation, he raised a nudging eyebrow, determined now to hear the whole of her story.

Silence stretched between them for several seconds, then she capitulated with a the-hell-with-it shrug. "While waiting for my lunch, I checked my finances," she said grittily. "The bottom-line balance indicated that it was time for me to go back to work—" she shrugged "—and here I am."

She had managed to surprise him, a rare accomplishment for anyone; he had long since been surprised by much of anything. Mitch glanced down at the bona fides on her application. A frown creased his brow when he looked up at her. "I don't get it," he admitted. "With your credentials, you could have secured an excellent-paying position in any major city." He refrained from adding that he was glad she hadn't. "Why Deadwood?"

She shifted in her chair, revealing her mounting impatience. "I think I've already explained that."

He agreed with a slight nod. "Been there, done that, tired of the grind. Right?"

"Yes." Her smile had a hint of smugness.

"But, if you're running out of money..." Mitch let his voice trail off, not yet ready to let her off the hook by quoting the salary he was prepared to offer her, for he definitely was going to hire her.

"I'm not running out of money," she corrected him. "I'm running a bit low. There is a difference."

"Point taken," he admitted, deciding he liked this woman's style. "But...why Deadwood?" he repeated, now merely curious about her choice.

She smiled.

His stomach muscles constricted.

"Believe it or not," she said, "I overheard the men seated in the booth behind me talking about it." She shrugged. "So, I figured...why not?"

Guts, style and insouciance. Some combination, and, thankfully, not in the least similar to Natalie, Mitch thought, tamping down an urge to laugh. He was looking forward to working with, matching wits with and, hopefully, gaining a more intimate relationship with this woman. But he didn't want to appear too eager or show his hand too soon.

"As I'm sure you couldn't help but notice, my assistant is in her third trimester of pregnancy," he said.

"It is pretty hard to miss," she responded dryly.

"Yes." He paused, allowed his concern for Karla to show on his expression. "I'm growing anxious about finding someone to replace her, she needs to rest more." He paused again, pursed his lips, just for effect.

She didn't betray knowledge of his "effect." She held his steady gaze with cool green eyes.

His admiration for her expanding, Mitch silently applauded her display of composure. "That being the case, the position is yours…if you still want it."

"I do." She nodded. "Thank you."

Then he quoted a salary figure.

That got a reaction from her. It was quick, but there, in the slight flicker of surprise in her eyes, her expression. She controlled it just as quickly.

"That's more than generous," she said. "When would you like me to start?"

Immediately, he thought. "As soon as possible," he said.

"It's Thursday." She raised a perfectly arched, dark red eyebrow. "Will Monday suit?"

"Fine," he agreed, somehow certain it would be a very long weekend.

Although she had endured the actual torture rather than allow her consternation to show, Maggie exited Grainger's office feeling as if she had been grilled to a turn by the Spanish Inquisition. She recalled the conversation she had overheard last night in a nearby restaurant. A woman who had interviewed for this position had stated a very adept description of Mitch Grainger. That young woman in the restaurant hadn't exaggerated; he was every bit as hard as bedrock, maybe harder, hard and tough, intelligent and probing, and physically attractive... devastatingly so.

After that nerve-jangling interview, Maggie felt as if his image was imprinted on her mind, never to be erased. And the image was more than a little disturbing.

The first thing Maggie had noticed about Mitch Grainger, even as he sat behind his desk, was his height. He was tall, at least six two, possibly three. He had the lean, well-toned body of a top-notch, worth-a-bizillion-dollars quarterback. His hair was dark, his eyes a piercing gray. His skin was sun-burnished. His clothes were expensive, impeccably tailored to his broad-shouldered, long-muscled frame.

Yes, indeedy, Mitch Grainger was sexy and good-looking…if one were susceptible to sharply defined features, cool reserve, an air of absolute command, blatant sensuality and quick, intelligent wit with attitude.

Fortunately, for Maggie's peace of mind, she was not so inclined. Within seconds of entering his office, she had labeled him an arrogant, chauvinistic ram, hiding inside the trappings of civilized clothing.

And she had just signed on to work for the man. The emotional side of Maggie urged her to run for the nearest exit. Her practical side reminded her that she needed the money, or she wouldn't be running very far for very long.

"How did it go?" Karla asked, equal measures of anxiety and hope in her tones.

Jarred from her less-than-encouraging introspection, Maggie dredged up a smile. "He hired me. I start Monday."

As if she had been holding it, Karla's breath

came out in a whooshing sound. "Oh, good," she said, a bright smile lighting her pretty face. "He was driving me crazy."

Great. Just what she needed to hear, Maggie thought, sinking onto the chair Karla indicated with a wave of her hand. Convinced her initial concern about Karla's obvious anxiety over finding her replacement was because the man was an absolute tyrant, she was almost afraid to ask "Why?"

"He thinks I should rest more."

"So he said," Maggie confided.

"Oh, he's so-o-o protective," Karla said, heaving a sigh and rolling her eyes. "This last week especially...just because my ankles have been swelling a little."

He was so-o-o protective? He noticed a little swelling in her ankles? Well, she guessed she could credit the man's supposed tyrannical behavior as the reason for Karla's overanxiousness, Maggie thought, her mental gears beginning to spin.

Why would an employer, a bedrock-hard employer at that, evince such concern...her gears ground to a halt at a sudden, most startling of questions: could Mitch Grainger be the father of Karla's baby?

Well, of course he could, Maggie chided herself. He was a man, wasn't he? A blatantly sensuous man.

For some inexplicable reason beyond her comprehension, she suddenly felt queasy.

"Is something wrong?" Karla asked, peering at Maggie with concern. "You're pale. Are you feeling ill?"

No, not ill, disgusted, Maggie assured herself, working up another smile. "No..." She shook her head and raked her mind for a reasonable response. "I...er, everything happened so fast, you know. It's exciting but a little unnerving, too." She managed a laugh, a weak one, but a laugh. Sort of. "I mean, who ever expects to get hired for a job—" she snapped her fingers "—like that?"

"I know what you mean." Karla laughed, too, for real. "But that's Mr. Grainger's way. He is decisive, forceful, and he has a tendency to be a bit overwhelming."

A bit? Like a bulldozer. Maggie kept her opinion to herself. All she said, dryly and wryly, to Karla was "I noticed."

The other woman giggled. "I think I'm going to enjoy working with you for the next couple of weeks, Maggie, and—" she paused, suddenly looking very young and uncertain "—I hope we can be friends."

Maggie felt a tug at her heartstrings. Off the top of her head, she'd guess Karla to be twenty-two, maybe twenty-three, four or five years her junior. Yet the girl appeared so much younger, so vulnerable, she made Maggie feel old, if only in experience.

"I'm sure we will be," Maggie said, reaching across the desk to take Karla's hand. "And, as a novice to the gambling business, I'm just as sure I'm going to need all the help you're willing to give me over the coming weeks."

Fairly beaming, Karla squeezed Maggie's hand. "With your experience, I'm positive you'll do fine."

Yes, she would, Maggie silently agreed. That is, if she could tolerate the bulldozer. And it was a big if. But, first things first.

"I was hoping you also could help me with something else," she said.

"Of course, if I can," Karla said. "What is it?"

"Well, right now, I've got a room at the Mineral Palace," she explained, her smile rueful. "But I can't stay there. I need to find a place to rent, a furnished room or small apartment. I don't suppose you'd know of any?"

"Yes, I do, and it's right in my building!" Karla exclaimed, laughing. "And I can almost guarantee you'll be able to have it. It's a bachelor apartment. And it's fully furnished but..." She hesitated, frowned, bit her lip.

"But?" Maggie prompted, her burst of anticipation doing a nosedive.

"It's on the third floor and there's no elevator...would that be a problem?"

"Not at all," Maggie assured her, laughing in sheer relief. "Where's the apartment house located?"

"It's right outside of town, but it's not a regular apartment house," Karla explained. "A long time ago, it was a private residence, a large old Victorian house that's been renovated into apartments."

Although Maggie immediately envisioned a somewhat shabby old house with mere remnants of its former elegance, she told herself that beggars couldn't be choosers. Besides, she had always loved Victorian-style houses, even the ones that had seen better days. Deciding to accept circumstances as part and parcel of her crazy adventure, she smiled to set the still-frowning Karla at ease.

"Sounds interesting," she said, feeling rewarded with the smile that chased the frown from Karla's face.

"Who do I talk to about seeing the place?"

Karla's smile grew into a grin. "The boss."

"The boss?" Maggie's stomach rebelled. "Mr. Grainger owns the building?"

"Yep." Karla nodded. "At least, his family does," she qualified. "His great-great grandfather built the house...oh, somewhere around the turn of the century, I think. It was several years after he had established his bank here and married the daughter of one of the partners or managers or executives or whatever of the Homestake gold mine."

"They own the bank, too?"

"No." Karla shook her head and frowned. "The way I understand it, Mitch's great-grandfather sold out the business in the twenties, when he got into buying real estate. Then the bank went under when the market crashed. Apparently, it was the land holdings that kept the family from ruin during the depression, for they managed to hang on to everything."

"Including the house that's now an apartment," Maggie inserted.

Karla nodded. "And this property." She waved a hand, indicating the casino building. "Both of which are under Mitch's control."

Wonderful. Maggie was hard-pressed to keep from groaning aloud. What to do? she asked herself, reluctant to go back into Mr. Grainger's office. While living in the same building as Karla would be nice, Maggie wasn't sure she wanted to both work for and rent from her employer. Besides, if her suspicions about Karla and him having an affair were correct, even though they somehow didn't seem to fit together, the idea of being around to witness their "togetherness" didn't appeal to Maggie in the least. And yet, she needed a permanent address, the sooner the better.

"I'll go talk to Mitch now," Karla said, settling the matter for Maggie by pushing herself out of her chair and turning to tap on his door.

Maggie opened her mouth to ask Karla to wait a moment, but before she could utter a sound, Karla had opened the door and slipped inside the office.

To her surprise, Maggie didn't have time to fume or to fidget, for within minutes, Karla was back, a triumphant smile on her face. She raised her hand to display a key clipped to a case dangling from her fingers.

"We're outta here," she said, motioning for Maggie to follow her as she skirted the desk and moved toward the outer hallway.

"But..." Maggie began.

"He gave me the rest of the afternoon off," Karla cut in breezily. "He told me to take his truck to run you out to have a look at the apartment. I'm to call him from there. If you like the place, I'm to use the truck to help you move your stuff...if you need help."

His truck? Frowning, Maggie scrambled out of her chair to hurry after the surprisingly agile woman. Should Karla be driving a truck in her advanced pregnancy? Never having been pregnant, she didn't have a clue.

They didn't go through the casino to the front entrance. Instead, at the base of the narrow stairway that led to the second floor, Karla turned to traverse another narrow hallway, leading to a steel door at the rear of the building. A burly uniformed guard stood posted next to the door.

"Hi, Karla, late lunch?" The guard smiled and gave Maggie a curious once-over.

"No." Karla grinned and shook her head. "The boss gave me the afternoon off." She turned to smile at Maggie. "Maggie, this is Johnny Brandon."

"Mr. Brandon," Maggie said, extending her right hand to be swallowed up in his.

Karla switched her glance back at the guard.

"Johnny, this is Maggie Reynolds. She'll be working here starting Monday."

"Pleased to meet you, Ms. Reynolds…and please, call me Johnny." The guard gripped her hand for a second, inclined his head, then shot a grin at Karla. "You've finally found someone to suit Mr. Grainger, huh?"

"Yes." Karla heaved a dramatic sigh, but ruined the effect with a giggle. "Finally. And now we're outta here, before he changes his mind about the afternoon off."

Chuckling, Johnny moved to open the door for them. "I can't see that happening. Nice to meet you, Ms. Reynolds."

"Maggie, please," she said, smiling as she followed Karla from the casino.

The exit led directly onto a parking lot. Trailing Karla, Maggie glanced around at the number of trucks parked in neatly aligned rows. The vehicle Karla stopped next to was not what Maggie had envisioned as a "truck," but a large dusty sports utility vehicle. But what a sports utility vehicle. Even with the coat of dust, the black behemoth fairly shouted *expensive*.

"Isn't it super?" Karla said, smiling at what Maggie knew must have been her bemused expression.

"And big," Maggie said, nodding. "No, huge."

Karla shrugged, and pushed a button on the key case, unlocking the doors. "These vehicles are almost a necessity in this mountainous terrain."

"What does it get, five miles to the gallon?" Circling the monster, Maggie slipped into the plush passenger seat, noting that plush described the entire interior.

"A little more than that," Karla said, grinning as she carefully slid behind the wheel. "But it drives like a dream," she continued, giving evidence that she had driven the vehicle before. "Like a luxury car, really." Firing the engine, she proved the claim by smoothly maneuvering the purring beast out of the parking lot.

"You know, I really don't need help moving my stuff, if I decide to take the apartment. We wouldn't have had to waste Mr. Grainger's fuel." Maggie turned her head to smile at Karla. "We could have used your car."

"No, we couldn't," Karla said, laughing. "Because I don't have a car."

"Then how do you get around—to shop, to work?" Maggie asked. "Is the house within walking distance?"

"Well I have walked, and I still could, if I

wanted, which I don't, at least not anymore.'' Karla smiled and shook her head. "No, Mitch drives me in to work."

Uh-huh, Maggie thought, growing more convinced about an intimate relationship between the two. Unbidden, and shocking, a vision rose in her mind of the bedrock-hard Mitch Grainger and the soft, puppy-friendly Karla, locked and writhing in a lovers' embrace. She immediately blanked the image. For some strange, confusing reason, she felt upset, almost hurt by the very thought of him making love to Karla.

Another thought rushed in, nearly as upsetting as the first, a horrifying thought that required immediate clarification.

"Does Mr. Grainger live in the house?" she asked, hearing the ragged threads of strain in her voice.

"Oh, no," Karla answered. "He has an apartment on the third floor of the casino, above the office."

Relief washed through Maggie, only to be followed by an odd and unwelcome sense of dejection at this further proof of their relationship. Why else, she reasoned, would he put himself out to fetch Karla back and forth?

Three

The house was beautiful.

Maggie fell in love with it on sight. It reminded her of the lovely old Victorian houses that had been converted into bed-and-breakfast inns in Cape May, New Jersey. But this house had been built on an even grander scale, and was a true mansion. It had a deep-roofed wraparound porch, intricate and lacy-looking decorative gingerbread and a copper-roofed tower on one corner.

Gazing up at the distinctive bell-shaped roof, Maggie quivered with anticipation at the realization that there were windowed tower alcoves on all three floors of the building. Having lived all her life in modern, boxlike apartments, first with her parents, then in the similar flat her grandmother had willed to her, Maggie loved old-fashioned places with nooks and crannies.

"So, what do you think?" Karla asked, breaking into Maggie's bemused near-trance.

"It's...magnificent," Maggie murmured.

"Big, too." Karla laughed. "Do you want to come in, or just stand here and stare at the outside of the place?"

"I want to come in," Maggie answered, grinning. "I can't wait to see the inside."

On entering the foyer, Maggie felt a pang of disappointment at the obvious but necessary changes that had been made to convert the once-gracious private home into apartments. Still, quite a bit of the former beauty remained in the original woodwork, including the hardwood flooring and the wide staircase attached to one wall. A hallway ran next to the stairway to the rear of the enormous house.

"As you can see, it wasn't at all difficult to section off for separate living accommodations," Karla said, motioning to the closed doors facing each other across the foyer. "This is my apartment." She moved to the door set into the stairway wall and inserted a key in the lock. "Come on in."

"Oh, you do have a tower alcove," Maggie said, eagerly following the younger woman. Once inside, she caught her breath on a soft "Oh…it's beautiful, like stepping back in time."

"Yes. I love it." Karla smiled.

"I can see why." Glancing around the generous-size living room, Maggie feasted her eyes on the period furniture and the curved, deeply padded window seat in the alcove.

The Victorian motif was carried through the rest of the apartment, even the small bathroom. Karla led the way into the kitchen at the back of the house. There, everything was bright with ultramodern white appliances.

"This room was originally the pantry and laundry room," Karla explained, moving to the sink. "Would you like a cup of coffee or tea?"

"I'd love a cup of coffee," Maggie said, then qualified, "But could I see the third-floor apartment first?"

Karla laughed. "Of course you can see it." Turning, she led the way back into the living room. "You might want to go on ahead," she said, grinning as she opened the door. "I'm a little slow lately going up the stairs."

Maggie's gaze rested on Karla's extended belly. "You don't have to go upstairs. I can go up alone. That is, if it's all right?"

"Oh, sure it's all right." Taking a key off the case Mitch had given her, Karla handed it to Maggie. "When you get to the top of the stairs, follow the hallway to the door at the back. Oh, and by the way, there's another enclosed staircase at the rear of the hallway, with an access door to the back parking area. I'll start the coffee while you have a look at the place."

At the second-floor landing Maggie found the door to the stairway leading to the third level. It was also enclosed, much narrower, but lit by a ceiling light and by the sunlight pouring in through lacy curtains at a window at the top landing.

Not knowing what to expect…a big old storage attic, or perhaps a large room sectioned off for servants' quarters, Maggie mounted the stairs. A wide hallway with sloping ceilings to either side ran to an enlarged room at the front. While she had expected the sloping roofs, she hadn't expected the storage cabinets built into the spaces beneath—nooks and crannies—or the size of the apartment beyond.

It was spotlessly clean, huge and wonderful and completely furnished, again with the same Victorian motif. To one side, the bedroom and bath were both sectioned off and private. To the other side one large room made up the kitchen and living area. A small round dinette table sat in the tower alcove, and a lace-curtained window overlooked the front of the house.

A strange sense of excitement stirred inside Maggie, a feeling almost as if she had found exactly what she had spent months unknowingly searching for.

A home…or a hideaway? Maggie didn't know, nor did she care. It felt right, and that was enough, enough even to put up with the bedrock-hard Mitch Grainger.

Picturing herself seated at the table, gazing out at the world while eating a meal, sipping a cup of hot chocolate on a cold night or a glass of iced tea on a hot afternoon, Maggie decided on the spot that she had to have the apartment, regardless of cost, or her new employer. With the salary figure he had quoted, she knew she could afford it, even though she had immediately thought of finding an inexpensive place and hoarding most of her money away.

Oh, well, she mused, slowly looking around, already feeling at home. She had to have it, and that was that.

Anxious to lay claim to it and move in her things, she gave a final longing glance at the alcove, then retraced her steps down to the ground level.

As promised, Karla had the coffee ready, along with a plate of packaged cookies.

"So, what did you think of it?" Karla asked, nibbling on a cream-filled sandwich cookie.

"I love it. I want it," Maggie answered, taking a careful sip of the hot liquid. "How much?"

Karla shrugged. "I don't know." She popped the last morsel of cookie into her mouth, chewed and swallowed. "You'll have to take that up with Mitch." She reached for another cookie, paused, sighed and pulled back her hand. "Better not." She sighed again. "I love sweets, but at my last doctor visit, I had put on five pounds. The doctor was not happy." She grinned. "She told me to lay off the junk."

"Must be rough when you have a sweet tooth," Maggie commiserated. "I don't, never did.'' She rolled her eyes. ''My downfall is pasta...with rich sauces.''

''Really?'' Karla laughed. ''I was planning to make a pasta dish for dinner. Why don't we move your stuff as soon as we're finished here, then have dinner together?''

Maggie frowned. ''Are you sure Mr. Grainger won't mind if I move in before paying the rent?''

''I told you he said I should use the truck to help you move your stuff,'' Karla reminded her.

''Well...all right. But I have a better idea,'' Maggie countered, mindful of Karla's condition. ''Most of my stuff is still in my car, as I only took two cases into the hotel and didn't even fully unpack them. If you'll run me into town, I'll grab my cases, check out of the hotel and follow you back here. Then you can rest, put up your feet, while I lug my stuff up to the third floor.''

''Oh, brother, I'm not an invalid,'' Karla protested. ''You sound just like Mitch.''

''God, I hope not,'' Maggie said fervently.

Karla giggled. ''He's really quite nice, you know.''

''Uh-huh,'' Maggie muttered, reserving her opinion and judgment. ''Anyway, I have eyes, and I couldn't help but notice your swollen ankles," she continued, deliberately changing the subject. "So, instead of your standing at the stove and cooking, when I'm finished lugging my stuff, I'd like to thank you for all your help by treating you to dinner at the restaurant of your choice."

"But..."

"No buts," Maggie said, cutting her off. "That's the deal." She grinned. "Take it or leave it."

Karla threw up her arms. "You win." She grinned back. "I'll take it."

"Good." Maggie shoved back her chair. "Then let's clear away the coffee things and get this show on the road."

The running and lugging were completed in less than two hours. Of course, Maggie didn't put a thing away, but simply dumped her four suitcases, a nylon carry-on and one cardboard carton in the middle of the living room. She did take a minute to retrieve her makeup case, though. Zipping into the bathroom, she freshened up, brushed her hair and swiped blusher on her cheeks and lipstick on her lips before dashing back down the stairs to collect Karla.

"Oh, I talked to Mitch on the phone while

you were carting your stuff upstairs," Karla said as they left the house. "He said you can take care of the rent payment on Monday morning, when you come in to work."

"Fine." Maggie masked a grimace with a smile, not wanting to reveal to the friendly and obviously trusting young woman how reluctant she was to face Monday morning, and working for Mitch Grainger.

The next three days flew by in a flurry of domestic activity for Maggie. For the first time since leaving Philadelphia, she actually unpacked every one of her suitcases, the nylon flight bag and the cardboard carton. She stashed foldables into the drawers of an old-but-solid and highly polished wood dresser and, after a brisk shake-out, hung suits, dresses, skirts, slacks and blouses in the roomy bedroom closet.

A soft smile on her lips, Maggie arranged the top of the dresser with the few personal items she hadn't been able to leave behind: a framed enlarged snapshot of her parents; a small hand-carved jewelry box; the white jade figurine of a tiger that had been the last Christmas gift she'd received from her grandmother; and a small, stuffed, gaily garbed clown Hannah had presented to her as a going-away present.

Deciding to pick up some groceries, Maggie headed downstairs and out to her car. Once in the parking area, she turned to glance back at the house. A soft 'oh' of pleasure whispered through her lips as she took in the beauty of the house once more.

Utterly charmed by the sight of the grand old house, Maggie didn't allow herself to so much as conjecture on the possible length of her stay in Deadwood. She'd been hired to stay until Karla was able to return to work—some four or five months from now. Perhaps she would stay on a little longer, to experience more of the changing seasons in this part of the country.

But that would depend a lot on Mitch Grainger, Maggie reasoned, suppressing a sudden shiver of indeterminate origin. Why the mere thought of the man should so affect her, she hadn't a clue. Yet, whenever he came to mind, or Karla mentioned him, a chill trickled the length of her spine.

And he came to mind often throughout the weekend, too often for Maggie's peace of mind. At odd, disconcerting moments, an image of him, in full detail and living color, invaded her consciousness. Primarily when she was in bed.

All of a sudden, he'd be there, filling her mind, her senses. She'd experience the weird sensation that she could actually *feel* him, was as aware of him as she had been in his office. She could almost feel the compelling pull of his intent gray eyes, the sensual energy that surrounded him like a magnetic force field.

It was really the strangest sensation, one she had never experienced before, and she didn't like it. The sensation unnerved her, made her feel chilled, then too warm, tingly and quivery all over.

In a bid to dispel her uneasiness about working closely with him, Maggie conjured defensive images of Todd and every other man she had ever come into contact with who had come on to her.

Her ploy didn't work; those other images left her completely unaffected. Only the image of Mitch Grainger had the power to make her heart race, her breathing shallow, her nerves twang, as if his long fingers plucked them like guitar strings.

It was all just too ridiculous, Maggie repeatedly chastised herself, firmly, if unconsciously, entrenched in denial about the root cause of her awareness of him. Still, deep down inside, she knew the energy was sexual, the attraction mutual.

By bedtime Sunday night, to Maggie's way of thinking, those three days had elapsed much too quickly.

Four

For Mitch, those days dragged much too slowly.

Like an animal's instinctive restlessness before an approaching storm, Mitch felt an inner expectancy, as if something momentous was about to happen. He felt charged, wired, restless, and the feelings were centered around one Maggie Reynolds.

It was the damnedest sensation, unlike anything Mitch had ever felt before in connection to any woman. It bothered him to the point where it interfered with his concentration on his work, and that bothered him even more.

What was it about this particular woman? Mitch asked himself at least two dozen times during those seemingly endless three days.

Unlike his former fiancée, with her near-perfect, symmetrical features, Maggie Reynolds was decidedly not a classical beauty, he continually reminded himself. Yeah, yeah, Maggie was striking, with that tall, slender but curvaceous body, that mass of red hair, those flashing green eyes, those full kiss-me-if-you-dare lips.

Well, Mitch dared, but why the hell should he want to? he wondered, too often. Yes, she was bright, and quick, and cool...oh, so cool.

And yet, her coolness of manner was different from the remote and off-putting detachment that had been integral to Natalie's personality.

In Maggie, Mitch sensed a coolness based on confidence, not instilled by growing up rich and pampered, but earned by intelligence and competence.

But Mitch instinctively felt there was even more to it than that. There was a wariness within the depths of Maggie's cool green eyes that spoke of something, he suspected, having to do with men in particular, and not simply reserve or even arrogance. What that something might be teased and tantalized him.

So then, a challenge? Was that her unusual appeal?

Mitch spent an inordinate amount of time mulling that one over. It was possible, he conceded, since a sense of challenge in regards to a woman was a new and novel emotion for him. By and large, Mitch knew he was rather blasé so far as women were concerned, simply because he had never had to go out of his way to attract any woman he had ever shown the slightest interest in, as well as those he had not.

But Maggie Reynolds was different. She had revealed not the slightest interest in him, nor so much as a hint of feeling a bit intimidated by him.

An image of Maggie slipped in and out of his mind at unexpected, inconvenient intervals. Always the same, the image of her was as she had looked while seated across the width of his desk from him. And she had looked anything but a nervous supplicant, anxious about an interview for the employment position she obviously needed.

The picture of self-containment and confidence, Maggie had met and maintained his deliberate and steady regard with a cool composure bordering on detachment.

A challenge? Oh, yeah, Mitch concluded. Maggie Reynolds presented a challenge he couldn't wait to accept.

By Sunday evening, the sensation of simmering expectancy inside Mitch had ratcheted up to rioting anticipation. Unused to the unfamiliar feelings, he prowled the confines of his spacious apartment two floors above the casino, disgusted and amused in turn by the novel, disruptive emotional, physical and mental effect of the inner heightened eagerness.

It was a relief when his private phone line rang, simply because of its distraction value. Mitch snatched up the receiver on the second ring. The sound of his brother's voice centered his attention.

"How are you, ole son?" Justin drawled in his usual low, sardonic tones.

"Compared to whom?" Mitch drawled back, a warm smile curving his lips and coloring his voice.

Justin chuckled. "Me, for one."

Despite his brother's soft laughter, Mitch frowned with sudden concern. "There's something wrong with you?"

"Now, Mitch, don't go tying your guts into

protective big-brother knots," Justin said. "I'm fine."

Mitch snorted at the big-brother reference. Less than two years separated them. But he was protective, he acknowledged. He always had been, not only of Justin and their sister, Beth, the baby of the brood, but of Adam, the eldest, who was even more protective of the rest of them. Come to that, a tightly knit group of four—rowdy angels, as their mother had lovingly called them—they were all protective of one another.

"But I do have a problem," Justin continued, "and I need a favor."

"Name it," Mitch said at once. "What's the problem?"

"It's Ben."

"Daniels? He isn't working out at the ranch?" Mitch asked in surprise.

Though the varied business enterprises of the Grainger Corporation had been headed by Adam since their father's retirement, Mitch still kept tabs on everything concerning his family. He knew full well the story of Ben Daniels. It had begun the year he turned twenty-two, two years before he had been given control of the Deadwood casino.

Thirteen years before, Ben, a seventeen-year-old orphan, had hired on as a wrangler on the Grainger homestead in Wyoming, where Mitch and his siblings had been born and raised. All of the Graingers, from Mitch's father and mother, straight down the line of the kids, even Beth, who was three years younger, had taken the tall, lanky Ben under their protective wings.

Over the years Ben had developed a real ability for handling horses. Although he wasn't to the level of Justin, whose talent with horses was damn near uncanny, Ben had a solid working ability.

As he matured, Ben's good looks formed into sheer masculine handsomeness, and he was hell with the women. Three years ago, the eighteen-year-old daughter of an influential banker became pregnant and named Ben as the father. Ben denied it, claiming he had never been intimate with the girl, and insisted on a DNA study. It never came to that for, distraught and terrified of her father, the girl had swallowed a lethal dose of her mother's sleeping pills.

The traumatic incident had nearly destroyed Ben. Depressed, he began drinking, heavily. Afraid he'd wind up destroying himself, Adam had fired him from the homestead ranch, then rehired and relocated him to the Montana horse spread Justin managed for the family.

But that had all happened three years before, and Mitch had believed Ben had overcome his depression.

"That's the problem," Justin said, breaking in to Mitch's surprised ruminations. "He's working out too well. Damned man don't quit."

"And that's a problem?" Mitch asked, thinking he should have that problem with—thankfully—a few of his less-ambitious employees.

"Hell, yes, it's a problem," Justin said. "At least in Ben's case it is. He goes nonstop, seven days a week, from before dawn until after nightfall. I don't think he's been off the ranch more than five times in the three years he's been here. You…"

"Just about the same could be said about you," Mitch cut in to observe about the brother who had always been something of a loner, but even more so after the breakup of his early, ill-fated marriage. "How long has it been since you left the ranch, had a vacation?"

"It's my place, Mitch, my home, even if it is a part of the family business," Justin retorted. "Besides, not that it's any of your business," he added in a one-upmanship tone, "but I took a short vacation last week, spent some time in Wyoming with big brother Adam, his gorgeous bride Sunny and our adorable niece Becky."

A soft smile softened Mitch's lips at the mention of the two-month-old baby; Becky *was* adorable. "I took a quick trip down week before last," he said, laughing. "I'm afraid ole Adam is in for a time of it in about fifteen or so years, because our Miss Becky is going to be a beauty."

"Yeah," Justin concurred softly. "Anyway, you should see Ben. He's honed down to nothing but muscle and bone. The man needs a break."

"So, give him one," Mitch said. "Tell him to take a vacation, get a little R and R."

"I did." Justin sighed. "He refused at first, but I made it an order and he finally agreed. That's where the favor from you comes in. Can you arrange a hotel room for him?"

"He's coming to Deadwood?"

"Yeah. Said if he's got to take a damn vacation, he may as well go there, hang out with you a little when you can spare the time, and lose some of the money he's stashed away over these past three years."

"If he's hell-bent on losing his money, why not go to Vegas, then?"

Justin grunted. "Ben said it's too crowded, too high-tech and too glitzy."

"He's got a point," Mitch conceded.

"So, can you arrange a room, say at the Bullock Hotel, on short notice?"

"Sure." Mitch hesitated. "How short?"

"He's leaving tomorrow morning, should arrive late afternoon or early evening."

Mitch shook his head. "That is short notice. Why did you wait so long to call me?"

Justin laughed. "I laid the law down just a half hour ago. Ben was not happy."

"Tough." Mitch laughed with him. "I'll see what I can do about the Bullock."

"Thanks. Ben'll contact you when he gets in."

They talked for several more minutes, discussing family business, ranching business, casino business.

"Oh, and Mitch, keep an eye on Ben for me. He seems okay now, but I'd hate to see him go off the rails again," Justin said before hanging up.

Wonderful, Mitch thought, frowning at the dead phone receiver. Now he was to play keeper to a thirty-year-old man. Thinking the role had better not interfere with his plans for Maggie Reynolds, he disconnected, punched in the number for the Bullock and secured a room for Ben without a problem.

Maggie drove Karla to work on Monday morning, as prearranged with Mitch Grainger when he drove Karla home from work the previous Friday afternoon.

Maggie and Karla had spent so much of the weekend together, their budding friendship had truly blossomed. Which was fortunate, Maggie figured, as her stream of chatter during the drive could be attributed to the easy camaraderie they now shared.

The nervy, almost queasy feeling had been incrementally growing inside Maggie with each passing day until, this morning, she couldn't seem to shut up.

"Are you feeling all right?"

Well, so much for the cover of easy camaraderie, Maggie thought, slanting a quick glance at Karla and seeing her quizzical expression of concern.

"Oh, sure, I'm fine," Maggie answered, in forced tones meant to reassure. "I guess I'm a bit nervous." A bit? Try a bunch, she thought, swallowing an anxiety-induced bubble of self-derisive laughter.

Karla's look of concern gave way to a smile. "I suppose that's understandable, with starting a new job," she said. "But, trust me, as I told you before, there's really nothing to be nervous about."

Trusting Karla was easy, Maggie thought, managing a smile for the cheery woman. During their gabfest over the weekend, Karla had been open and candid about herself, her life, even her reasons for not telling her parents about her pregnancy. She'd been open about everything—with one exception. Not once had Karla mentioned the circumstances surrounding her pregnancy, or the man who had fathered the child growing inside her.

So, of course, in light of Maggie's suspicions as to the identity of that man, and that tingly, almost electrifying sensation she had experienced while in his company, it was trusting Mitch Grainger she had doubts about. The troubling thing was, she didn't have anything concrete on which to place any of those doubts. All she had were her feelings, the vibes her senses had picked up while she had been in his office.

Her senses might have been wrong.

Yeah, and she might win a million-dollar lottery.

Maggie sighed as she pulled onto the employee parking lot. Crunch time. She'd soon know if she had been wrong, at least so far as that charged atmosphere was concerned.

"The first day's always the hardest," Karla said as she opened the outer office door. "So, the sooner we get started, the sooner it'll be over."

"Makes sense to me," Maggie agreed, catching the scent of fresh-brewed coffee as she followed Karla into the room. She'd skipped breakfast, and coffee, to allow herself more time to choose just the right clothes to wear—she'd tried on and discarded three perfectly suitable outfits before settling on a favorite skirt suit. The distinctive aroma of coffee set Maggie's senses clamoring for a strong dose of caffeine.

Alas, it was not to be. Karla sent them crashing with the information that, not only had their esteemed employer started the coffee—a cause for speculation in itself—it was decaf.

"Sorry," Karla said, her smile rueful. "But Mitch insisted we switch to decaffeinated after I told him I was pregnant...he said the caffeine was bad for the baby."

Uh-huh, Maggie mused, her suspicions deepening. But she smiled and shrugged. "No problem," she said. "It wouldn't hurt me to cut down on the caffeine, either." Other than to further irritate nerves already jangling like discordant bells.

"Have a cup," Karla invited as she headed for the door to the inner office. "And a pastry." A wave of her hand indicated a selection of Danish pastries and sweet rolls arrayed on a tray next to the coffeemaker.

Mouth watering, stomach rumbling, Maggie was perusing the goodies on the tray when she heard Karla tap on the door and speak to "the boss."

Mitch knew the minute Karla and Maggie entered the outer office. He knew because he had planned it that way, by leaving his own office door open a crack.

Karla and Maggie were chatting. Mitch caught Karla say something about the first day being the hardest. The statement was certainly true in his case: it was his first day with Maggie in the office, and he was already getting hard.

Damn fool, Mitch cursed himself, disgusted with his body's immediate response to the muted sound of her voice, the mere idea of her presence. It had been years, long years, since his body had broken free of his mental control.

Sitting still, Mitch blanked out the chatter from the other room and drew slow, deep breaths, exerting his considerable willpower over his physical reaction. It required a lot of deep breaths, but he won the battle.

And not a moment too soon, for he had just returned his attention to the printout sheet on his desk when Karla tapped against his door and pushed it open another inch.

"Ready for coffee, Mitch?" she asked.

"Yes, Karla. Thank you."

Mitch was beginning to absorb the data on the sheet when Karla entered the room. He raised his head to smile and again thank her, only it wasn't Karla, it was Maggie crossing to his desk, a steaming cup in her hand.

"Good morning," he greeted her, slightly amazed by the cool, even tenor of his voice, considering the zing of intense awareness that shot through him.

This morning, Maggie definitely had dressed to impress; at least, her appearance impressed him. Her glorious mass of red hair had been tamed, smoothed back, away from her face. Her pin-striped navy suit was businesslike and smart, the jacket tailored, the skirt not too short, not too long. Beneath it she wore... What? All Mitch could see in the open vee of her buttoned jacket was skin, pale skin, as soft and creamy-looking as her face.

He was nearly undone by the sight of her.

"Good morning." She smiled.

Mitch had to fight against the urge to jump from his chair, leap over the desk, take her in his arms and claim her smile with his mouth.

Craziness. Pure craziness.

"Where do you want this?"

"Wherever." Coming to his senses, he motioned for her to set the cup anywhere on the desktop.

Maggie bent to set the cup near to hand and Mitch caught a brief glimpse of the shadowed valley between her breasts revealed by the slight gap in the jacket lapels.

Moisture rushed to his mouth. Heat pooled in his loins. Mitch told himself he was in big trouble.

"Will there be anything else, sir?" Her voice was too cool, too composed. It rankled him.

"Mitch," he said with firm determination, wanting to hear his name from her lips.

She blinked...with patently contrived surprise. "I beg your pardon?"

Sure you do, Mitch thought, feeling that exciting sense of challenge surge through him.

"I prefer working on a first-name basis... Maggie."

"But...I...I just started today," she said, as if that said it all.

Mitch cocked an eyebrow. "Your name will change tomorrow, or the next day, or next week?"

"Of course not." Her gorgeous green eyes glittered, shot fiery sparks at him.

Mitch loved it. "Neither will mine," he pointed out in tones designed to add fuel to her fire. "You'll still be Maggie. I'll still be Mitch."

She narrowed her eyes. He fought an impulsive bark of laughter. Oh, yeah, they were going to clash, and he was going to enjoy every minute of it.

"If you insist...Mitch," she said through gritted, sparkling white teeth.

His name from her lips hadn't had quite the sound he had wanted to hear, but, hey, Mitch told himself, anything was better than nothing.

Any concession from her, however slight and reluctantly given, was a win.

"I do insist," he drawled, wondering at the excitement shimmering through him over what was in reality such an inconsequential exchange.

She heaved a sigh, conveying impatience. The deliberate action lifted her breasts into prominence...and Mitch's excitement level to uncomfortable heights. He swallowed a groan of combined frustration and self-ridicule.

Never, never had he experienced anything remotely similar to the feelings this woman so effortlessly stirred in him. It was damned annoying.

"Will there be anything else?" she repeated, minus the formal address, and his name.

"Just one other thing," he said, plucking another sheet of paper from beneath the printout. "I faxed your former employer Friday for confirmation of your references." He glanced down at the piece of paper. "I received this faxed reply less than an hour ago."

"And?" she asked.

Leaning back in his chair, Mitch raised his head to meet her steady, confident regard. "Confirmation in spades," he said. "One might even say a rave review."

Maggie inclined her head. "Thank you." Though her tone was even, bare of so much as a hint of smugness, her eyes glittered with the gleam of justification.

Mitch allowed her the moment of self-satisfaction, for he had harbored some doubt about the veracity of her credentials, and the verification of them proved she had earned it. Then, the moment over, he moved his hand, just enough to rattle the paper, and threw her a curve.

"Along with the superlatives, your former employer expressed his disappointment, surprise and bafflement at your sudden decision to leave the company." Watching her closely for any reaction, he caught the slight stiffening of her body, the quick alertness in her eyes. "I must confess to my own share of curiosity as to your reasons."

"I believe I've already explained," Maggie said, her voice tight, militant.

"Ah, yes," Mitch murmured, thrilling to the green glare of challenge in her eyes. "Been there, done that."

"Yes." Her reply came close to a hiss.

There was more to it than that. Mitch knew it as sure as he knew that winter brought snow to the Dakotas. Too much time had elapsed between the date she had left Philadelphia and when she had arrived in Deadwood. His gut feeling was that Maggie was on the run from something...or someone. He opted for the someone, and that the someone was a man.

"Will there be anything else...Mitch?" she repeated for the third time, her tone now hard, her eyes as sharp as shards of green glass.

Cancel any doubts, Mitch thought. It had to have been a man. If it were anything else, something unsavory or illegal, Maggie would be on the defensive, but she wasn't. Just the opposite, in fact. Maggie was quick to go on the offensive, cool, collected and defiant.

Magnificent.

While Mitch itched to plumb the depths of her defiance, he decided to give her a break and back off for a spell. Besides, if he was a betting man, he'd bet the casino that should he push too hard, she'd shove back, just as hard, very likely with a charge of employer harassment.

The thought made him smile.

Maggie narrowed her eyes.

"You're satisfied with the apartment?" The change of subject caught her off guard, as he had figured it would. She blinked again, drawing his attention to her eyelashes, her long, lush eyelashes. "Everything in working order?"

"Yes, everything works." She nodded. "And I'm completely satisfied with it." She jerked, as if having just remembered something important, and made to turn away. "If you'll tell me the rental fee, I'll go write out a..."

Mitch stopped her with a sharp hand motion. He quoted the figure, then quickly added, "But you can write the check later."

"All right." She raised russet eyebrows, and once again repeated, "Will there be anything else?"

"Just one thing," he said. "After you and Karla have had your coffee, tell her I said she's to give you a tour of the place, introduce you to the other employees."

"Yes, si—" she began before catching herself up short. She drew a breath. "Mitch," she finished, her soft, enticing lips curving into a wry half smile.

That half smile indicated that she might have discerned his intentions...at least so far as testing her mettle. As for his ultimate intent, that of having her soft and warm and eager in his arms, in his bed, he felt positive she hadn't figured that one out yet.

But she would, and soon. Maggie was quick and bright, she'd reach that conclusion very soon.

Chuckling to himself, Mitch watched the smooth movement of Maggie's trimly rounded hips and long legs as she crossed to the door. But he was no longer chuckling seconds later, after she had closed the door behind her.

He was aching, in all sorts of uncomfortable places.

Damn thing was, Mitch thought with a sense of both amusement and amazement, he was enjoying the ache, and looking forward to more of the same.

Oh, yeah, he was in big trouble.

Five

He had been baiting her. From their very first meeting, Mitch Grainger had been baiting her.

But… Why?

The question left Maggie in an emotional pickle; she couldn't decide whether to laugh or curse. Never had she dealt with a man so darn confusing. On one hand, Mitch Grainger was arrogant, imperious and irritatingly confident and self-contained. On the other hand…

Come to think of it, what was on the other hand—other than the fact that he was obviously intelligent, attractive as the devil, and exuded sheer masculine sexual magnetism? Maggie mocked herself, uncertain exactly what it was about him that sparked her sense of humor.

The man was absolutely impossible, she thought, smiling at Karla as she left Mitch Grainger's office.

Karla returned Maggie's smile with a frown. "Everything okay?" she asked anxiously. "You were in there an awfully long time."

"Everything's fine," Maggie said, thinking *coffee, coffee, even without caffeine,* as she made a beeline for the coffee machine. "Mr. Grainger told me he had checked out my references." She turned to flash a grin. "Said I checked out in spades."

Karla grinned back. "I just knew you would." The phone rang. "Have your coffee and a pastry," she said, waving at the table before snatching the receiver from the cradle and saying brightly, "This is Karla."

Maggie was munching away happily on an iced cinnamon roll when Karla hung up the phone. It was then she remembered Mitch's instructions.

"Oh, I almost forgot. No, I did forget." Grimacing, she paused to take a sip of the hot brew.

"Mr. Grainger said I was to tell you to give me a tour of the place."

"Oh, good." Karla laughed. "I was just feeling the need to get up and move around a little." The phone rang. She rolled her eyes. "We'll escape as soon as you're finished." Reaching for the phone with one hand, she indicated an identification badge like the one she wore with the other hand, and again snatched up the receiver.

They escaped a few minutes later, the badge bearing Maggie's full name pinned to her lapel.

"From now on, you must wear that at all times in the building," Karla said.

"Right." Maggie nodded, then frowned. "Who'll answer the phone while we're gone?" she asked, casting a worried look at the closed door to Mitch's office.

"If I don't pick up by the third ring, Mitch will," Karla said, leading the way out of the office.

Wonder of wonders, a C.E.O. who'll deign to answer his own phone, Maggie thought, unable to recall any one of her previous employers who would do so. If she were out of the front office, even for a quick trip to the rest room, some lesser executive's secretary was pressed into service.

Why that unimportant tidbit of information about Mitch's apparent willingness to fend for himself should impress her, Maggie hadn't a clue—and yet, it did.

Though it nagged at the back of her mind, Maggie had little chance to examine her odd emotional reaction to Mitch's obvious baiting of her, for Karla began the tour with the first door along the long hallway.

The door led into another set of offices, similar but smaller than Mitch's and Karla's. The front office was manned by a young, nice-looking guy named Roger Knolb. Karla introduced him as the assistant to the assistant manager of the casino, one Rafe Santiago. Rafe was second in command to Mitch.

"You'll have to meet Rafe later," Karla said, waving to Roger as they left the office. "He works the night shift and doesn't come in till around five."

Maggie gave her a puzzled look. "Then why is Roger here now, so early?"

"To handle the regular daytime minutiae," she explained. "Don't forget, most of the rest of the business world keeps nine-to-five hours. Rafe spends most of his time down on the casino floor, as Mitch's eyes, you might say."

They progressed from one room to the next, the rest rooms, the records office, the security office and the money-counting room, where Karla halted one step inside the door, right next to a keen-eyed security guard. Though Karla gave a brief explanation, it really wasn't necessary. The procedure was self-explanatory. Maggie observed the activity in awe, never before in her life having seen so much money in one place.

From the second level, they descended to the main floor. As she had on the office floor, Karla introduced Maggie to every employee they encountered. While every one of them was friendly, they also stirred speculation in Maggie, for every one of them, from the pit boss to the bartender, referred to their employer by his given name. Everywhere they went, it was Mitch this and Mitch that, in tones both casual and respectful.

Odder and odder, Maggie mused.

"Is something bothering you?" Karla asked as they made their way to the far side of the casino floor. "You look puzzled about something."

"It doesn't bother me," Maggie said, quick to clarify her thoughts. "It's just…well, it seems a little unusual to me that all the employees refer to Mr. Grainger by his first name."

"Oh, that." Karla laughed. "My understanding is that Mitch has always worked on a first-name basis with his employees. He's never played the 'Big Man' role. And so far as I know, at least most of the employees not only respect him, they genuinely like him."

"But...doesn't that easy, casual manner instill the temptation to take advantage?" Maggie asked.

Karla smiled. "With anyone else, it might, probably would. But everyone knows exactly where Mitch stands. He's fair and generous, but he demands absolute loyalty. You see, he has a thing about trust." She paused, an odd, fleeting shadow dimming her soft eyes, and she gave a delicate shudder. "But make no mistake, Mitch can be an unholy terror with anyone who breaks his trust."

How ironic, Maggie thought. The man had a "thing" about trust...whereas she had come to believe that she couldn't or shouldn't trust any man.

"Intimidating, huh?" Maggie said, wondering what had caused the brief, sad-looking shadow in Karla's eyes, her shudder.

"I'll say." Karla giggled, her sunny disposition restored. "I was so intimidated by him, I was here a long time before I could bring myself to using his first name, and that was only a couple of months ago."

A couple of months ago? Maggie thought in astonishment. Then, that could only mean...

She slid a sidelong glance at Karla's protruding belly. That could only mean she was completely off base in her suspicion that Mitch was the father of Karla's baby.

Which meant that Mitch's concern for Karla was that of a concerned and caring friend as well as her employer, and that Maggie had been condemning him without cause.

The feeling of relief that swept through her was bewildering in its intensity. Why she should feel such relief, Maggie couldn't, or more precisely wouldn't, examine.

Mentally shying away from any deeper meaning in her startled reaction to Karla's laughing remark, Maggie told herself she felt relieved simply because her suspicions were laid to rest and would make working with Mitch a lot less stressful.

From the casino floor, they went to the restaurant where they learned that Mitch had already ordered lunch.

Mitch raised his head at the sound of the outer office door opening, the murmur of feminine voices.

They were back. An anticipatory thrill shot down Mitch's back, tingling the base of his spine. *She* was back.

He grunted in self-disdain when he caught himself straining to distinguish Maggie's voice through his closed office door. At that moment, a tap sounded on the wood panel.

Not wanting to take a chance on being caught with his expectations exposed, Mitch lowered his head and fastened his gaze on the balance sheet in front of him.

"Come in," he said, certain it would be Karla delivering his lunch, hoping it would be Maggie.

The doorknob turned. The door was pushed open. "I have your lunch order from the restaurant upstairs...Mitch."

Maggie.

Mitch hadn't had to hear her voice; he had known it was her the minute she stepped into the room. He had felt her presence, felt as well the same explosive sexual-energy attraction crackling between them he'd felt from the beginning. And she had felt it, too. He could see the awareness of it in her eyes, the infinitesimal quiver of response of her body.

Ruling his expression into a bland mask, Mitch lifted his head. "Thank you, Maggie."

Collecting the pile of printouts and correspondence, he set it to one side, clearing a portion of his desk. Shoving back his chair, he rose, intending to relieve her of the carryout container and drink cup she was holding.

"Don't bother," she said, quickly moving forward to set the containers on the desk. "And you're welcome," she continued, standing straight and alert, as if prepared to bolt the instant he told her she could go. But that flash in her eyes, that minute quiver of her body gave her away.

Oh, yeah, Maggie felt that sizzling attraction as sharply as he did, and she didn't like it. But she would, Mitch promised himself. Eventually, she'd love it, revel in it, every bit as much as he knew he would.

Amused by her wariness, Mitch flicked a hand at the deeply padded chairs in front of his desk. "Have a seat."

Her beautiful green eyes flared with consternation. "But...your lunch will get cold."

Good try, he thought, silently applauding her. "Doesn't matter. It's already cold."

She frowned.

He relented...a little bit. "I ordered a cold sandwich and a cold drink." He inclined his head at the closed cardboard container and tall, lidded waxed paper cup on the tray. "So, please, sit down, Maggie." Though politely phrased, he made it a direct order.

Still she hesitated, uncertainty flickering in her eyes, her expression.

Standing firm, Mitch stared her down—all the way down into the chair placed farthest from him. Conquering an urge to laugh, he reclaimed his seat.

"That's better." He arched a brow. "You and Karla have had lunch?"

"Yes."

Oh, Lord. Her voice sent those fiery fingers girding his hips into overtime. Mitch nodded and cleared his throat. "We can talk while I eat." His hand moved to hover over the closed container. "If you don't mind?"

She answered with a quick shake of her head. He missed the swirl of her glorious red hair, now confined in a neat plait at the back of her head. Mitch found himself fighting an impulse to leap up, circle the desk, pull the pins anchoring the strands and spear his fingers into the silky-looking russet mass.

His fingers tingled.

Enjoying the sensation, too much, Mitch swallowed a groan of despair. This was crazy, he thought. Never had he experienced this urgency of desire, this need to be one with a particular woman.

Those green eyes were watching him, shadowed by... What? Mitch asked himself, probing those emerald depths. Fear? Confused awareness? Yes, both, he decided.

Knock it off, Grainger, before you scare her away, he berated himself, wondering what in hell had happened to his normal control.

Flipping open the take-out container, he picked up a triangle of the stacked turkey club sandwich. "Would you like some?" he asked, in what he considered remarkably calm tones, considering his semiarousal and emotional upheaval.

"No, thank you." A near smile kissed her lips; he envied the smile. "As a matter of fact,

I had a turkey club sandwich for lunch, too. It was very good."

Too bad, Mitch mused, biting into the layered sandwich. He would have liked watching her eat.

"You wanted to talk?" Maggie raised her eyebrows.

Not really, what he really wanted was to… Down boy, Mitch cautioned himself, feeling fiery fingers dig hungry claws deep into his groin.

Nodding, he finished chewing and swallowed before answering. "Yes. How was your tour of the premises?"

"Interesting." She gave another half smile, "And a little confusing. And not only the general operation of the business. Karla introduced me to so many of the other employees, all the names ran together. The only ones I remember are the first two, Roger and Rafe, and the last one…Janeen."

Chewing another bite of the sandwich, Mitch nodded again. "It'll take a while," he said, after again swallowing. He washed it down with the cola in the tall cup, trying to think of something else to say to keep her in the office. "You'll learn the ropes soon enough."

"I'm sure," she agreed, then fell silent once more.

"And everything's okay with the apartment?" Damn, Mitch thought, he was reaching, and he knew it. He had asked her that earlier. "Nothing you need?"

"No, everything's fine." Then she frowned. "But about the rental payment...?"

He waved her concern away. "Make the check out to Grainger, Corp. and give it to Karla. She'll take care of it."

"All right." Maggie inched forward on the chair. "Is there anything..."

"No," he interrupted, giving up—for now. "Tell Karla I'll have some tapes to be transcribed later, after I've finished going through the correspondence."

Frustrated, Mitch watched Maggie walk out of the office, unaware that, had she quickly turned back, she'd have seen not only the sexual hunger revealed in his silvered gray eyes, but poignant longing, as well.

Quietly closing Mitch's office door behind her, Maggie was relieved to see Karla busily concentrating on the computer terminal.

Eyes wide with wonder and confusion, Maggie reflected on those emotional and physical electrically charged minutes she had spent in Mitch's company. While she had been aware—too aware—of the force field humming between them before, this time the very air surrounding them seemed to have crackled with the power of the magnetic attraction. It seemed that each time she was near him, the voltage increased.

Nothing anywhere near the conflicting sensations she had experienced during those last few minutes had ever happened to her before. She felt so...so strange, so churned up by myriad feelings of apprehension, incipient panic, simmering excitement and sheer, sizzling sensual tension.

Several times, when Mitch's blatantly passion-fired eyes had pierced hers, as if he were trying to see into the very depths of her mind to her soul, Maggie had literally ceased to breathe, to think.

On the surface, the conversation had all been so casual and mundane. But beneath the surface, Maggie's senses had been bombarded by silent messages.

Without a word, or a move out of line, Mitch had transmitted his desire, his intentions. He wanted her, in the most basic way a man wanted a woman.

It was scary...yet excitingly so.

Needing a few precious seconds to collect herself, Maggie stood silent, inches outside Mitch's door, drawing deep, calming breaths into her oxygen-starved body.

Raising one hand, she stared numbly at the tremor in her fingers. She was trembling inside, too, trembling and...

Again Maggie's breath caught in her throat. She was trembling and aching, tight and hot and moist in the sensitive heart of her femininity.

She wanted him.

The realization battered its way through the barrier of Maggie's self-constructed denial. She had wanted him from the moment she walked into his office that first day and looked into his eyes to feel the power of his masculine attraction to her.

Forewarned by the woman in the restaurant that Mitch Grainger was tough, hard as bedrock, she had been prepared to dislike him on sight. And Maggie had told herself repeatedly over the ensuing days that she had disliked him. She had spent the weekend avoiding the truth that, from that first moment, she had felt irrevocably drawn to him.

How had it happened? Why had it happened? Maggie asked herself, bewildered by her uncharacteristic response to him. She had believed herself sorely lacking in sensuality. She didn't even particularly like sex, had never experienced anything remotely similar to joyous ecstasy while engaged in the act of lovemaking.

Still, her body pulsated with a hollow, aching desire to be one with Mitch Grainger.

What in the world was she going to do? Maggie's first impulse was to bolt, not only from the office, but from the building, straight to the apartment to gather her stuff and hightail it out of Deadwood.

With trembling fingers, Maggie plucked her handbag from the corner of Karla's desk, where she had placed it before entering Mitch's office with his lunch. On shaky legs, she took a step toward the door, and freedom.

"Oh, Maggie," Karla exclaimed on a short laugh, stopping Maggie in her tracks. "I didn't hear you come out of Mitch's office." Her smile gave way to a frown. "You look a little upset. Aren't you feeling well?"

"Yes, I'm fine," Maggie said, raking her

mind for an excuse, any excuse. "I just need to go to the rest room," she improvised.

"Oh…" Karla giggled. "I know the feeling." She flicked a hand at the door. "So…go, you know where it is."

Maggie was through the door like a shot, nearly colliding with Frank, one of the guards, and another man who were right outside. "Oh, excuse me, Frank," she said, feeling foolish as she circled him and the other man. "I'm kind of in a hurry."

Frank chuckled. "Nature calling, huh?"

"Afraid so," she said, her face growing warm with embarrassment. "Too much coffee," she explained, continuing along the hallway to the door marked Women.

Once inside, Maggie slumped back against the door, her pulse racing, her breathing erratic, her body trembling. Staring straight ahead, she was shocked at the sight of her stark reflection in the long mirror above the marble-topped line of sinks.

Startled to her senses by her own pale, distressed image, Maggie drew a deep breath and stiffened her spine. Eyes narrowing, she moved closer to the mirror.

This is nuts, she thought, glaring at her reflection. *You're reacting like a twittery teen at the prospect of her first real date.*

But, what to do about it? About Mitch?

The impulse to run swept over her again. Exerting every atom of willpower she possessed, Maggie quashed the thought out of existence.

Damned if she would run, she lectured herself. She had been running for months, only to learn, finally, that she couldn't run from herself. Her anger, her uncertainties were always with her.

Well, she had decided to stop running, hadn't she? Maggie reminded herself. She had settled into the apartment, determined to stand firm, to face and deal with whatever life threw at her.

But…Mitch Grainger? Could she deal with him? Or, more important, her wildly sensual reaction to him?

Worrying the questions, Maggie gnawed at her lip, only then noticing she had eaten off her lipstick along with her lunch. She could use some color in her cheeks, as well.

Pull it together, she advised herself, turning on the cold water tap to bathe the still-racing pulse in her wrists. Turning off the tap, she dried her hands with a paper towel, then dabbed at the moist line of perspiration on her brow and at the back of her neck.

Cooler, calmer, feeling more composed, Maggie removed the small makeup pouch from her handbag and set to repairing her appearance.

Minutes later, Maggie critically studied her renewed reflection. She allowed herself a faint smile of satisfaction for the effort at camouflage. The shine on her forehead, nose and chin had been concealed by a few pats of translucent pressed-powder foundation. Her cheeks glowed with healthy-looking, if artificial, color, the muted red applied to her full lips was outlined with a darker hue.

Warpaint on, Maggie squared her shoulders. She would not run. She was done with running. She would stay and face not only Mitch Grainger, but her own overwhelming attraction to him.

Curving her lips into a pleasant smile, Maggie turned and marched back to the office.

Six

Moving back into the office quietly so as not to disturb Karla, Maggie slipped into a chair in front of the desk. Taking her checkbook from her bag, she wrote out the rental payment on the apartment. She was tearing the check from the book when Karla turned away from the screen to smile at her.

"Oh, I'm glad you're back," she said, pushing her chair back and easing out of it. "Now I have to go…urgently." She grinned. "You can man the phone."

"Mitch told me to give the rent payment to you," Maggie said, holding up the check.

Already at the door, Karla said, "Lay it on the desk, I'll take care of it when I get back."

Man the phones. Great, what'll I do if the darn thing rings? What'll I say? Sorry, but I'm new and don't know diddly about the business yet? Now, that would make a sterling impression, Maggie thought, grimacing as she moved around the desk and settled into Karla's chair. She had just decided that her best bet was to pray the phone didn't ring, when the darn thing did.

Maggie warily eyed the phone through the second ring, then recalling Karla saying that if it wasn't answered by the third ring Mitch would pick it up, she grabbed the receiver.

"This is Maggie," she said, in the same manner as Karla always answered.

"Maggie? What happened to Karla?" the caller, a woman, asked in an ultracool, rather haughty tone.

An old hand at dealing with all types of calls, from all types of people, Maggie was less than impressed, but scrupulously professional. "Karla is out of the office at the moment," she responded pleasantly. "May I help you?"

"Yes," Ms. Haughty snapped back. "You

may put me through to Mitch." Not a request; an order.

As if, Maggie thought, raising her eyebrows. "I'll see if Mr. Grainger can take your call," she said, ever so sweetly. "Whom shall I say is calling?"

"Natalie Crane." The woman's superior tones suggested her name alone opened all doors.

"Please hold." Witch, Maggie added to herself, immediately hitting the hold button. She waited with calm deliberation for a full thirty seconds before buzzing Mitch.

"Yes, Karla?"

The sound of his voice reactivated the quiver inside Maggie. For an instant, her mind went blank, her throat went dry. Idiot, she chastised herself, clearing her throat.

"Karla?"

"It's Maggie," she quickly responded. "Karla's out of the office."

He chuckled. "Ladies' room, huh?"

"Yes." She had to smile.

"What can I do for you, Maggie?"

The ideas that sprang to her mind didn't bear thinking about. Shocked at herself, Maggie rushed into speech. "There's a call for you on line two...a Ms. Natalie Crane."

A pause, then he said, "Get rid of her," in a hard-sounding near growl, before disconnecting.

Oh, my, Maggie thought, so much for opening all doors. Happy to oblige, she released the hold button. "I'm sorry, Ms. Crane, but Mr. Grainger is in conference and can't take your call right now. May I take a message?"

"Yes," Ms. Haughty snapped. "Tell him I expect him to return my call as soon as he is out of conference."

Maggie winced as the receiver was slammed down at the other end of the line. "Well, goodbye to you, too," she murmured, smiling with satisfaction.

"Who was that?"

Not having heard the office door open, Maggie started at the sound of Karla's voice. "Oh, Karla," she said, her smile widening. "Feel better?"

"Umm," Karla nodded, and grinned. "At least for another hour or so. Who were you talking to?"

"An unpleasant woman named Natalie Crane," Maggie drawled. "She demanded to speak to Mitch."

Karla made a face. "The Popsicle Princess."

"Popsicle Princess?" Maggie laughed. "Why do you call her that?"

Karla laughed with her. "Because she's cold as ice, and has very little substance." Her laughter gave way to a frown. "What did Mitch say?"

"He refused to talk to her." She lowered her voice. "In fact, he told me to get rid of her."

"I'm not surprised," Karla confided. "He can be utterly unrelenting at times."

A terror and unrelenting, Maggie mused, suppressing a shudder. Wonderful. The strange thing was, the shudder was made up of equal parts of trepidation and...and...surely not a sense of fascination and excitement? Of course not, she assured herself, while at the same time speculation whispered through her mind about whether some of those unrelenting times might occur when he was in bed, with a woman. More to the point, was Natalie Crane one such woman?

Although Maggie tried to contain her curiosity, she had to ask, "And he's unrelenting with this particular woman?"

"Yes." Karla sighed. "She's called here several times, but he absolutely refuses to speak to her."

Unrelenting indeed, Maggie mused, her curiosity unanswered by Karla's response. But, telling herself it was really none of her business, Maggie refrained from questioning Karla further on the subject.

"Is his visitor still in there?"

Jarred from her musings by the question, Maggie blinked. "Visitor?" she repeated, getting up and moving around the desk so Karla could sit down. "He has a visitor?"

"Yes." Karla nodded, settling into the chair. "Frank brought him in right after you went out." She frowned. "Didn't you see them?"

"Oh, yes," Maggie said, her smile wry. "I nearly ran smack into Frank. But I was in such a rush, I didn't notice the man with him."

"You're kidding," Karla exclaimed. "Gosh, I'd have taken notice of him in a crowded room."

Maggie laughed. "Good-looking, huh?"

"I'll say." Karla heaved a dramatic, exaggerated sigh and placed a hand on her chest. "Be still, my heart."

"Wow," Maggie said, playing along with the fun. "I can't wait to see…" She broke off when the sound of men's voices preceded the opening of Mitch's door.

The man who emerged from the office ahead of Mitch was good-looking, tall and lean, but the sight of him didn't set Maggie's heart to fluttering. That feat was accomplished by Mitch, coming to a halt in the doorway, his silvered eyes piercing hers before shifting to Karla.

Mitch introduced the man as Ben Daniels, an old friend of the Grainger family. As greetings and handshakes were exchanged, Maggie couldn't help but notice the flare of keen awareness in Ben's eyes each time he looked at Karla.

Interesting, Maggie thought. She wondered if Ben's attention was personal in nature or mere curiosity at Karla's obvious pregnancy and equally obvious lack of a wedding ring.

"Karla, Ben will be in town a couple of weeks on vacation," Mitch said. "I told him you had some brochures for the local attractions you could give him."

"Oh, sure, have a seat," she invited, tearing her gaze from the man to reach for the bottom desk drawer.

"Thank you, ma'am," Ben said, lowering his long frame into one of the chairs in front of her desk.

"I'm going to get back to work, Ben," Mitch said. "Stop by anytime, and good luck at the tables." A slow grin curled his lips, and Maggie's toes. "Except mine, of course." With a casual wave of his hand, he turned away.

Beginning to feel like the third wheel on a bicycle, Maggie moved to go to the small table she had used the previous week to fill out the job application.

"Oh, Maggie, is there any coffee left?" Mitch asked, turning back into the doorway.

"Yes." Maggie glanced at the pot, noting that it had been sitting, with the warmer plate on, since that morning. "But it must be bitter by now," she added. "Would you like me to make a fresh pot?"

"Yes...if you don't mind?" His tone and one arched brow had a sardonic cast.

"Not at all," Maggie said.

"Thank you." He again turned from the door.

"You're welcome." Crossing to the coffeemaker, Maggie could hear Karla explaining to Ben Daniels the self-explanatory information contained in several different brochures.

The two were still discussing the pros and cons of the various sights of interest when, a few minutes later, Maggie carried a fresh cup of coffee into Mitch's office.

"That smells good, thank you," Mitch said as

she set the cup close to hand on his desk. Inner amusement gave his gray eyes a teasing glimmer. "But I miss the caffeine kick."

Maggie laughed aloud. "I know what you mean. I fortified myself with two cups of the real thing at lunch."

"Lucky you. I guess that's what I should have done." He took a careful sip. "But this'll do."

Taking that as a dismissal, Maggie nodded and turned to leave. "If you want a refill just…" she began, breaking off when she suddenly remembered the earlier call. "Oh, yes," she said, turning back to face him. "Ms. Crane left a message requesting you return her call."

In the process of taking another sip of coffee, Mitch muttered something that sounded suspiciously like a suggestion as to what Ms. Crane could do to herself.

"I beg your pardon?" Maggie said, positive she had not heard him correctly.

"Never mind." The glimmer in Mitch's eyes took on a devilish glint. "I really don't think you'd want to hear the remark repeated. I wouldn't want to shock your delicate sensibilities."

So, she hadn't misheard him, Maggie thought,

giving him a droll look, and a dry-voiced response. "I suspect I've heard worse."

"Hmm," he murmured, around the rim of the cup he'd raised to his mouth. He swallowed deeply and held the cup out. "Did you mention something about a refill?"

"Yes." Stepping forward, she reached for the cup. The tips of her fingers brushed the backs of his. The brief touch of his skin against hers caused a prickling sensation. It took all Maggie's will to keep from pulling her hand back, out of harm's way. "I'll...er...be back in a minute," she said, grasping the cup and hurrying from the room.

Maybe it was her imagination, but Maggie could have sworn she heard the rich sound of his muffled laughter.

To her surprise, Karla and Ben were still deep in conversation. Moving quietly, Maggie crossed to the coffeemaker and refilled Mitch's cup. To her amusement, neither Karla nor Ben appeared to take notice of her as she returned to Mitch's office.

Once again, Maggie walked to his desk and set the cup close to hand, her spine tingling in response to the intentness of his steady gaze monitoring her every step.

Damn, how was it that this man could make her feel all nervy and quivery just by looking at her? Maggie wondered, steeling herself to meet and hold his consuming stare.

"Thank you."

The low, sexy sound of his voice shot adrenaline into her system. "You're welcome," she replied, despairing her own breathy, whispery tones. "Will there be anything else?"

"Yes." He smiled, slowly, sensuously, sending a silent message that raised the short hairs at her nape. Picking up a sheaf of papers, he held them out to her. "This batch of correspondence requires only a general form-letter response. Karla will show you how it's done."

Wonder of wonders, a boss who'll answer the phone and sift through the correspondence, Maggie thought, careful not to touch him as she took the papers.

Noting her reluctance to so much as brush his fingers with her own, Mitch's eyes danced with deviltry.

Torn between annoyance and amusement, Maggie beat a hasty retreat. This time she was certain she heard his soft laughter following in her wake.

Shivering with sensitive awareness, of herself

as a woman, of Mitch as a man in pursuit, Maggie breathed a sigh of relief as she shut his door behind her.

Fortunately, Karla didn't hear or even see her. Alone now in the office, the pregnant woman sat still as a stone, staring into space, a bemused expression on her pretty face.

Maggie moved to the side of the desk. "Karla?"

"Oh, Maggie." Karla blinked and blushed.

"You look strange," Maggie said with concern. "Are you feeling all right?"

"Yes..." she said, her cheeks glowing with color. "Yes, I'm fine. Really." She laughed. "Ben's invited the two of us to dinner. Please say you'll go."

"Well, of course I'll go, but..."

"I think he's terrific," Karla quickly added. She glanced down at her protruding belly and sighed, her color fading. "And I believe he's interested in you."

Maggie couldn't help smiling at the very idea. It had been obvious to her that Ben had taken an immediate shine to Karla. "I seriously doubt that," she said. "He barely looked at me. Perhaps he would just like some feminine company," she suggested. "Since he's here on his own."

"Maybe you're right," Karla agreed, brightening. "He's so nice, soft-spoken and gentle."

"He's a hellion," Mitch said with hard-voiced conviction.

Neither woman had heard him open his door. Maggie jumped. Karla squealed in shocked surprise.

"Sorry if I startled you," he apologized, while sounding not a bit sorry.

"That was a terrible thing to say about Ben," Karla reproached him, her eyes shadowed with disappointment. "I thought you said he was a family friend."

"He is, but that doesn't change the fact that he was always a hellion and a devil with the ladies," Mitch retorted. "Though I will admit that Justin claims Ben has changed his ways the past few years."

"Justin?" Maggie asked, frowning at the unfamiliar name, although it was really none of her business.

"Justin Grainger." Karla supplied the answer. "Mitch's brother. He runs the family horse ranch in Montana."

"Ben works for Justin," Mitch added.

"Okay, I've got the picture," Maggie said, puzzled by the whole conversation, though she did have some suspicions. "But why did you want us to know about Ben's reputation?"

Mitch favored her with a hard stare. "I overheard Karla say he had invited the two of you to dinner."

Bingo. Maggie arched a brow. "So?"

His eyes narrowed. "I just thought you should know that he has a reputation so far as women are concerned."

"It's only for dinner, Mitch," Karla protested, her dejected tone a clear indication to Maggie that if he said she shouldn't go, she wouldn't.

Like hell, Maggie thought. There was no way she was going to allow Mitch to dictate to either her or Karla as to how and with whom they spent their free time.

"And we're going," Maggie stated, her voice firm with stark challenge.

Hope flared to life in Karla's eyes, cementing Maggie's determination. It was all so silly, really, she thought, glaring at Mitch. What earthly harm could there be in having dinner with the man?

To Mitch's credit, he gave in gracefully. "Of

course, I can't stop you from going. What you two do on your own time is your business."

"That's right, it is." Maggie continued to hold his steady stare, which hadn't softened a whit.

"Just be careful," he advised, turning to go back to his office.

"I always am. And I'll take care of Karla, too." Maggie's wry assurance stopped him in the doorway.

"Hey," Karla yelped. "I can take care of myself."

"Right," he drawled, his gaze dropping to her distended belly.

Karla blushed.

Maggie bristled. "We all make mistakes," she snapped in Karla's defense, while reflecting on her own mistake in trusting Todd, convincing herself she'd been in love with him. "I'd wager even you have made your share."

"A few," he admitted, closing the subject by stepping into his office and shutting the door.

"Wow," Karla said in admiration. "I've never heard anyone talk back to him like that before."

"Oh, for heaven's sake," Maggie said, rolling her eyes. "He's a man, not a god."

"He's the boss," Karla reminded her.

"Not of my free time, or yours," Maggie retorted. "And not over whomever we choose to spend that time with. However, we're on his time now, so I guess we'd better get to work."

Dammit, he really screwed that one up, Mitch thought, cursing his heavy-handedness. He should have known Maggie would defy him, even on her very first day in the office. Hell, hadn't she been silently challenging his authority since the first day she walked into the office? And hadn't her open defiance been one of her attractions?

Despite his frustration, Mitch had to chuckle. But his chuckle dissolved into a low growl at the very real possibility that Ben, like Mitch himself, had instantly developed an appreciation for Maggie's many attractions. Why else would he have so quickly invited the women to have dinner with him?

Mitch had already dismissed the notion that Karla might be the reason for Ben's interest. Not because Karla was unattractive—she was a lovely young woman, inside and out. But, as she also was very pregnant, it stretched credulity to conclude that Ben's gaze had skipped over Maggie to land on Karla.

No, Mitch was convinced Ben had designs on Maggie, and the idea of them, possibly alone together in Maggie's apartment after Karla had retired for the night, bugged the hell out of him.

His imagination ran wild, and rather erotic, throughout that night...and the other two nights Ben escorted the two women during that week. Mitch knew about the successive dates, because the women talked freely about them. And, for all he knew, the three of them might well have gone traipsing off together over the weekend, as well.

By the next Monday, Mitch was not in the best of moods or frame of mind. Seething inside at having his own plans for Maggie usurped by Ben's appearance on the scene, he reacted by presenting a cool, remote demeanor in the office.

Looking bewildered and apprehensive, Karla fairly tiptoed around him.

Maggie, conversely, went about the business of learning her duties with commendable competence and a calm reserve belied by the glitter of defiance in her green eyes.

In regard to her competence, Mitch had expected no less, after receiving that rave review from her former employer. Yet even so, he was impressed by her efficiency, her quick grasp of the day-to-day running of the business.

As to the blatant defiance in Maggie's eyes, her thinly veiled look of challenge each time their gazes met and locked, that both thrilled and annoyed him.

It was a maddening situation for Mitch, as never before in his life had a woman so irritated him, while at the same time arousing within him such deep instincts of physical hunger and possessiveness.

Something had to crack, and soon, Mitch decided. He only hoped that something wouldn't be him.

What on earth was the matter with the irascible man?

Maggie asked herself that same question about Mitch Grainger at least a dozen times during those first two weeks of her employment with him.

She was beginning to wonder if Mitch could possess multiple personalities. It was the only thing she could think of to explain his sudden, inexplicable switches.

With each successive day, Mitch was proving

more difficult for Maggie to characterize. But he was definitely more complex than she had first believed. Bedrock-hard and tough? Yes, that he was. Somewhat arrogant and intimidating? That, too. A man definitely in control? In spades.

On the other hand Mitch was not above preparing the morning coffee before she and Karla had arrived for work. He'd also answer the phone and sort through the mail whenever they were out of the office on some errand.

In addition, it quickly became obvious to Maggie that there was a regularity to Mitch's leaving his office for an hour or two every other day or so. The third time he did so, she voiced her curiosity about his purpose.

"Oh, he's making the rounds of the place, the other offices, the casino floor, even the bar and restaurant...keeping contact with the employees," Karla told her. "Not checking *up* on them," she quickly clarified. "But checking *in* with them, keeping the lines of communication open."

On a first-name basis, Maggie had thought, recalling her surprise on hearing everyone refer to Mitch that way. A two-way street of the trust and loyalty thing. Commendable...and also very smart.

Almost against her will, Maggie felt a growing respect for the man, both as an employer and a male.

Yet, at the same time her respect for him was growing, he continued to unsettle her. And the most baffling thing of all for Maggie was the complete change in his approach to her, from his initial droll, teasing attitude, to one of withdrawn, near icy remoteness.

Yet for all his surface coldness and hard-edged tones, there was still a smoldering passion blazing from his silver-sheened eyes every time he captured her gaze.

It was unnerving, because it excited Maggie so very much. It stirred her up inside, made her feel feverish and chilly at the same time.

Maggie found the job as personal assistant to the C.E.O. of a gambling casino an interesting departure from her previous employment. But working for the icy-voiced, hot-eyed Mitch, eight hours a day, five days a week, was sheer torment with a generous dash of delicious danger. Each time she entered his office she was never quite certain of what he might say or—even more unsettling and secretly more exciting—what he might do.

For Maggie, each morning she walked into the

office was like stepping onto a tightrope. And it amazed her that Karla seemed serenely unaware of the energy simmering in the atmosphere.

But then Karla, while scrupulous in teaching Maggie every nuance of the job, was floating in a rosy cloud of infatuation with Ben Daniels.

That Ben was equally infatuated with Karla was obvious. In fact, by their second evening out with him, Karla had accepted Maggie's first impression that Ben's interest had always been for Karla.

And yet when, after their third dinner date with Ben, Maggie had suggested begging off on future evenings out so that Karla and Ben could have some time alone together, Karla had objected. Her past experiences with the still-undisclosed father of her child continued to make her wary of Ben's ultimate intentions.

While she fully understood Karla's apprehensions, Maggie's impression of Ben was that of a down-to-earth, honest and dependable man. And her initial impression of him went up a notch when he had gently suggested to Karla, as Maggie herself had numerous times, that she tell her parents about her condition.

But then, impressions could be deceiving, she reminded herself. Hadn't she trusted Todd?

Her second week in the office was pure torture for Maggie, and she began to rue her own expertise. Wanting to save Karla as much of the legwork as possible—since her expanding condition was obviously making it noticeably more difficult to get in and out of her chair—Maggie took on the responsibility of responding every time Mitch called for one of them to come into his office.

Merely crossing the threshold into his office became an ongoing torment, for Maggie was struck, weakened, by the electrically charged magnetic waves of physical attraction emanating between them. The sensuous sensations aroused within her were breathtaking, exciting, demoralizing.

On each occasion, Maggie exited Mitch's office feeling shaken, hungry, yearning for...

It didn't bear thinking about.

By Friday, Maggie was seriously considering flinging herself into Mitch's arms, offering herself up to the heated passion in his eyes, if only to end the sensual agony.

But, of course, Maggie didn't do any such thing. Quitting time Friday did finally arrive and, along with it, Ben Daniels. He was taking her and Karla out one last time as he was leaving to return to Montana early the next morning.

Although Ben had made a solemn promise to Karla to return to Deadwood in December and to be with her for the birth of her baby, Karla's spirits were low at the prospect of Ben's imminent departure.

Maggie was laughing and chattering away with Ben, who was equally animated, in hopes of lightening Karla's dejected mood, when Mitch's office door suddenly opened.

"Hi, Ben," Mitch greeted the other man, rather coolly, in Maggie's opinion. "Heading out tomorrow?"

"Yeah." Ben sighed, but worked up a smile. "So tonight Karla, Maggie and I are going to live it up."

"I'm sorry, but I'm afraid I have to interfere with your plans." Avoiding Maggie's surprised look, he turned to Karla. "A fax just came in that necessitates an immediate and lengthy response. I need you to stay late, Karla."

"We'll wait," Ben offered at once. "Won't we, Maggie?"

"No," Maggie was quick to assert, noting the gleam of disappointed tears in Karla's eyes. "You two go on ahead. I'll stay," she volunteered, wondering at the flash of bewilderment in Mitch's eyes. "That is, if it's all right with you?"

"Yes, of course," Mitch said, his voice sounding odd, almost stunned.

"Oh, but..." Karla began, in token protest.

"No, buts," Maggie cut in. "I know where you're going. Maybe I can catch up with you later."

"Well...if you insist," Karla said uncertainly, looking at Ben for guidance.

"Are you sure, Maggie?" Ben asked. "We really don't mind waiting."

"Go, go," Maggie said, exasperated by their display of reluctance, when she knew they wanted to be alone together, especially this last night of Ben's vacation.

"See you, Ben," Mitch said, shooting a puzzled glance between Maggie and Karla before turning back into his office.

"Yeah, see you," Ben called after him. "Ready, Karla?" he asked, taking her arm.

Karla looked undecided.

"Will you go already?" Maggie said, heaving a noisy sigh. "You're wasting time. I'll never get done here at this rate."

"Well..." Karla hedged.

"Go," Maggie ordered.

Grinning, Ben gave Maggie a thumbs-up as he hustled Karla out the door.

Grinning back, Maggie responded with a happy nod. But her grin faded with the shutting of the door behind them.

The question of whether she could handle the job before her should have been uppermost in her mind. It wasn't. No, what took command of her thinking was whether she could handle her employer. But it wasn't a fear that she couldn't handle him that gave Maggie pause, but the very real possibility that she wouldn't want to.

Taking a deep breath, and drawing her composure around her like a shield, Maggie followed Mitch into his office.

He was standing in front of his desk, his expression contemplative. A slow smile tugged at his lips as Maggie crossed to him.

"Alone at last."

Seven

Alone at last?

Momentarily stunned by Mitch's murmured remark, Maggie stared at him with wary suspicion.

Had his claim about the urgent need to respond to a late-arriving fax been just a ploy to get her alone?

Excitement flared to life inside her. Yet even as it came into her mind, Maggie rejected the question. Mitch had had no idea that she would offer to remain, had in fact asked Karla to stay.

So, then, why had he said…

"Don't freak, Maggie," he drawled, making a half turn to pick up the fax on his desk. "Trust me, I have no intentions of bushwhacking you."

"I wasn't about to 'freak'," Maggie informed him, arching a brow in disdain. "And I don't *trust* any man," she said with hard emphasis.

He went stone still for a moment, as if in personal affront, then a wry smile flickered over his lips and he raised one dark eyebrow. "Not even Ben Daniels?"

"Ben is very nice, charming and good company," Maggie said, wondering what Ben had to do with anything. "But, he is still a man."

"I see," he murmured. "You've been bushwhacked before, and the wounds inflicted are still raw."

Well, that was a fairly accurate description, Maggie reflected. She had felt bushwhacked when she'd read that damned note Todd had left for her, and the emotional wounds were still raw, despite her acceptance of never really having been in love with him in the first place. But, naturally, she wasn't about to admit as much to Mitch.

"Is disclosure about my personal life, past and present, part of my job description?" she countered, mirroring his single raised eyebrow.

"No, of course not," he conceded. "What you do on your own time is entirely your own business." He managed a small but genuine smile. "So long as it's legal."

"Glad to hear it," Maggie drawled. "That being the case," she continued, pointedly glancing at the fax he was holding, "I suggest we get to the business at hand."

Mitch actually chuckled. "You don't rattle easily, do you?" he said, gliding a molten, silvery look over her.

"I don't rattle at all," she retorted, knowing it was a bare-faced lie, as the heat, the blatantly hungry glitter in his eyes, had her hot and bothered and rattled something fierce.

"All right." Giving a brisk nod, he raised the fax. "This came in a short time ago. It's from Adam. He needs some information from us...a lot of information, and he needs it by Monday morning."

Naturally, by the end of her second week on the job, Maggie knew that Adam Grainger was the president of the Grainger Corporation, the head honcho of its diverse operations. Taking the fax sheet Mitch held out to her, she carefully read the terse, concise instructions, concluded that Mitch was right, his brother did want a lot of information.

Rereading the fax, Maggie raised her eyebrows.

"Adam recently picked up some dependable murmurings about the financial difficulties of a riverboat casino," Mitch said, answering her silent question. He named the parent group of a chain of casinos.

Unfamiliar with any but the most publicized of the casino groups and owners, the name meant nothing to Maggie, and she admitted as much.

"Doesn't matter," Mitch said. "What does matter is that Adam got word that the group was planning to file bankruptcy. He contacted the president of the group this morning, suggesting the possibility of a full takeover by Grainger Corp." He smiled. "They must be eager to unload, because a meeting was set up for Monday morning. Naturally, Adam intends to be well armed with comparison data, thus this rushed request."

Naturally, Maggie thought. She was inordinately pleased by the confidence implied by Mitch's comprehensive explanation, when he could have simply ordered her to retrieve the information without giving her a reason.

"Then, I guess I'd better get to work," she said.

As expected, gathering and retrieving the requested data proved to be a lengthy process. Immersed in the work, Maggie was only peripherally aware of Mitch moving around in his office. The sound of his voice as he spoke on the phone wafted to her through the open doorway.

Sometime later, she saw him leave his office and exit through the door to the hallway, vaguely thinking he was off to make one of his periodic swings through the casino floor.

"Time for a break, Maggie."

Not having heard him reenter the office, she started at the sound of his voice, clueless as to how long he'd been gone. "I've just finished gathering the info. I was ready to start faxing it." Turning away from the computer screen, she saw he was carrying a tray, laden with covered dishes.

"I've brought us some dinner." He held the tray aloft. "Leave that for later and come eat."

Grateful for the opportunity to stretch her stiff

neck, back and legs, Maggie stood. She followed him into his office, to the small round table between the two narrow windows that looked out onto Main Street.

Mitch set the large tray on the table, then pulled out one of the deeply padded leather captain's chairs for her. "You relax," he ordered gently. "I'll play server."

Settling into the comfortable chair, Maggie gave him an impish smile. "Will you expect a tip?"

"Certainly." Smiling back at her, he proceeded to transfer the covered dishes, utensils, two cups and a tall thermos of coffee from the tray to the table.

"Okay, don't bet on a draw for an inside straight," she quipped, deadpan, expecting him to laugh.

Setting the tray aside, Mitch seated himself opposite her before replying, his tone serious. "You'll have to do better than that...because I never gamble on games of chance."

Surprised by his remark, Maggie blurted out the first thought that sprang to mind. "You run a casino and you never gamble?"

"That's right." He smiled with wry humor. "Life itself is enough of a gamble for me."

"Incredible," she murmured, lifting the cover off the plate he'd set before her. She inhaled the mouth-watering aromas of filet of sole in lemon butter, chunks of roasted potatoes and green beans with slivered almonds. "Thank you for this," she said appreciatively. "It looks and smells wonderful."

"You're welcome," Mitch replied, standing to pick up the thermos and circle the table to pour her coffee. "And here's the best part." He grinned. "It's caffeinated."

"Pure decadence," she said, laughing.

His grin was infectious. *He* was infectious. As he bent over to pour the steaming brew into her cup, Maggie caught the heady fragrance of his spicy cologne, and the even more heady scent of musky male.

Decadence, indeed. He was more tempting than the beautifully prepared food on her plate. In that instant, Maggie was uncomfortably aware of an earthy hunger more powerful than her body's need for mere food and drink.

"I had considered a crisp white wine to go with the fish," Mitch was saying, returning to the chair opposite her. "But figured you'd prefer the coffee."

"You figured correctly," Maggie said, thinking the look of him, the scent of him, the nearness of him was enough to fog her senses.

"I wanted you clearheaded."

Maggie nearly choked on the bite of fish in her mouth. Could he mean...? No. Surely not, she told herself. He must have been referring to the fax still to be sent, not a desire for something intimate between them.

"Of course," she agreed, after managing to swallow the mangled bite of sole. "Understandable."

She raised her cup to her lips.

He smiled...a slow, sexy smile.

Maggie scalded her tongue on the hot coffee.

As the meal progressed, Maggie grew steadily more nervous and churned up inside. It didn't help matters that she couldn't seem to stop glancing at his mouth every time he took a forkful of food or a sip from his cup. He had a beautiful male mouth, the upper lip thin, the lower slightly fuller, more sensuous. She felt she could almost taste it along with her food and drink.

It was pure heaven.

It was sheer hell.

It was finally over.

Barely tasting the food she'd consumed, Maggie was amazed that she had cleaned her plate of every morsel. Even so, she still felt hungry, empty and needy.

Get back to work, to reality, Maggie scolded herself. Setting her napkin beside her plate, she pushed back her chair, stood and began clearing the table.

"Leave it," Mitch ordered. Rising, he circled the table to pluck the plate from her suddenly trembling fingers.

"But..." Maggie began, her voice trailing away as she looked up, stopped breathing and got lost inside his silvery eyes.

"I'm going to kiss you, Maggie."

It was a fair-enough warning, Maggie allowed. He didn't move or lower his head, giving her a moment to protest or retreat if she chose to do so. She didn't. Instead, she raised her head to give him her response, and better access to her mouth.

"Yes, please."

Something flickered in his eyes. Surprise? Delight? Maggie didn't know, nor did she care, for he slowly lowered his head to claim her mouth with his own.

Shooting stars. Exploding rockets. And yes, the earth moving under her feet. Maggie felt certain she experienced every one of those phenomena, plus sensations too numerous to count.

She wanted, she needed...more.

So, obviously, did Mitch. His arms coiled around her, drawing her into intimate contact with his hardening body. His mouth devoured hers. His tongue thrust deep to scour the sweetness of her mouth.

Curling her arms around his taut neck, Maggie vaguely heard a low groan of need, but wasn't sure if it came from his throat or her own. She could taste the coffee he had drunk, and the distinct, mind-clouding flavor of pure Mitch. Wanting more and more of his taste she clung to his mouth, to him. She couldn't breathe. She didn't care. At that moment, she'd have happily died in the all-consuming fire of his kiss.

But, apparently, Mitch had a different kind of death in mind for both of them. Pulling his head back, he stared at her, his eyes molten silver with passion. Loosening his hold, he moved away, toward a door set into the wall a few feet behind them.

Maggie blinked in confusion. Where was he going? she wondered. Of course, she had noticed the door before, and had assumed it opened into a storage area, or perhaps even Mitch's private bathroom.

"Come with me, Maggie," he said, extending one hand to her, while grasping the doorknob with the other. "Please."

He wanted her to go with him into a closet...or a bathroom? But, even as the question flashed through her mind, Maggie took a step forward and slid her hand into his.

The door opened to reveal an enclosed staircase, and it was then Maggie recalled Karla saying that Mitch had an apartment on the third level.

Butterflies were doing bumps and grinds in her stomach, but she allowed Mitch to lead her up the carpeted stairs.

The staircase opened onto a spacious landing. A large living area was located to the left and a hallway ran straight to the back of the building.

Maggie barely had time to see the living area, getting a mere glimpse of large, overstuffed furniture in midnight blue and white. With a tug on her hand, Mitch drew her to an open door along the hallway.

Legs trembling, she preceded him into his bedroom, flinching when he swung the door shut behind them.

Alone at last.

The echo of his words of a few hours ago rang inside her head. Only here and now, they were really alone...together...in his bedroom. The king-size bed loomed enormous in Maggie's sight, blurring her vision to any other furniture, the overall color scheme.

An instant of panic gripped Maggie at the touch of his hand on her shoulder. She froze for long seconds, motionless with indecision.

What did she think she was doing? a scared inner voice demanded.

Oh, don't be such a wuss, go for it, a braver voice insisted.

She fought the urge to bolt, with the stronger urge to stay. Would being with Mitch, in the most intimate of ways, be any different? She gulped a strangled breath and turned to face him.

"You can change your mind, Maggie," he said, his features taut with self-imposed control.

Her gaze lowered to his mouth, those lips that had turned her gray matter to soggy granules. Excitement leaped like a flame inside her, spreading like wildfire throughout her entire being. She wanted that mouth, those lips on hers, doing crazy, erotic things to her.

"Don't look at me like that." His voice was soft, harsh.

"Like what?" Her voice was barely there.

"Like you want to devour me."

"I do." In that instant her decision was made. "But only if you promise to devour me in return."

Exhaling the breath she hadn't realized he was holding, Mitch groaned and pulled her into his arms. "That's a promise I'll be happy to fulfill," he murmured, lowering his head to take her mouth.

The devouring process had begun.

Heat consuming her, Maggie was only vaguely aware of Mitch moving her toward the bed, of his fingers plucking the pins from her hair, of his hands divesting her of her clothes, of her own hands tugging at his attire. But within minutes, they stood next to the bed, facing each other, the trappings of civilization littering the floor around them.

"Beautiful," he said, slowly gliding his hot-eyed gaze over her body.

"Yes, you are," she whispered, returning the compliment with an appreciative examination of his tall and fit muscular body, the awesome length of his manhood.

He chuckled. "Men aren't beautiful," he scoffed, raising his hands to cradle her breasts with a near reverent touch. "They're beautiful."

"They're too small." She sighed, quivering as his fingers stroked the tingling, tightening tips. "They barely fill out a B-cup bra."

"They fill my palms." He closed his hands around her breasts, claiming them for his own. "Perfect."

Obeying the boldest impulse she had ever had, Maggie slid her hand down his torso and curled her fingers around him. "So are you."

Mitch drew in a sharp breath, thrust his hips forward, closed his eyes and groaned. "I think we'd better lie down...before I fall down."

"Yes," Maggie agreed in a wavery voice, feeling rather light-headed herself.

Mitch paused long enough to toss the comforter and top sheet to the foot of the bed. Settling her in the center of the mattress, he sought, captured her mouth as he stretched out beside her.

Maggie's mind was on the verge of taking a leave of absence when a thought popped in out of nowhere. Tearing her lips from his, she cried, "Mitch, the fax!"

"Screw the fax," he growled, stabbing the

corner of her mouth with the tip of his tongue. "On second thought, I'd much rather scr..." He shook his head. "No, not with you. With you, I want to make love."

Thrilled, shivering in anticipation, Maggie caught his head with her hands, speared her fingers into his luxurious dark hair. "Does making love include devouring?"

He laughed, a rich, free-sounding roar. "Of course."

"Then, get on with it," she commanded, laughing with him as she drew his mouth to hers.

Eight

Mitch propped himself up on his arm and looked over at Maggie, who was curled up beside him, sound asleep. His mind still on stun, Mitch studied her face and her form in awed astonishment.

Maggie had not been a virgin. Mitch had not expected her to be untouched, not in her late twenties. But, to his complete surprise, he had quickly realized that she was woefully untutored, a near innocent to sensual play. To his delight, she had proved not only willing but eager to learn and had shyly, yet trustingly following his lead.

For Mitch, Maggie's wholehearted responsiveness to his every suggestion acted upon him like the strongest aphrodisiac. Reciprocating in kind to his every touch, every caress, she had unconditionally surrendered to him, and in turn, he had unconditionally surrendered to her.

In the end Maggie had cried out his name in tones of amazement and disbelief while in the throes of utter release. Her cries of pleasure, and the speculation that she had never experienced such an all-consuming release, had heightened his own satisfaction.

At thirty-five, Mitch was far from a novice in the art of sensual pleasures. Yet, for all his worldly experience, never had he known—lived through, died through—such an intense, mind-and-body-shattering sexual encounter, as he had with Maggie.

His body was still pulsating in reaction to the gut-wrenching intensity of his climax. His heart was still thumping, his nerves still thrumming like a vibrating guitar string, his breathing still shallow and irregular.

Damn...he loved it, loved it so much, he replayed the scene in bits and pieces in his pleasure-addled mind.

His gaze surveying Maggie's sleep-softened features, Mitch relived the taste of her creamy skin, the tickle of her eyelashes against his lips, the moist sweetness of her mouth, her tongue, joined in carnal hunger with his.

His chest tightening, Mitch slid his gaze to her hair, spread like strands of living flames in wild disarray against the pillow—*his* pillow. And it had been his fingers, coiling, curling, grasping those strands that had caused that tale-telling disarray.

A sudden dryness parched his throat. Mitch's gaze moved on to her satiny shoulders and lower, to her breasts. Their deliciously tempting tips were still tight and hard from the attention lavished upon them by his tongue, his greedily sucking lips.

Desire reawakening his body, Mitch trailed his gaze lower still. He followed the neat indentation of her slim waist, the alluring flare of her hips, the gentle roundness of her belly, the parted juncture of her thighs.

Sweet heaven.

Mitch closed his eyes. Perspiration sheened his forehead. He was quivering, actually quivering in response to the passion roaring through him.

With every fiber of his being, Mitch wanted, needed to experience that heaven again.

Sliding his rigid body down the enticing

length of hers, he lowered his head to bestow the most adoring and intimate of kisses on the portal of her sweet heaven.

Maggie roused to an aching, fiery sensation in the core of her being. Sensual energy recharged her depleted body. Not fully awake, but luxuriating in the new sensation, she moved in sinuous response, parting her thighs and arching her hips.

Soft laughter, followed by a quick, hot caress against the most sensitive part of her femininity brought her fully awake, shockingly aware.

"Mitch...no," she protested, stiffening.

"Maggie...yes," he murmured, delving deeper.

She wanted to resist, felt compelled to resist, but the sensations swirling through her from his ministrations defeated her resistance, turned it into raging desire. Writhing, helpless within the grip of erotic pleasure, she grasped his head, dug her fingers into his hair, arched her hips high and gave herself up to the hungry fire of his mouth.

Tension unlike anything Maggie had ever experienced wound tighter and tighter until, gasping, pleading, fearing she'd go mad from the pleasure, the tension snapped and a torrent of even more intense pleasure cascaded through her.

Her breathing labored, Maggie lay exhausted. At least she thought she was exhausted, beyond the slightest movement, until she heard the faint but unmistakable noise of tearing foil. Mitch surged up over her and into her, further intensifying the diminishing pulsations.

It was fast, and furious. And to Maggie's utter disbelief, she once again went soaring into ecstasy, and promptly into the enfolding blanket of slumber.

"Maggie... Are you dead?"

Mitch's soft tones roused her consciousness, his teasing aroused her amusement.

"Yes."

"Too bad." His voice held silent laughter. "I guess I'll have to drink the coffee I brought for you."

"Coffee?" Maggie pried open her eyes to see him standing next to the bed, a cup in each hand. He looked devastating, clad in nothing but faded jeans that rode his slim hips. "Caffeinated?"

"What else?"

Inhaling the aroma rising from the steaming brew, Maggie groaned in appreciation as she levered herself up, then yelped with the realization that she was stark naked.

"Will you hand me my blouse?" she asked, yanking the sheet up to her neck.

"Why?" he drawled, grinning at the fierce frown she'd produced. "I've seen...and tasted...it all."

"I could say the same of you, yet you're covered," she muttered. "Mitch, please," she pleaded, feeling her face, her entire body grow warm with embarrassment at the flood of memories, her abandonment... How long ago?

"Oh, all right, Little Ms. Modest," he grouched, his silvery eyes gleaming with amusement.

Sighing with relief, Maggie clamped the sheet under her arms. Wriggling into a sitting position, she watched him as he set the cups on the nightstand and turned to a chair, where her neatly folded clothes lay draped over the high back, obviously placed there by Mitch.

"What time is it, anyway?" she asked, quickly shrugging into the blouse he tossed to her.

"Ten-twenty," he said, handing a cup to her. "Why, are you going somewhere?"

Cradling the cup in her palms, Maggie raised it to her lips and took a careful sip of the aromatic brew. "Hmm, lovely," she murmured, taking another sip before answering his question. "If you'll recall, I told Karla and Ben I'd join them if it didn't get too late...which, of course, it now is."

"Does not being able to join them bother you?"

Giving serious concentration to her caffeine intake, Maggie wasn't looking at him. But the tight edge to his tone snagged her attention, drew her gaze to his face. His expression was closed and every bit as tight as his voice.

"Bother me?" she repeated, frowning. "No, it doesn't bother me. Why should it?"

Mitch's lips curved into what she felt sure was supposed to be a smile. It had more the look of a grimace. "Come on, Maggie," he said chidingly. "What is one supposed to think? Ben's been hanging around here since he arrived. He escorted you out to dinner, Lord knows how many times the last two weeks. And even though he has kindly included Karla in on the outings, it's obvious to anyone with eyes in their head that he's attracted, one might even say extremely attracted, to you."

Maggie nearly choked on her coffee. Fortunately, she managed to swallow before bursting into laughter.

"What the hell's so damn funny?" Anger flashed in his eyes.

"You," she said, stifling her mirth. "And your all-seeing but clouded vision."

"Meaning?" Mitch demanded, bristling.

He looked so affronted, so rattled by his failure to intimidate her, Maggie had to fight another gurgle of laughter. "Meaning," she said, sweetly, "you obviously missed the real truth."

He actually growled. "Explain."

"Ben is not attracted to me, Mitch." She heaved a dramatic sigh. "He's crazy about Karla."

He looked both stunned and shocked. "But… Good Lord, Maggie, she's pregnant."

"No!" Maggie exclaimed, widening her eyes in a parody of astonishment. "How did it… Well, I know how, but… When did this happen?"

"Cute." Mitch somehow managed to sound annoyed, amused and relieved at one and the same time. "And you don't mind…about Ben's interest in her?"

"Why should I mind?" She shook her head. "I mean, other than a natural concern about whether Ben's interest in her is genuine."

"Understandable, of course, but…" He

shrugged. "I thought you were attracted to him."

Now it was Maggie who felt affronted, really insulted. They had just had sex...which, to her at any rate, had seemed more like making love. Could Mitch seriously believe she would go to bed with one man while feeling attracted to another?

To Maggie, it was patently obvious that that was exactly what Mitch believed. Damn his hide.

"I see," she said, her cool tone reflecting an inner chill of pain. Setting her empty cup on the night table, she clutched at the sides of her blouse with trembling fingers and slid her sheet-draped legs over the edge of the mattress. "If you'd turn your back, please," she said, not looking at him, "I'd like to use the bathroom."

"What's wrong?"

"I have to leave," she muttered, staring at the carpet, and absently noting it was plush, a deep chocolate brown. "It's getting late."

"It's not that late. Maggie, what's wrong?"

"I told you," she said to the carpet. "I must go. I need to clean up and dress."

"Look at me, Maggie." It wasn't a request, but a direct order.

From the boss to the... Maggie shook her

head in denial of the ugly word that sprang into her mind.

"Damn it, Maggie," he exploded, stepping closer to her. "What's wrong?"

She saw his feet crush the carpet before she felt his hands grab her shoulders to pull her upright. Suddenly furious, she jerked her head back and glared at him.

"I'm mad as hell, that's what's wrong."

"What?" Mitch looked bewildered. "Mad about what?"

Chin tilted at an aggressive angle, Maggie lashed out at him. "How dare you insinuate that I'd go to bed with one man, while feeling attracted to another?"

"I didn't... I..."

"You did." Exasperated, irritated, Maggie raked him with a withering look. She hadn't felt so incensed since June, when she'd discovered that note. Inside her mind, she was no longer seeing just Mitch, but Todd and every other insensitive male she had ever met.

"Maggie...I swear I don't know what you're talking about." His hands tightened on her shoulders. She shrugged out of his hold and sidestepped away from him.

"Men." On a roll, she practically spat the word at him. "You're all alike, taking what you want from whomever you want, without a thought or care for any pain or mental damage you might inflict."

"What pain?" Mitch gave her a helpless look. "What mental damage have I inflicted—" He broke off, his eyes narrowing. "Who did this to you…hurt you?" he asked—demanded—in icy tones. "Was it Ben?"

"Ben? Again?" Maggie threw her hands in the air. "I told you I'm not interested in Ben that way."

"Then who?" Mitch persisted. "And don't hand me that bull about me insinuating anything unsavory about you. I meant no such thing. It's more than that…much more. Isn't it? You're attacking me for something some other son of a bitch did. Aren't you?"

Maggie sighed, deflating as fast as she had blown up. She had overreacted, and she knew it. "Yes," she admitted, hastening to add, "but I did feel as though you were casting aspersions on my character."

"I wasn't." His voice was hard with conviction. "He hurt you very badly?"

She smiled with wry self-knowledge. "He hurt my pride," she confessed, her face flaming as she suddenly realized she was standing there stark naked from the waist down. If she hadn't felt so vulnerable, it might have been funny, she with only her chest covered, Mitch with only his...bottom concealed. "May I get dressed now?" she said, shifting uncomfortably.

"You're not going to tell me, are you?"

"Mitch, I feel like a fool, standing here half-dressed like this," she snapped, patience wearing thin. "Will you please point me toward the bathroom."

"Right there." He indicated a door on the far wall. "But I expect some answers when you're finished."

Dream on, mister. Maggie didn't bother verbalizing the thought. Scooping her clothes from the chair, she dashed for the bathroom.

Twenty minutes later, after making free with his shower in the luxurious black-and-white-tiled bathroom, Maggie strode back into the bedroom. Her confidence was restored by the armor of being fully clothed.

Mitch, on the other hand, apparently felt well protected by the indomitable force of his personality. He sat sprawled in a wing chair, still clad in nothing but the jeans, unbuttoned at the waist.

The sensuous sight of him had Maggie reeling from an erotic blow to her senses.

She sucked in a steadying breath.

He smiled, slow and sexy. "You look fantastic...but I liked you better the other way, with your gorgeous hair all wild and tangled, and your lips red and pouty from my kisses, and your beautiful green eyes shadowed by passion."

Good heavens. Maggie's legs went weak. Heat seared through her, tingling the tips of her breasts, drawing moisture from the core of her being. It was crazy, sheer madness. Nevertheless, she wanted him. Again. So soon.

He held out a hand. "Come to me, Maggie," he murmured in a low siren-song voice.

Every living cell in her body urged her to obey his whispered plea, relive the ecstasy to be found in his embrace, his possession.

She actually took one step toward him, before common sense came to her rescue, warning her that if she surrendered to him again, she'd be a goner, defenseless against his potent kisses. She shook her head in denial, of him and herself. Until she felt certain she could trust him...

"Maggie, trust me," he crooned, as if he could read the turmoil of her conflicting thoughts.

She shook her head again. "I told you before, I don't trust any man. And now, since we—" she glanced at the rumpled bed, then quickly looked away "—I no longer trust myself."

"He really did a number on you, didn't he?" His voice harsh with disgust, Mitch sprang from the chair to confront her, his hands planted on his slim hips.

"Yes," she admitted, holding her ground, facing him with challenge. "But, you see, I allowed it by doing a number on myself," she conceded.

"How?"

Maggie smiled, faint and self-deprecatingly. "By convincing myself I was in love with him."

Speculation silvered his eyes. "You weren't in love with him...whoever the hell he is?"

She squared her shoulders and raised her chin. "No, I wasn't in love with him," she confessed. "I was feeling desperate. I was tired of the upwardly mobile mania. My biological clock was running. I longed for a child, a family, a man I could trust to provide those things." She shrugged. "It was easy to convince myself I was in love."

"You wanted marriage," he concluded.

"Yes, I wanted marriage," she said, a wry smile twisting her lips. "And I believed I was going to get what I wanted," she added, feeling a need to at last purge herself, her mind of the humiliating experience. "Everything was arranged. Then, two weeks before the big event, he eloped with his employer's daughter, and heir. He left me a note, and a mess to clean up."

"The bastard," Mitch growled.

"That's precisely what I said." She smiled. "I went wacky for a while. I slashed my damned wedding gown into ribbons, quit my job, rented out my apartment and simply loaded my car and started driving. I finally wound up here, in Deadwood."

"I'm glad you did."

"I'm sure you are," she said dryly, shooting a pointed look at the bed. "And now I'll be on my way." Swinging around, she headed for the door.

"Wait a damned minute," he said, his hand clasping her arm to stop her in her tracks, turning her to face him. "Where are you going?"

"Home, to my bed..." She smiled, almost.

"I'd rather you slept here, in *my* bed." His soft voice enticed her senses.

Maggie drew a slow, steadying breath. "I don't think so," she said, shaking her head. "I lost my head there for a while, but it's back in place now. This—" she flicked a hand at the bed "—won't happen again."

"Not even if you find you can trust me?" he asked, raising a hand to cup her face.

Maggie's breathing went haywire. He was going to kiss her. She knew he was going to kiss her. She knew as well that she should stop him, step away from him...run away from him. She neither stopped him nor ran. She parted her lips for him.

Mitch's mouth was gentle on hers, sweet, undemanding, demoralizing.

"Maggie?" He lifted his head to stare into her eyes. "If you find you can trust me?"

She swallowed and pulled her scattered senses together. "Maybe. We'll see."

"Good enough." Releasing his hold on her arm, and her face, Mitch stepped back. "I'll follow you home."

"No." Maggie shook her head. "That's not necessary."

He sighed. "Don't argue, Maggie. Just give me a few minutes to get dressed."

Maggie didn't argue, but as soon as he had crossed the room and entered the bathroom, she called, "Don't forget that fax for your brother."

Then she ran.

Exasperating woman. Fumbling with the top snap on his jeans, silently cursing, Mitch pushed open the bathroom door and strode to the clothes closet, determined to pull on a shirt and shoes and tear after Maggie.

He was stamping into buff-toned desert boots when he heard a car start up in the employees' parking lot.

"Dammit," he muttered, kicking off the boots. No point in going after her now. Letting the boots lie where they fell, he turned to the nightstand to collect their coffee cups, and stopped still at the sight of the rumpled bed.

A shiver-inducing thrill, immediately followed by a searing streak of heat, shot through him at the vivid recollection of the activity that had caused the wild disorder of bedding.

Lord, she was magnificent, this woman who had presented a challenge to him from the first day she had walked into his office. Was it really only a little over two weeks ago? Mitch asked himself. It seemed more like months, or years that he had spent watching Maggie, learning her mannerisms, her particular personality traits, listening for the sound of her voice, her laughter...wanting her.

And now that he had tasted the fullness of her, tapped the depths of her sensuality, reveled in her surrender, Mitch instinctively feared he would never again live to see a day dawn that he did not want to be with her, in and out of bed.

It was a sobering consideration. It was a mind-

and life-altering thought, most especially since Maggie, the woman who didn't trust any man, just might decide on the spur of any moment to cut and run.

Maggie was afraid. She was afraid to trust not only men, but herself. Because one lapse in her judgment had allowed her to lead herself down the proverbial garden path.

And yet, by his observation—and he had made almost a science of observing her—she had revealed not only a quick wit and sharp intelligence, but a warm, caring personality. She showed genuine affection, with a strong strain of protectiveness toward Karla...which he highly approved of. In addition, everyone she had come in contact with in the casino appeared to like and respect her.

All of which was a clear indication to Mitch that the cool, savvy, challenging, almost militant front she presented was simply that—a self-protective facade.

And beneath that facade was a many-faceted woman, a woman confident and comfortable wearing many of life's hats.

Maggie wanted a child, a family life...

The matter needed more serious thought.

Grabbing up the cups, Mitch left the bedroom and headed for the kitchen. If he was going to engage in some mental and emotional probing and come up with some viable solutions, he needed caffeine, lots of caffeine.

By 3:00 a.m. he was tired but wide awake. His hair was ruffled from repeated raking of fingers and he fairly sloshed with the two pots of coffee he had drunk. But his mental and emotional state was resolved as he stumbled down to his office to at last send the fax to his brother.

As impossible and improbable as it seemed to him, and after much soul-searching, Mitch had finally faced the singularly amazing fact that he was in love with Maggie Reynolds. He was deeply, irrevocably and forever-after in love with her.

Who would have thought? Certainly not Mitch. He had long since decided that love, romantic love, was for, well...romantics, of which he was not one.

But there it was, romantic love, in all its gut-wrenching glory, figuratively laughing its ass off at him. Okay, let it laugh. Better yet, hopefully, he'd laugh along.

But now, Mitch acknowledged, his work was really cut out for him. For now, he had to not only prove to Maggie that she could trust him, but love him back in return.

It was enough to make a strong, iron-willed man weep.

Of course, Mitch wasn't into weeping over his troubles, or anything else. He never had been. He was into taking whatever action was required to remedy the situation.

With his eyelids heavy, but his brain alert on caffeine, Mitch retraced his steps to his bedroom. Shucking out of his clothes, he crawled naked into the tangled bedding and set about devising a strategy to lure Maggie back into the bed next to him...for the rest of her natural life.

Nine

It was raining, hard. Fortunately, it was Saturday. At least she didn't have to go to work and beard her personal dragon in his den, so to speak, Maggie thought as she dragged her weary, sleep-denied body from the bed. She had a headache, most likely from the battering her brain had taken throughout the long night of mental taxation. She also ached in some, no, a lot of very delicate places.

And it was all thanks to her personal, bedrock-hard dragon, she reflected. She now had firsthand knowledge of how very hard, and gentle, Mitch could be.

What to do? What to do?

Sick and tired of the endless question, Maggie started a pot of coffee. Then she headed for the bathroom to beat her protesting body parts into submission with a hot shower.

Fifteen minutes later, she felt marginally better, so far as her aching muscles went. Dressed in jeans and an oversize Penn State University sweatshirt, Maggie sat curled up on the kitchen window seat, a steaming cup of coffee warming her cradling hands.

Three sips of the brew made her feel almost human. Perhaps some food. Maggie made a face. Perhaps not. So, okay, she advised herself. Drink the coffee and think it through.

Then again, what was to think about? She had felt an immediate attraction to Mitch, an attraction she had thought was purely physical in nature. Think again.

Mitch was scrupulously honest, not only fair but generous with his employees, and genuinely concerned for their well-being. In retrospect, Maggie had to laugh at her original suspicions about Mitch being the father of Karla's baby. He actually acted more like Karla's father, monitoring her increasing condition, making sure she ate right and wasn't overdoing the office work, insisting she stay off her feet when her ankles swelled.

Maggie had quickly come to appreciate Mitch's sense of humor, revealed in the teasing gleam that lit his eyes, the occasional droll remark, the laughter that rang out, free and clear of any malicious content.

And Mitch was fantastic in bed. The errant thought induced a delicious tingle inside Maggie. Good heavens, she never dreamed she could feel the sensations she had experienced in his bed. Of course, she was sadly inexperienced, since Todd had been her one and only lover...and he had hardly aroused her, never mind set her on fire. For Maggie, sex with Todd had been a functional exchange, uninspired and finished quickly.

With Mitch... Maggie sighed. With Mitch the physical act had been an enlightenment, a feast of sensual delights, a shared journey through exotic realms.

Every living cell in her body cried out to share that journey with Mitch again. Share the closeness, the laughter, the passion, the feeling of being joyously alive.

By her third cup of coffee, Maggie admitted that she could very easily fall in love with

Mitch...if in fact she hadn't already fallen in love with him. If she dared.

But Mitch had a thing about trust.

Maggie winced. She had a thing about trust, too. Her thing being that she had good reason to doubt the sincerity of any man's avowed trustworthiness.

What to do? What to do?

Maggie was back at square one.

Hugging her knees, she stared out the window at the pouring rain, noticing that autumn had come to South Dakota. The leaves on the trees behind the house, colorful mere days before, were drying. Many had already fallen to the ground. There was a chill in the air she could feel through the windowpane.

Maybe it was time to hit the trail, go home to Philadelphia before winter set in.

She sighed again. The shame of her situation was that she really liked being here. She liked the town, the surrounding terrain. She liked her work. She liked her apartment. She liked Karla, and the other employees she had come to know over the previous two weeks. And, despite her initial misgivings, she liked Mitch, the man.

The man wanted her.

And she wanted him.

A part of her demanded she give it time, explore the possibility of a workable and satisfying relationship with Mitch. Another part of her, the wary part, urged her to pack up and take off before she got hurt again.

But she couldn't go, at least not yet, Maggie told the wary part. She had to stay, wanted to stay until after Karla's baby was born. So she'd stay...awhile.

But she'd have to play it cool, Maggie told herself. Resisting Mitch wouldn't be easy, but she would have to keep him at arm's length. And maybe, with any luck, she might discover that she could place her trust in him.

One could always hope.

Maggie took her tired body, and her hope, back to bed.

The phone woke her late in the afternoon. It was still raining, and almost dark.

"Where have you been hiding all day?" Karla's cheery voice brought full wakefulness.

"Right here," Maggie said, covering a yawn with her hand. "I was having a nap."

"Did Mitch keep you at it very late?"

A loaded question if Maggie ever heard one. She played it straight. "Not too late," she answered, her tone neutral. "I left around ten-thirty." Which was true. "But I didn't sleep well, so I went back to bed." Also true. "Did you and Ben have a nice evening?"

A pause, then Karla said, "Oh, yes, we had a lovely dinner, and then we just talked."

"May I ask what about?"

"Sure," Karla said, her voice light, happy. "I'll tell you everything over supper."

Maggie smiled, and pushed a swath of hair from her eyes. "We're having supper together?"

"Yep, chicken and salad, and it's almost done." Karla laughed. "You have twenty minutes to get up, get dressed and get yourself down here."

Maggie produced a not entirely fake groan. "Nag."

Karla laughed again. "Did I mention that the chicken is in a pasta dish...with mushrooms and other good stuff?"

Laughing to herself, Maggie threw back the covers. "Start the coffee, I'll be down in fifteen."

"Oh, that was so-o-o good," Maggie complimented the cook, sighing with repletion as she set her napkin aside. "Where did you find the recipe?"

"I'm so glad it turned out right, and that you liked it," Karla said, smiling with pleasure for the compliment. "I got it from one of those TV cooking shows."

"It was wonderful," Maggie said, feeling stuffed, and curious. "So, was your dinner last night as good?"

"Yes." Karla nodded. "But later was better."

"Later?" Maggie prompted.

Karla nodded, looking shy. "We...Ben and I came back here after dinner to talk."

Alarm flared inside Maggie, concern for her innocent friend. Ben was a mature man, after all, a virile, healthy male. "And...er, what did you talk about?"

"Us...Ben and me." Karla's cheeks bloomed with becoming pink. "He said...he's in love with me."

"Karla..." The alarm bells were clanging, and Maggie didn't know how to proceed, other than directly. "He didn't...you didn't...?"

"Go to bed with him?" Karla said it for her. "No, I didn't. I wanted to," she quickly added. "I know I'm in love with him—Ben's so wonderful. And I really wanted to make love with him before he had to leave but..."

"But?" Maggie repeated, fearing that the couple had tried but that Karla had found it uncomfortable.

"He wouldn't."

The simple statement rocked Maggie's precepts of the male gender. *"He wouldn't?"*

"No." Karla pouted. "He said he was afraid he'd hurt me or the baby."

"Well, good for him," Maggie said, breathing a silent sigh of relief. "Is he still planning to come back here and be with you through the birth?"

"Yes." The pink in her cheeks deepened to red. "And he promised he'd make up for last night...after we're married."

"He proposed?"

"Not really." She giggled. "He just said we're getting married, that we'd do it as soon as it could be arranged. But he had to go back to the ranch first and talk to his boss."

What was wrong with the telephone? Maggie wondered with cynical suspicion. Not wanting to upset Karla, she kept her mouth shut.

"Oh, Maggie, I'm so happy. I couldn't wait another minute to tell you. That's why I called." She laughed. "And, you'll be surprised to hear, I was so happy, I called my folks, too. Told them everything. They're coming to Deadwood the week before my due date to be with me when the baby comes."

"Oh, Karla, I'm so glad you called them. And I am happy for you," Maggie said, jumping up to hug her friend, glad she had kept her suspicions to herself.

"Have dinner with me." It was Wednesday, and the third time that week Mitch had asked that same question. Over a week and a half had elapsed since the memorable night they had been together. And though she had maintained a pleasant, outwardly friendly demeanor, Maggie had kept a cool and deliberate distance between them.

"Mitch, I..." Maggie began.

"Wait," Mitch interrupted her, certain she was about to refuse him, again. "Just dinner, Maggie, no strings, no pressure for anything more. I promise."

"I don't know." She hesitated, her gaze steady on his, her eyes revealing an inner conflict.

Encouraged, Mitch forged ahead. "Maggie, it's only dinner. I'm inviting you to have a meal with me, not an orgy," he said, even though, with the constant memory of those incredible hours they'd spent together tormenting him, an orgy sounded pretty good to him. Especially considering how difficult he was finding it to keep his hands off her.

Maggie didn't frown, or go stiff and cold with rejection. She laughed. More encouraging still.

"If I say please?"

"Well..." She smiled. "If you behave yourself."

With a sorrowful expression, he placed a hand on his chest over his heart. "You wound me."

"I seriously doubt it," she drawled, arching a brow and looking suspicious. "Where?"

Mitch knew exactly what she was asking. "Not in my apartment, if that's what's worrying you."

"It was," she admitted.

"But we were so good together, so..." Mitch caught himself up short, but it was too late, the impassioned words were out, dangling there in the sudden silence.

Maggie didn't respond or even react. She simply sat there, still as death, staring at him.

Damned fool, Mitch berated himself. He'd screwed up, big time, and it would serve him right if she told him to take a flying leap off a high cliff. He knew how she felt, knew she didn't trust him.

The results of winging it, he supposed. After crawling back into bed the night they had been together, Mitch had scrapped the notion of forming a strategy to win Maggie's trust, and eventually her love. He'd decided to just be himself. For if she couldn't come to trust him, love him, for what and who he was, the whole thing would be pointless. Maybe he should have gone with a strategy. Too late now, he thought, his path was set.

"Maggie, I'm sorry. Not about us being good together. I'm not sorry about that, because we were, more than merely good, more like fantastic. But I am sorry for bringing it up now, when I know you don't want to discuss it."

"You're right, I don't wish to discuss it." She moved her shoulders in a minishrug. "But you're also right about being good together—we were."

"But…then why…"

The simple act of raising her hand silenced him. "I don't know where you're coming from, what you want from me—" a wry smile brushed her lips "—other than sex."

"It was more than sex, Maggie." Mitch paused, then admitted with blunt honesty, "Okay, to begin with it was the sexual attraction… I felt it, and you felt it, too." He gave her a hard stare. "Didn't you?"

"Yes." She met his stare with commendable directness. "And it rattled me."

He smiled. "I know."

"It still does."

His smile softened. "I know. That's why you've been keeping your distance from me, even though the attraction is still there, just as strong."

She nodded in agreement but didn't return his smile.

"Then, don't you think we should explore this attraction? We could spend time together, away from this office and get to know each other. Not in bed," he quickly assured her, "even though I'll admit I want that, too."

"You're suggesting a platonic relationship?" Maggie's voice and expression were skeptical.

"For a while...hopefully a short while...until we see if we have anything else going for us."

Maggie studied him, quiet, pensive. Too long.

"Well, what do you say?" he said, impatience riding him. "I did promise I'd behave."

She sighed, smiled and said, "Okay."

And not a second too soon, because Mitch couldn't hold his breath any longer.

"I loved that movie," Maggie exclaimed, laughing. "It was so off-the-wall."

"I'll say." Mitch laughed with her. "You can't get more off-the-wall than the Frankenstein monster dancing and singing 'Putting on the Ritz.'"

Maggie nodded. "I must have seen it a dozen times," she confessed.

Mitch grinned. "Me, too."

His grin sent a shiver down Maggie's spine. Wrapping her trembling fingers around her coffee cup, she raised it to her lips. Dinner was over. She had enjoyed every bite of the meal; she had enjoyed Mitch's company more, even though he did send hot and cold chills through her.

Ever since Mitch had picked her up at the apartment—he wouldn't hear of her meeting him somewhere, then driving home alone afterward—his behavior had been above reproach. He had opened the car door for her, usurped the restaurant host by holding her chair for her, and had broken the initial awkward silence by recounting amusing anecdotes.

Nervous at the outset, she had been nearly overwhelmed by the sheer masculine attraction of him. She yearned for him, and the yearning both scared and annoyed her, rendering her almost incapable of anything but the most monosyllabic responses to his attempts at conversation.

But her vocal ice was broken the first time he

made her laugh. From then on, talking got easier. The evening became less a strain and surprisingly enlightening.

Maggie would never have dreamed that two people from different parts of the country with completely different lifestyles could have so much in common. And yet they did.

She had already known, of course, that they both preferred caffeinated coffee. But, over the course of the meal, she had discovered they shared a passion for sunsets over sunrises, mind-teasing mystery stories, cheeseburgers and pasta. Their mutual appreciation of zany comedy was the latest discovery.

"I want children."

Mitch's bald statement startled Maggie out of her things-in-common amazement. "What?"

"I said, I want children." He shrugged. "I just thought I'd make that clear up front."

"Okay," she said warily. "And your point being...?"

"You told me...that night...that you had convinced yourself you were in love, because you wanted to step off the career treadmill, have a home life, a family. I wanted you to know that I want those same things."

So had Todd, or so he'd said, Maggie thought, her mellow mood rapidly dissipating. But all she'd been to Todd was a convenient bed partner, until something better came along. The old resentment flared, fueled by new resentment for Mitch, for ruining the pleasant evening.

"I...ah, think I'd like to go home now," she said, her voice tight, her body trembling.

"Maggie, I'm not him." Mitch's voice was harsh with frustration.

"I know that." Carefully setting her cup in the saucer, she folded her hands in her lap.

"Then cut me some slack." He raked long fingers through his neatly brushed hair. "Dammit, Maggie, you're driving me nuts. I want you, you know that. But I want more than a couple nights in bed with you, or a couple months. I want it all. I know I promised not to pressure you, but..." He broke off, cursing under his breath. "I'm bungling this, I know. But, you see, I've never been in this position before. I've never been in love before."

Love. Maggie blinked. Love? Impossible. Wasn't it? They barely knew each other. Yet, she had felt the same emotional stirrings. Had felt she could easily fall in love with him if, that is, she didn't already love him.

Maggie was very afraid that she was in love with him. And it scared the hell out of her. He scared the hell out of her. What if she were to commit herself to him, and then... No. She shook her head. She wouldn't be able to bear it if Mitch were to walk out on her.

"I want to go home," she repeated in an agonized whisper, denying an inner longing to find a home in his arms.

"Maggie, trust me, please," he implored her, his voice raw. "I won't hurt you."

"I...need time."

"How much time?"

"I...don't know."

"All right. Take all the time you need. I'll wait." He sighed. "I have no other choice."

The atmosphere in the office the next day was rather strained, although Mitch made a gallant effort at maintaining a normal workday appearance.

Though she tried to emulate his in-office professional attitude, Maggie was miserable. Her heart was torn between the desire to take a chance, grab hold of Mitch, accept whatever he offered, and the chilling fear of again losing everything.

They circled around each other like two magnetized metals, fighting the attraction drawing them together.

Off in her own rosy world of planning a future

with Ben and the child she was carrying, Karla was unconscious of the drama being played out between Mitch and Maggie.

On Friday, Maggie sighed in relief, tension easing as lunchtime approached. It was Karla's last day of work. With Mitch's ready approval, Maggie had planned a surprise baby shower for her during the lunch break. He had even bent the rules a little, not only by extending the lunch hour for the other female office workers on the second floor, but by shifting break periods for the women friends of Karla's on the casino floor and in the restaurant, so they could join the party. He had also made arrangements for the restaurant kitchen staff to cater the affair and provide a decorated cake.

By prearrangement, Mitch called Karla into the office ten minutes before noon. The moment the door closed behind her, Maggie went into action. Ushering the tiptoeing women and servers into the outer office, they got to work, stringing streamers, positioning a pink-and-blue-striped umbrella, setting out the food and drinks.

Within fifteen minutes, everything was in place. Maggie alerted Mitch with a short buzz of the intercom. Karla exited his office to cries of "Surprise!" Flabbergasted, she laughed, then burst into tears. Shaking his head at the mysterious emotions of pregnant females, Mitch beat a hasty retreat, making himself scarce by doing a regular sweep of the premises.

It was great fun. There was a lot of laughter and teasing, mingled with a few scattered tears. When it came time to open the pile of gifts set before her, Karla rummaged in her desk for a pair of scissors. Finding none, she glanced at Maggie.

"I think there's a pair in Mitch's office. Try the top-center desk drawer."

Maggie zipped into the office and to his desk. She found the small pair of scissors, but that wasn't all she found. Shoved into one corner was a ring. It wasn't just any old ring, but what appeared to Maggie to be an obviously expensive and elaborate engagement ring.

Frowning, she removed the scissors, closed the drawer and returned to the party. But a niggling concern dampened her spirit.

Although the party lasted less than two hours, it seemed to drag much longer for Maggie. It ended when Mitch strode back into the office. Taking their cue, the employees drifted back to work, the women from the restaurant taking the food and drink carts with them. Maggie began clearing away wrapping paper and stacking the gifts.

"You two might as well call it a day," Mitch said, smiling into Karla's flushed, bemused face. "I've asked Frank to come help you carry your loot to the car."

"Oh, but..." Karla began in token protest.

Troubled by the possible connotations concerning the ring she had seen in his desk, Maggie stayed silent.

"No buts," he decreed. "The excitement has tired you. Go home and rest." He ended the discussion by walking into his office and shutting the door.

Frank arrived with another security guard in tow, and between the four of them, they managed to transfer the gifts to Maggie's car in one trip.

It wasn't until after they were in Karla's apartment, the gifts piled on the sofa and Karla settled in a chair, that Maggie tentatively broached the subject of the ring.

"Oh, that." Karla made a face.

"It looked like an engagement ring," Maggie ventured. "A very expensive engagement ring."

"It is...or was," Karla said, nodding. "Mitch was engaged for a few months to the daughter of a prominent local family. The wedding date was set, but..." She shrugged.

Maggie felt a chill. Not another man who

made commitments, then broke them at will? She had to know.

"What happened?"

Karla sighed. "It was a misunderstanding on Miss Crane's part."

Miss Crane? The name rang a sharp peal in Maggie's memory. She'd taken a call from a Natalie Crane, demanding to speak to Mitch. And Maggie remembered his harsh order for her to get rid of the woman. The chill intensified inside her.

"I felt terrible about it," Karla continued.

Maggie frowned. "What did you have to do with it?"

"It happened right after I found out I was pregnant," she explained. "I was upset, afraid to tell my parents. I didn't know where to turn." She sighed again. "So I cried my troubles out to Mitch...literally. Trying to comfort me, he held me in his arms and let me cry on his shoulder. We didn't hear Miss Crane enter the office. She saw me in his arms, heard me mention the baby and naturally assumed the worst. She threw the ring at him and ran out."

"But...surely he went after her...explained the situation?" Maggie asked.

"No." Karla shook her head. "I offered to go see her, explain the circumstances, but he wouldn't let me. He said it was over, and that was that.''

"I see," Maggie murmured, very much afraid that what she saw was the picture of a man, a bedrock-hard man, who could discard women as easily as he could a rumpled shirt. The very idea caused a sharp pain in her heart.

After coaxing Karla to lie down and rest, Maggie climbed the stairs to her apartment, where she curled up on the window seat to do some heavy thinking.

She loved him, Maggie acknowledged. And this time, the emotion was for real—it wouldn't hurt so badly if it weren't. But fear and trepidation riddled her thinking. An impulse to hit the trail was strong and compelling. At the same time, an equally strong impulse urged her to stay, confront Mitch with her knowledge of his previous engagement, hear whatever he had to say for himself.

But she was so afraid to trust again. If she were to have her trust thrown back in her face, she knew that something inside her would shatter.

Her ruminations were interrupted by Mitch's phone call later that afternoon.

"Hi, is our little mother okay after all the tears and excitement?"

"Yes," Maggie answered, her stomach lurching at the sound of his voice, a longing for him tugging at her emotions. "I think she's having a nap."

"Good. How about you and I having dinner?"

"Mitch...I..." Maggie paused to swallow against the emotional tightness in her throat.

"Maggie, what is it?" His tone had an edge of anxiety. "What's wrong?"

In that instant, Maggie made a decision. She was tired of running. She had to know, even if the knowing squashed her emotionally. "We must...talk."

"I'll be right over," he said at once.

"No." Maggie gave a sharp shake of her head, even though he couldn't see her. "I don't want Karla to start wondering why you're here. I'll go there... You're still at the office?"

"Yes, but..."

"I'll be there in a few minutes."

A few minutes. Her words echoed in Maggie's head all the way to the casino. Within a few short minutes her whole world could change.

Mitch was standing by the window, waiting for her. His expression was somber, his body rigid with tension.

"What's this all about, Maggie?"

Maggie crossed directly to his desk, slid open the top drawer. "This afternoon, quite by accident, I saw this." She lifted the ring with two fingers.

"It is, or was an engagement ring," he said, walking toward her to pluck the bauble from her fingers. "Rather garish and ostentatious, isn't it?"

Since that had been her own private opinion, Maggie had to agree. "Yes."

"What about it?" With a careless flick of his fingers, he tossed it back into the drawer and closed it.

"I asked Karla about it."

"Of course." He smiled, a wry twist of his lips. "And immediately jumped to conclusions about me. None of them favorable. Right?"

At his cool tone, Maggie suddenly recalled Karla's words, telling her about Mitch's thoughts on trust. And she knew, without his spelling it out, that he was daring her to test it, test him...while simultaneously, he would test her.

"I'm afraid so," she confessed, facing him squarely. "I've been burned before, Mitch."

"Not by me," he pointed out in hard tones.

"Yet," she retaliated.

His chest expanded, then contracted on a sigh. "What the hell do you expect me to do? I'm sure Karla told you the sorry details. What more is there to say?"

"You tossed Miss Crane aside as easily as you tossed that ring into the drawer," she cried accusingly.

"She didn't trust me," he retorted angrily. "So why should I have given a damn?"

The trust thing. Still, something didn't ring right to Maggie. A question niggled. "But I just indicated a doubt in your trust. Where's the difference?"

"I love *you*," he declared, in less than loverlike tones. "I never loved her. As I believe I already told you, I've never loved any other woman."

"Oh," Maggie murmured, feeling confused and extremely flattered at one and the same time. "And loving me, you're willing to be patient with my doubts?"

"Hell, yes," he said, hauling her into his arms. "Maggie, you've been hurt. I understand that. And you're cautious. I understand that, too. But I love you. And I want you. In bed. Out of bed. In my life. And because of that, I'll be patient until you admit to me, and yourself, that you love me, too. The trust will follow."

This man was too good for her, the dimwit who had been ready to settle for a man she hadn't truly loved, Maggie conceded...to herself. But, whether or not she deserved him, his love, she wasn't about to be so foolish as to let him get away from her. She was going to grab him and hang on tight—for the rest of her life.

Putting action to thought, Maggie coiled her arms around his neck and clung.

"I already love you, Mitch," she said, her body springing to vibrant life at the touch, the feel of him pressing urgently against her. "That's why I was so damned scared."

"I knew that," he murmured, with supreme self-confidence. "That's why I only panicked a little bit when you said we had to talk."

Laughing together between rapidly heating kisses, Maggie and Mitch made their slow, sense-arousing way up the stairs to his apartment, to his bed.

Two weeks before Christmas, Karla, now Mrs. Ben Daniels, gave birth to a healthy, squalling son.

Staring through the nursery window at the red-faced baby, Mitch circled an arm around Maggie's waist and drew her close to his side to whisper in her ear.

"I want one of those," he murmured, indicating the baby. "Marry me, Maggie."

Tears glistening in her eyes, Maggie turned her head to smile at him. "I thought you'd never ask."

The sound of Mitch's joyous laughter rang through the hospital corridors.

* * * * *

SILHOUETTE DESIRE

AVAILABLE FROM 16TH NOVEMBER 2001

CHRISTMAS WEDDINGS

MONAHAN'S GAMBLE Elizabeth Bevarly

Sexy Sean Monahan aimed to make Autumn Pulaski break her no-man-for-longer-than-four-weeks rule. And when the four weeks were over, her rule had been replaced...*by wedding bells?*

A COWBOY'S GIFT Anne McAllister

Rugged Gus Holt was sure he could win over his pregnant ex-fiancée. Mary *would* be his by Christmas—if he could just work out how to gift-wrap forever!

FIRST LOVE, ONLY LOVE

A SEASON FOR LOVE BJ James

Men of Belle Terre

Maria Delacroix had been forced to flee her home and leave her first love. Now she was back, but someone was determined to destroy her. Could the tall, dark Sheriff protect her and give them a future—together?

SLOW FEVER Cait London

Freedom Valley

Returning to her home town meant that Kylie Bennett had to face Michael Cusack, her first love—who'd never shown any interest in her...*until now.* Had his passion been simmering for all these years?

JUST ONE TOUCH

THE MAGNIFICENT MD Carol Grace

Sam Prentice, prestigious MD, had been Hayley Bancroft's first love until they'd been cruelly driven apart. Now he was coming home, and time hadn't dimmed the memory of Sam's loving touch and fiery kisses...

THE EARL'S SECRET Kathryn Jensen

Just one touch was all it took for Jennifer Murphy and Christopher Smythe to feel an intense passionate attraction. But this union could only be temporary, unless the Earl could divulge his secret...

AVAILABLE FROM 16TH NOVEMBER 2001

SILHOUETTE®

Sensation™

Passionate, dramatic, thrilling romances

LOVING LIZBETH Ruth Langan
STRANGERS WHEN WE MARRIED Carla Cassidy
SPECIAL REPORT Lovelace, Price & Cowan
THE BRANDS WHO CAME FOR CHRISTMAS Maggie Shayne
DAD IN BLUE Shelley Cooper
MAD DOG AND ANNIE Virginia Kantra

Special Edition™

Vivid, satisfying romances full of family, life and love

MATERNAL INSTINCTS Beth Henderson
THE DELACOURT SCANDAL Sherryl Woods
JUDGING JUSTINE Penny Richards
FATHER FOUND Muriel Jensen
THE COWBOY'S GIFT-WRAPPED BRIDE Victoria Pade
HER WILDEST WEDDING DREAMS Celeste Hamilton

Superromance™

Enjoy the drama, explore the emotions, experience the relationship

TEXAS VOWS: A McCABE FAMILY SAGA Cathy Gillen Thacker
SECOND TO NONE Muriel Jensen
'TIS THE SEASON Judith Arnold
CHRISTMAS BABIES Ellen James

Intrigue™

Danger, deception and suspense

LULLABY AND GOODNIGHT Susan Kearney
MYSTERY BRIDE BJ Daniels
THE OUTSIDER'S REDEMPTION Joanna Wayne
TO DIE FOR Sharon Green

NEW for November
SUPERROMANCE™

Enjoy the drama, explore the emotions, experience the relationship

FIRST BORN SON — Muriel Jensen
HER SECRET, HIS CHILD — Tara Taylor Quinn
THE WALLFLOWER — Jan Freed
THE WOMAN IN BLUE — Janice Kay Johnson

4 NEW titles a month

SPECIAL INTRODUCTORY PRICE –

£2.99

Normal price – £3.49

For a more satisfying read try Superromance this month!!

Available at most branches of WH Smith, Tesco, Martins, Borders, Eason, Sainsbury's, and most good paperback bookshops.

SUPERROMANCE™

Enjoy the drama, explore the emotions, experience the relationship

Superromance is a fantastic new Silhouette® series that is starting this month.

Longer than other Silhouette books, Superromance offers you emotionally involving, exciting stories, with a touch of the unexpected.

4 GREAT NEW TITLES A MONTH

SPECIAL INTRODUCTORY PRICE –

£2.99

Normal price - £3.49

Available at most branches of WH Smith, Tesco, Martins, Borders, Eason, Sainsbury's, and most good paperback bookshops.

MORE DESIRE™
FOR YOUR MONEY

NEW Silhouette Desire® has doubled
in size to offer you
double the romance and
double the passion for less money!

3 BRAND NEW DESIRES
every month with
**2 FULL LENGTH NOVELS
IN EACH BOOK**

For the great price of
£4.99
Previously £2.80 per book

Get more Desire and great value every
month from November with Silhouette

*Available at most branches of WH Smith,
Tesco, Martins, Borders, Eason, Sainsbury's,
and most good paperback bookshops.*

Watch out for our fantastic
NEW LOOK DESIRE™
series in December

2 FULL LENGTH NOVELS IN 1 FOR ONLY £4.99

Available from 16th November

*Available at most branches of WH Smith,
Tesco, Martins, Borders, Eason, Sainsbury's,
and most good paperback bookshops.*

Available from 19th October 2001

Winter
LOVING

TWO HEART-WARMING LOVE STORIES

FROM
DIANA PALMER
JOAN HOHL

*Available at most branches of WH Smith,
Tesco, Martins, Borders, Eason, Sainsbury's,
and most good paperback bookshops.*

The Christmas that changed everything

Mary Lynn Baxter   Marilyn Pappano
Christine Flynn

Available from 16th November

*Available at most branches of WH Smith,
Tesco, Martins, Borders, Eason, Sainsbury's,
and most good paperback bookshops.*

FREE!

1 Book
and a surprise gift!

We would like to take this opportunity to thank you for reading this Silhouette® book by offering you the chance to take another specially selected title from the Desire™ series absolutely FREE! We're also making this offer to introduce you to the benefits of the Reader Service™—

- ★ FREE home delivery
- ★ FREE gifts and competitions
- ★ FREE monthly Newsletter
- ★ Books available before they're in the shops
- ★ Exclusive Reader Service discount offers

Accepting this FREE book and gift places you under no obligation to buy; you may cancel at any time, even after receiving your free shipment. Simply complete your details below and return the entire page to the address below. **You don't even need a stamp!**

YES! Please send me 1 free Desire book and a surprise gift. I understand that unless you hear from me, I will receive 3 superb new titles every month for just £4.99 each, postage and packing free. I am under no obligation to purchase any books and may cancel my subscription at any time. The free books and gift will be mine to keep in any case.

DIZEB

Ms/Mrs/Miss/Mr .... Initials ....
BLOCK CAPITALS PLEASE

Surname ....

Address ....

....

.... Postcode ....

Send this whole page to:
UK: The Reader Service, FREEPOST CN81, Croydon, CR9 3WZ
EIRE: The Reader Service, PO Box 4546, Kilcock, County Kildare (stamp required)

Offer not valid to current Reader Service subscribers to this series. We reserve the right to refuse an application and applicants must be aged 18 years or over. Only one application per household. Terms and prices subject to change without notice. Offer expires 31st May 2002. As a result of this application, you may receive offers from other carefully selected companies. If you would prefer not to share in this opportunity please write to The Data Manager at the address above.

Silhouette® is a registered trademark used under licence.
Desire™ is being used as a trademark.